THE ANNULET OF GILT

Books by Phoebe Atwood Taylor
available from Foul Play Press

Asey Mayo Cape Cod Mysteries

THE ANNULET OF GILT
ASEY MAYO TRIO
BANBURY BOG
THE CAPE COD MYSTERY
THE CRIMINAL C.O.D.
THE CRIMSON PATCH
THE DEADLY SUNSHADE
DEATH LIGHTS A CANDLE
DIPLOMATIC CORPSE
FIGURE AWAY
GOING, GOING, GONE
THE MYSTERY OF THE CAPE COD PLAYERS
THE MYSTERY OF THE CAPE COD TAVERN
OCTAGON HOUSE
OUT OF ORDER
THE PERENNIAL BOARDER
PROOF OF THE PUDDING
SANDBAR SINISTER
SPRING HARROWING
THREE PLOTS FOR ASEY MAYO

Writing as Alice Tilton

BEGINNING WITH A BASH
FILE FOR RECORD
THE HOLLOW CHEST
THE LEFT LEG

PHOEBE ATWOOD TAYLOR

THE
ANNULET
OF
GILT

An Asey Mayo Cape Cod Mystery

A Foul Play Press Book

THE COUNTRYMAN PRESS
Woodstock, Vermont

Copyright © 1938, renewed 1966 by Phoebe Atwood Taylor

This edition is published in 1986 by Foul Play Press, a division
of The Countryman Press, Woodstock, Vermont 05091.

ISBN 0-88150-078-X

Printed in the United States of America

10   9   8   7   6   5   4   3

THE ANNULET OF GILT

$1.$ ASEY MAYO spotted them first from the top of Cannon Hill, where he paused to shift before plunging his roadster through the wallow of muddy ruts ahead. Those dripping little figures that trudged along the shore lane were the Pilgrim Camera Club of South Pochet, a trio no less indefatigable than the surf pounding the beach beyond, and no less persistent than the rain beating against his windshield.

"Motto," Asey murmured, "results. Emblem, a fiery hornet's nest—"

What victim they might be pursuing in such weather, or what calamity might be drawing them so far from home, Asey didn't even bother to guess. The motives directing the Pilgrim Camera Club resembled those of the anonymous person who once painted the old Baptist Church with scarlet and yellow stripes; while the coat of paint itself was admittedly divine inspiration, the color scheme definitely was not.

The club's results, too, were almost always as spectacular as the striped church. You had to give the youngsters credit for their studies of that famous camera-smasher, Hector Colvin, and for the masterly shots that collared Pochet's bank robber. And after their intimate views of the new submarine tests off Provincetown, the navy department still rang like a gong at the names of the Budd twins and Noah Snow.

In short, cameras in the hands of those boys bore more than a flitting likeness to the thumbscrews of an inquisition torturer.

The trio melted expertly into the bushes as Asey's roadster swung through the gate of young Bill Porter's driveway.

"Ahoy!" Asey stuck his head out into the rain and called to them.

The lilacs quivered innocently in the wind.

"Twins!" Asey assumed his most penetrating quarterdeck bellow. "Pink! Pokey! Noah!"

At the third roar, they slithered out and swarmed delightedly over the car.

"Asey, when'd you get back? Geeps—"

"Last night," Asey told them. "And what's the idea, slinkin' away from me like this?"

"Not from *you*," Pink said. "We weren't hiding from *you*, Asey. We thought you were Bert Blossom!"

"To think," Asey said, "that Bert took on the job of constable because he thought it'd be a snap—what have you gone an' done now?"

"Not a thing, not one darned thing," Noah answered righteously. "It's an injustice, the way he keeps chasing us like we was gangsters or kidnappers or something! We're pretty sick of being persecuted, we are!"

"You poor downtrodden things," Asey said, surveying their grinning faces. "Noah, you're gettin' as freckly as the twins, and they're gettin' pug noses like yours. Protective colorin', I s'pose—look, you crawl inside here an' tell me what Bert's chasin' you for today."

"It began at the Inn," Noah slid across the leather seat, "with those Garths—"

"What Garths?" Asey demanded.

"Oh, a fellow and a girl at the Inn. We always take pictures of people at the Inn, you know, for the 'Record.' We get forty cents—"

"I know," Asey said. "Pilgrim Pix. But about these Garths. Are they Hector Colvin's relations?"

"Geeps," Pokey said. "Geeps! Maybe *that* was the trouble! We didn't know that! The girl—her name was Carol—she'd of let us take her picture, but the brother said we was imposing on his privacy, and chased us off. And then when he found us in his closet, he sent for Mrs. Hoyt, but she couldn't calm him—"

"Not then," Pink corrected him. "We beat it that time. It was when he found us under his bed he sent for her, and she sent for her husband, and *he* called Bert—"

"But we didn't wait for Bert to get there," Noah said blandly. "We left and went over to Hector Colvin's house—"

"And then Hector, he called Bert," Asey said. "Don't you realize you bring on Hector's high blood pressure? You kids just ask for trouble when you harry him—but say, Colvin's gone off on his yacht, hasn't he? He wanders abroad always, this time of year."

"He's gone," Noah said, "but he's rented his house to these foreigners, this blonde woman, and an older woman— geeps, you'd just ought to see the rings she wears, Asey!

And all those servants in green shirts, with daggers in their belts—only they're sashes, not belts. And—"

"Noah," Asey said, "you been readin' a book!"

"Honest. And one of 'em wore earrings. And this blonde, she had on pyjamas, like." He paused and lowered his voice. "Of gold cloth!"

"Gold nothing," Pokey said. "It's brocade. I could of told you that. Sis's got a coat of it. And the daggers were curved, sort of, Asey. At the tip. And—"

"I'll swallow the Garths," Asey said. "They haven't been here since they were children, and you couldn't of made them up. But blondes and daggers! Why, you know perfectly well that Colvin hasn't opened that old ark of a house for years. He lives on the yacht. Blondes in gold at Hector Colvin's! Pooh. A couple of poohs!"

"But it's true," Noah said. "The people came yesterday, and we heard about 'em last night, so we came right over today, only we stopped first at the Inn. And those servants in the green shirts, they wouldn't even let us past the door. Wouldn't even take our card!"

"So," Pink said, "we sneaked in the back way with the carpenters. The place's been fixed up a lot in the last two weeks, and they're still hammering around. But those servants chased us out, and the tall one—he's about ten feet high —he grabbed our bikes, and they called Bert. And Bert said last Saturday if he had any more complaints about us, he'd take our cameras away, and now he's chasing us in his car."

"That's why we hid when you came," Noah continued as

Pink stopped for breath. "Mickey Ryder says that Bert's boiling mad. I don't know why. We didn't take any pictures, did we? We just tried to. You can't treat people like gangsters and kidnappers just because they try to take pictures, can you? And we already been run out of *here,* twice. We want—"

"Pink!" Asey pointed a rigid forefinger at a limp bundle that had slipped from under the twin's rain coat down on the floor of the roadster, "Pink, what have you got there? That's a *hand* sticking out of that brown paper!"

The three writhed with laughter, and displayed a life-sized baby doll.

"Maybe," Noah said, "maybe Bert thinks it's real, too. He heard—but it's just for the bombardment of Shanghai. Or Madrid. Whichever works out best. That's all we want over here—"

"So," Asey said. "Just a little bombardment, huh? Now you looky here, you imps. When you start bombardin' my friends the Porters—"

"Asey, you don't understand," Noah said. "You been away—how long, a month? Well, you drive along, and you'll see. An' you'll get Mrs. Porter to let us take pictures, won't you? I know she'd let us, but we can't find her, and that architect—do drive up to the house, Asey!"

"Do," Pokey urged. "Drive right up, Asey—"

"Quick," Pink chimed in. "Uh—go on. Now. Quick—"

"You're awful sort of eager an' hurried, all of a sudden," Asey commented. "I—oh. That's a car you're starin' at in the rear view mirror. Bert Blossom's, huh?"

"He's waiting on the top of Cannon Hill for us," Noah said. "Pulled his car off the road—I just noticed the fender when the rain let up a little then. Wonder how long he's been there?"

"If he'd seen you here," Asey said, "he wouldn't be waitin' on the hill. Bert ain't a very subtle man. Mind you," he leaned over and pressed the starter button, "if you smother inside my closed rumble seat on your way home, it's your own fault. An' if he catches you takin' any bombardment pictures, I shan't say a word to save you."

The Pilgrim Camera Club gazed up at him with such mute and honest affection that Asey felt a little embarrassed.

"So," he started the roadster along the winding drive, "you three water spaniels— God A'mighty, what happened to this place?"

He slowed down beyond the windbreak of evergreens to contemplate the devastation that had been one of Cape Cod's show places.

The old elm trees that had died the previous summer had been cut down, and their roots widely extracted. Yawning chasms freshly dug by a steam shovel indicated that the elms were to be replaced by new, and apparently larger trees.

"See, shell craters. Isn't this swell for the bombardment of Shanghai?" Pink fingered the camera case hanging from his shoulder strap. "And see where they're digging that big new garden, where that old wire fence is down? Well, that's trenches—"

The ell on the rear of the house looked as though it had

been blown away by a direct hit, the chimneys were down, the garage sat jauntily on piles.

"They're renovatin'," Noah said. "The—"

"Uh-huh," Asey said. "I gathered as much—but what's those subway entrances over yonder?"

"Oh, they keep trying to dig a new well," Noah explained, "but they keep running into this rock ledge. Now you see, Asey, we'll drape the doll around—oh, geeps, there's that ole architect! An' if we get out of the car here, then Bert'll see us—"

"Stay put," Asey said. "I'll talk to this feller. An' Bert Blossom can sit an' drip up on the top of Cannon Hill, an' watch me to his heart's content—"

Pochet's constable, he thought as he buttoned up his oil-skin coat, certainly might think up wiser methods of coping with the Pilgrim Camera Club than sitting on spongy hilltops, peering at them from afar.

But of the two people concealed in the cluster of pines on the top of Cannon Hill, neither was Bert Blossom.

The tall man in the wet green blouse, with the little curved dagger in his belt, passed the binoculars to the woman standing beside him.

"That is the man," he said, as Asey strode across what was left of the Porter's front lawn.

The woman, whose amazingly blonde hair was crammed under a tight green beret, shrugged her shoulders, nearly shrugging off the oversized black rubber raincoat that protected her glittering pyjamas from the rain.

"No," she said. "That is not Warner."

Both spoke English without any accent, but with a precision and an intonation that sounded strange among the pines and the bayberries.

"Then what," the man demanded irritably, "were those boys doing with their cameras? Who is this man? He has hidden the boys in his car!"

"Probably a fisherman," the woman said. "And the boys took no pictures, Johann—"

"How do you know? And fishermen don't drive cars like that one! That is a Porter sixteen."

The woman shrugged again and held out the binoculars.

"I am wet," she said, "and very very tired of your alarms. Those children wanted to take pictures of us because we are foreigners, and strange—"

"But they came back, again and again and again!"

"They are American children, remember," the woman said. "Come. I am going home." She shivered. "I am so wet!"

"Very well, I'll take you," Johann said grimly, "and then I shall return to this place. Perhaps that man is not Warner, but I have seen him before. Say what you will, I have seen that man before!"

Noah Snow and the twins were chortling when Asey came back from his conversation with the architect.

"Bert's gone," Noah said. "The big goon! Backed his car down the hill, even, so's you wouldn't see him an' ask him later what he was there for. Geeps, you got a way with you, Asey! Say, can we take the bombardment pictures now? Where you going?"

"Betsey Porter's hereabouts," Asey said, "an' I want to talk with her. An' when I blow the horn twice, mind, I'm ready to leave."

He drove the roadster as far down toward the shore as he could, parked by a pile of lumber, and dashed through the rain to the end of the wharf and the glorified shed which the Porters still referred to as The Old Boat House. Their more accurate friends called it Porter's Country Club.

But no country club atmosphere greeted Asey when he opened the door.

The place was choking with smoke from wet logs that had fallen from the andirons to the hearth. In one corner, a red-faced carpenter coughed as he planed viciously at a board. Beside him, a motor lathe hummed. Dismal funnels of rain trickled from the roof and overflowed the bowls set about like checkermen on the floor. The shutters clattered, and the tide banged up against the wharf. Above all the din and confusion, a screeching radio shook the windows with the praise of canned codfish cakes.

Near the fireplace, in a wicker chair without cushions, Betsey Porter slept like an exhausted child.

"Now," howled the radio, "Chums, the makers of Chums' Yummy Codfish Cakes, bring you the weather report. For Maine, New Hampshire and Vermont, rain. For Connecticut and Rhode Island, rain. For Massachusetts, rain. For Boston and vicinity, rain. For Cape Cod, Nantucket and the islands, rain. Coastal conditions, Eastport to Sandy Hook, rain. A trough-like disturbance continues to overspread New England—"

Betsey Porter sat up straight as Asey snapped off the

radio, turned off the lathe, and kicked the smoking logs into the ashes.

"Asey, it *is* you—how wonderful to see a human face! Asey, was that the weather man? What did he think?"

"He seemed," Asey told her gently, "to think rain."

Betsey closed her eyes and shuddered.

"They call this May," she said. "May. It *was* May, one day last week. It was almost June. Since then it's been Little America in a monsoon. Is it that trough disturbance still overspreading all New England?"

"It continues," Asey said.

"I know every inch of that trough," Betsey moved her chair away from a new leak. "Most of it's fallen on me, personally. In fact, quite a bit seems to have dropped on you—how well you look, Asey!"

"Oh, it's the latest thing," Asey said. "Wet corduroy an' a drenched duck coat. All us well dressed men—"

"I meant you, not your clothes," Betsey said. "You look so cheerfully healthy and unworried—what did that newspaper call you? Not detectivish, but—"

"The best one lately," Asey said, "called me a lithe hayseed sleuth. I keep wonderin', what's a lithe hayseed?"

Betsey laughed. "What do you think of our new wing?"

"So it's a wing, is it?" Asey asked. "Wing to you, maybe, but to me an' the Pilgrim Camera Club, it's the bombardment of Shanghai. Bill might have let me in on this renovatin', I think."

"My bright husband," Betsey said, "didn't dare tell anyone. Putty in the hands of that architect, that's what he was. He only broke the news to me last week. Seemed he was so busy, so terribly terribly busy, that *I* had to come down and see to his beastly renovations. He said it would be a nice change for me. Cape Cod in Maytime. He envied me the birds and the bees and the sun, and the peace of it all—"

She winced as the carpenter's plane hit a new high in discordance.

"The peace, the quiet—must you," Betsey turned around and raised her voice, "must you make that noise? Can't you plane in any key but F minor? Can't you *stop* planing, for heaven's sakes!"

"You said," the carpenter picked up a file, "you wanted this book case done if I had to stay here all night, didn't you? Well, if you want this book case—" he left the sentence ominously unfinished and went to work with the file.

A dangerous gleam appeared in Betsey's eyes.

"Put that down!" she said. "And pack up your tools—"

"But you told me," the man looked uneasily at Asey, "you wanted the book case—"

"And never," Betsey continued, "let me see that hideous face of yours again."

"But—"

"Dispose of him, Asey, please. Before I really lose my temper and start throwing things."

The carpenter fled.

"And in another minute," Betsey said, "I should have chewed hunks out of him—oh, Asey, this new wing has got me down! Five blessed days of this rain, and the house like that—and I simply can't get anything done, Asey! The roads are so gooey, the trucks stick—my beach wagon's stuck in Melcher's Hollow. Why do they always tear roads up in May?"

"It's an old New England habit," Asey said. "Come May, the roads get mended—"

"Oh, I know, I know—but those carpenters and all the rest, Asey. They could do *some* work, but they won't. They keep sneaking off to that blonde at Hector Colvin's, damn her hide!"

"Who is this blonde?" Asey asked. "Who *is* she? An' what's she doin' at Colvin's?"

"Oh, Hector's gone off the loose end and let his house to this exotic blonde," Betsey said, "after all these years of apparently blameless living—of course he's away on his yacht, but even so! And the carpenters come here, and snarl at me, and grudgingly stick in a tack, and then they simply trample each other in the rush to get back to Hector's and fix Hector's blonde up all snug and waterproof. And meanwhile, the old Porter place floats in mud. Asey, the way I feel now, you could put me next to a cucumber, and I'd automatically pickle it. This—oh, this shambles!"

"Who," Asey inquired, "is supposed to be doing the work for you?"

"That idiot architect hired Santos from Weesit. He claims that everyone else was tied up with contracts. He won't be forceful because he's afraid Santos'll quit cold, and Santos knows it—and if something doesn't get done soon, we'll just have to tear the whole house down and start from scratch. There's no reason why they can't at least put tar paper on the ell! But Hector Colvin's blonde has to be kept dry and happy. Until she finally arrived in person, they did make an occasional feeble effort, but since yesterday—"

"Why don't you ask the blonde for the loan of her lads until they get you temp'rarily settled?" Asey asked.

Betsey drew a long breath. "I did. Let me count a hundred before I go into *that*. Oh, have you a match?"

Asey chuckled as he lighted her cigarette.

"Oh, it's all terribly funny," Betsy said. "Hilarious, that's what. But don't you laugh too hard, because I have this feeling that you're the man that's going to put on tar paper, and oversee Santos, and get the trees in and the garden planted. Lithe Hayseed Sleuth Again Proves Versatility. Just Jack-of-All-Trades, says Modest Mayo—before I forget it, Asey, what's an annulet?"

Asey stared at her.

"What's that?"

"Look out," Betsey said, "that match is going to burn your fingers. An annulet. What is it?"

"Something to wear around your neck, an' it keeps evil spirits away an' good ones in," Asey said. "Or maybe the other way around. Why?"

"You're thinking of amulet," Betsey said. "This is an a-n-n-u-l-e-t," she spelled it out. "Two n's instead of an m."

Asey strolled over to the window. "It's a ring, isn't it? That coat of arms I got hanging in the hall at home, that's got a ring in one corner, a thin circle, sort of. Seems to me that's what old Professor Harriman, that friend of Bill's, called an annulet."

"Mayo, the fact collector," Betsey said admiringly. "No item too small, no item too remote. Maybe it is a ring, I wouldn't know. I never heard the word in all my twenty-seven years until I got that letter from Terry Warner to-day. He said—what's the matter, Asey?"

"I was just watching the Pilgrim Camera Club," Asey said. He hoped that Betsey wouldn't come to the window to investigate, for the Pilgrim Camera Club wasn't even in sight. "Warner, did you say?"

"Remember him?"

"Warner," Asey continued to look out the window. "Wasn't he the government inspector at the Porter factory when old Cap'n Porter turned out cars an' engines in the war?"

"That's the one," Betsey said. "He used to come down to see the Cap'n here, once in a while. He had the most beautiful uniform, with a Sam Browne belt. I was ten, and I fell in love with him. I knit him a sock, but the war was over before I got the mate done. Anyway, I had a let-ter from him today—isn't it amazing, the way people turn up? He said he was thinking of spending the summer on the Cape, would I look around for a quiet place for him, and he sent his regards to you, and then he said something about asking you if you remembered the annulet. Now if an annulet's a ring, what on earth did he mean?"

"Piston rings," Asey said promptly. He had been an-ticipating some such question. "We once chased a car load through six states."

"What a terribly remote way of saying something," Bet-sey remarked. "Were you at the Porter factory during the war, Asey? It's funny, but I can't seem to remember you in uniform, or what you did. What did you do?"

"Towards the end of the war," Asey said, "I went to the factory to play with the tanks they was startin' to make, but things ended before we really got goin'. Most of my work in savin' democracy was carried on in a sub-chaser galley, peelin' spuds."

"How silly," Betsey said, "to think of your wasting time like that, while young squirts like Warner were officers. I wonder," she added, "how old he is now."

"Forty-nine," Asey said, and then added rather quickly, "or fifty, or fifty-one. Prob'ly fat an' bald, an' a grandfather. Got his address, Bets? I think I just might know of the right place for him."

Betsey kicked the pile of mail at her feet. "The letter's in this mess somewhere. Here—no, damn it, it's gone. That fool carpenter probably put it in the fire with his shavings. But Warner said he'd be down very soon, Asey. He was in Boston, at the Parker House. Lord, hear that rain! By tomorrow, that ell will be pulp, what's left of it. I could ruin that blonde!"

"You haven't got to tellin' me about that lady," Asey reminded her.

"She's really very beautiful," Betsey said. "Looks younger than I do, and she's probably ten years older. I never saw a more superb figure—did I tell you about my beach wagon getting stuck?"

"Uh-huh," Asey said, marvelling at the flexibility of Betsey's mind.

"Well, it stuck," Betsey continued, "so I walked from the Hollow to Hector's house. I had on a sheepskin coat under my oilskin coat, and Bill's oilskin pants over slacks, and hip rubber boots. And mittens. And a sou'wester. You get the picture? There was quite a lot of mud around, too. And I got met at Hector's by dozens and dozens of these myrmidons—you couldn't really call 'em plain servants. Not exactly liveried, but dressed in comic opera chorus clothes, if you know what I mean. I got shunted from one lot to another—really, by comparison the court of St. James is just gaily informal. Finally I got marched into this room where the blonde was."

"What's her name?" Asey asked.

Betsey shook her head. "I haven't the faintest idea. I just asked for whoever was in charge, and no one mentioned her by name. There was a lot of bowing and scraping—anyway, I asked her pleasantly if she'd be good enough to let me borrow her workmen—who were also supposedly my workmen—long enough for them to make my house impervious to the elements. I was very charming and plaintive, pointing out that tomorrow was Sunday—those beasts said they wouldn't work on Sunday, by the way. I outlined the situation to her in my best manner, trying to look as if I wasn't aware of all the drip I was making on the rug."

"And what did the lady have to say?"

"She said, no. Regally, with one eye on my boots. No, says she, and waves to the myrmidons, and they all lined up in a sort of phalanx and bore me to the door. You'd ought to have seen Betsey getting the bum's rush."

Asey grinned. "I'd like to of," he said sincerely. Knowing Betsey, he felt that the time would undeniably come when the blonde would regret the scene. "I'd of enjoyed it, Bets. All that glamor, an' you—"

"Glamor my eye!" Betsey retorted. "It was just so much third rate musical comedy. Hector's been hanging around stage doors, I think. And the servants—well, they just all reminded me of my fruit man. And I still think that 'Yes' would have been a more regal and courteous answer for the blonde to make. Anyway, that's that. Tomorrow you can take charge of the Porter renovations—"

"But who *is* this blonde?" Asey asked. "Who is she? What is she?"

"I suppose she's a passing fancy of Hector's," Betsey said. "And she apparently comes high. He must have spent a young fortune modernizing that ark—"

"I mean, what nationality is she, an' the rest of the bunch?"

"Frankly, I wouldn't know," Betsey said. "She spoke English with a bit of a lilt, and the servants were on the guttural side, but none of them were definitely one thing or another. I didn't pay much attention to their accents, anyway, I was so mad and so wet and so confused by all the trappings. The last time I was inside Hector's, it looked like a high class funeral parlor, and it's now department store modern, with a million miles of squashy broadloom, and the walls all velvet. You could peddle foundation garments or cold cream for moddom in practically any corner—"

She stopped as someone outside banged at the ship's bell that served as a knocker.

"Betsey! Betsey Porter! Where are you?"

Before Betsey could answer, the door swung open and a small good looking girl panted in.

"Carol!" Betsey got up. "I'm so flattered at your tramping all the way—Asey, this is Carol Garth, remember? Hector's niece. Turned out to be very beautiful and very bright. She and Lewis came to the Inn yesterday—come over to the fire and dry out. You look sodden."

"I am," Carol said, shaking hands with Asey. "Sodden, and—look, Bets, I—this Cape isn't what it used to be when I was a child!"

"You're telling me?" Betsey said. "May was May, in those days, and look at it now, all mud and trough disturbances—Carol, you look scared!" she snapped on a bridge light. "Good Lord—here, sit down. What's the matter? What's happened? What's that you've got under your arm, a hat?"

"I'm just scared to death," Carol held out a broadbrimmed Stetson, and Asey took it quickly. His face, Betsey noticed, was suddenly very grave.

"Asey, that looks like one of your own hats," Betsey said. "One of your own special Stetsons—"

"It is," Asey told her.

He did not add that two hours ago, it had been on the bureau in his bedroom.

"Where'd you pick this up, Carol?"

"This man on the beach," she said in a small voice, "at the foot of the dunes. He was wearing it."

"An' who," Asey inquired, "put the bullet hole through it?"

"I guess," Carol said, "that's what the man who was wearing it rushed off to find out—"

2.
ASEY twirled the soaking Stetson around on his forefinger.

"When'd all this happen?" he asked.

"When did it happen!" Betsey mimicked his calmly restrained tones. "When—oh, Asey! Don't tell me you're going to sit there and dissect this little incident in that sort of detached voice, with murderers or something racing madly around my beach!"

Asey pointed out to her that the hat, and not the man, seemed to have been pierced.

"An' how long ago was it?" he asked Carol.

"I can't tell you exactly. I was up by the beach dunes, the big ones that slope from Cannon Hill. I'd been ploughing along the lane, but the ruts got so bad that even the beach and the sand seemed the better idea. And it got so dark! And Bets, I didn't know it was such a terrific distance over here. I walked it often enough as a child, and it wasn't anything at all. Oh," she leaned back in the chair, "I'm limp!"

"I should think that you might be," Betsey said with vigor. "Practically winged—Asey, *do* something!"

"From the dunes over here," Asey said. "Let's see. You couldn't have run all the way, even in decent weather. Took you twenty minutes, I'd say. Did you hear the shot?"

"I suppose I must have, but I didn't separate it at first

23

from the noise of the breakers and the wind. I'd just caught sight of this man, and then he suddenly turned and ran toward the thick dune grass, and his hat came blowing toward me—I just reached out and grabbed it, and then I saw the hole, and remembered the noise. Look, is this sort of thing common on the Cape these days? I'm sure people weren't shot at on the beach in the old days." Carol wet her lips. "I can't seem to take this in my stride. I'm still scared. Somehow I wasn't half so frightened till I got here—"

"I marvel that you're here at all," Betsey said. "Personally, I'd just be a jellied heap on the nearest bit of seaweed—Asey, what'll we do?"

"I don't know," Asey said truthfully, "what we *can* do."

"Why, we've got to find out who's wandering about shooting who, haven't we? Things are a shambles here, but I'm not going to have any free lance sniping in what amounts to my own back yard! What would Bill Porter say if people got shot all over his beach? I won't have it. Asey, who'd you give that hat to?"

"No one."

"You mean someone stole it? That's awful, that's much worse! Asey, someone thought they were shooting at you! Pull down those shades, fix the shutters—*do* something!"

"If you want me to call in the lawr," Asey said, in the slow drawl that so irritated Betsey, "I s'pose I could sally forth an' drag Bert Blossom here."

Betsey sighed. "That lump!"

"An' what use he'd be," Asey continued, "I wouldn't

know. I wouldn't even know what to tell him he was wanted for. I grant you that there'd ought to be some step you could take when people shoot hats off other people's heads—"

"I get your point," Betsey said. "There should be a step, but Bert isn't it. Carol, my dear," she added with lavish irony, "just you forget the whole business. Put it out of your mind. Tch, tch, just a friendly little shooting, nothing to bother your pretty head over!"

Carol joined Asey's laughter.

"But he's right, Bets," she said. "What good would it do to call out the militia now? In the half hour that's intervened, the person with the gun has had time enough to put three towns between him and the beach. And the man in the hat wasn't hurt. The whole thing wouldn't have come up if I hadn't happened to grab that hat. But I can tell you this much, I shall *not* walk back to the Inn."

"Asey'll drive you," Betsey said. "Maybe someone'll see his yachting cap and put on another William Tell act for you—"

"Then you'll be a witness too," Asey said. "Remember your stuck beach wagon. You don't get back to town yourself unless you walk, or I take you. Tell me, Carol, how come you're back on the Cape after all these years?"

Betsey, about to comment acidly on his deft changing of the subject, looked at Asey and suddenly decided to hold her tongue. It occurred to her belatedly that no matter how hard he was trying to minimize the incident, Asey had no intention of letting this shot-at hat slip into oblivion. Asey was going to take steps, but in his own way, and at his own time. And by himself.

Betsey lighted a cigarette. Particularly, she thought, by himself. He probably was yearning to do something, but he didn't want to leave her and Carol there alone, and Carol had to be talked back to normal. The girl was still white and breathless, and her right eyelid twitched nervously.

"Just sort of vacationin'?" Asey added.

Carol hesitated.

"Well, yes and no. Brother and I remembered some things we thought we'd like to have from the cottage. Stuff left there when we were children. Both of us happened to have some free time, so down we came. And now we're—well, we're stymied by this strange blonde person that Uncle Hector's given the place over to."

"You, too?" Betsey said. "Why, Carol, you never told me that you'd had any truck with that blonde!"

"We were a little embarrassed about it, Lewis and I. You see, she won't let us into our own little cottage, or even the grounds, until she's consulted with the lawyers and they approve. So—"

"The nerve of the piece!" Betsey said. "I'd jump over the walls, in your place. Why, the cottage is yours!"

"Yes, of course. But if we start any bickering, and if people start rousing uncle with cables and phone calls and all," Carol said, "then Hector'll ask, with perfect logic, why we didn't let him know we were coming, and why we chose to come when we knew he'd be abroad. We don't want to make issues, and uncle's so inclined that way."

Asey grinned. Hector Colvin's temper was legend.

"Do you," he asked, "happen to know who this blonde woman is?"

Carol shook her head. "She startled Lewis and me. Uncle's such a strait-laced, conservative soul, you wouldn't expect him to have anything like her about the house. As Lewis said, uncle's tenants aren't our business, but we do rather resent her making such a mountain of our visit, and the poor worthless little trinkets we came for, and the stuff Vivian wrote Lewis about."

Betsey and Asey exchanged glances at the mention of Carol's much married mother.

"If it weren't for Vivian's things," Carol continued, "Lewis and I would leave. It's just not worth all this perfectly tremendous to-do."

An uncomfortable little silence followed. Betsey was dying to ask questions about Vivian Garth, but she didn't know just where it would be tactful to begin.

"You're wondering about Vivian?" Carol said with a smile. "Don't hold in, Bets. I haven't seen her—oh, I haven't seen mother half a dozen times in the last eighteen years. The last I heard, she was married to a Spaniard."

"I wanted to ask you about her last night," Betsey said, "but it seemed so sort of rude—how many times *has* Vivian been married, all told?"

"Lewis says seven, but I make it eight. It depends on whether there were two Russians, or only one. I think that a White general came after the Georgian prince, but Lewis doesn't seem to think that she really ever got down to actually marrying that particular general."

"But there was a general somewhere, wasn't there?" Betsey asked.

"Oh, there was a French one, with a goatee. He died. And then there was an American colonel who got to be a general. He used to be a friend of father's. Of course, all I know about mother," Carol said, "is what I read in the papers. It seems funny just to call her mother. She's a complete stranger. I've never seen much of Lewis either, for that matter. Once in a while we met in the Grand Central, en route to camps or schools or something. Hector and the trust brought us up—that is, their secretaries did. We were a lot of files. Garth Children: Medical and Dental. Garth Children: Education. Garth Children: Clothes and Entertainment."

"It sounds about as attractive as a switchboard," Asey remarked.

"It was awfully efficient," Carol said, "but I was glad when I got to be twenty-one two years ago. So was Lewis— he got free first, of course. Anyway, after all those years of Hector's remote control, we still rather steer clear of him. That's why we came here when we knew he'd be away. We knew that our touching Vivian's things would rouse him, too."

"While we're on the topic," Betsey said, "Hector and your mother never got along, did they?"

"They simply loathe each other," Carol said. "Of course, no brother and sister could be more completely different. Uncle thinks Vivian's a bad, lewd thing, and says so, and she thinks he's a stick and a prig, and she says so. Their early life at home must have been one interminable battle. But that's enough of why Lewis and I are here. How long we stay depends on the whim of the blonde—and on Lewis's office, and—"

She stopped short as Asey strode over to the door and opened it wide.

"Come in, you three," he said. "I thought I heard you rustlin' out there. This is the Pilgrim Camera Club—did the dark finally stop you?"

"That an' the rain," Noah said. He looked at Betsey and Carol, and prodded Pink. "Get goin', you," he ordered. "Go on—"

Pink stepped forward, made a dancing school bow to Betsey and another to Carol.

"How do you do, Mrs. Porter, thank you for letting us take the bomb—I mean, the pictures of your place. We'll bring you some prints." He paused briefly to draw another breath, and turned to Carol. "Uh—Miss Garth, how's for that shot? The one we didn't get this morning?"

Asey rubbed his chin as Pink bowed again. This was a side of the Pilgrim Camera Club with which he had never before come in contact.

"Good Lord," Betsey said in amazement, "it's the first time I've seen such manners in a child for—which twin are you?"

"Pink, ma'am."

"Where," Betsey said, "did you learn that superb bow, Pink?"

"Aw," Pink said, "dancing school in Boston. We come

from there. But we got poor and came down here to live last fall, and—" he stopped as Pokey's elbow bit into his ribs.

"Let me tell you," Betsey said, "it's a far better bow than Bill Porter ever made—"

"Geeps, did *he* used to have to do it?"

"Sure he did," Betsey said, "and he tripped all over the place. Carol, for that bow, I think you should break down and give 'em a picture."

"They could have had it this morning," Carol said. "I was flattered to have my picture wanted. But you irritated Lewis so. If only you'd bowed and scraped like that to him, and called him 'sir'—he loves being called 'sir.' So does Uncle Hector. But of course, you'll never get any pictures of him—"

"We got 'em," Noah said, briskly zipping open a knapsack. "They bought this outfit, the Colvin pictures did."

"Oh, so you're in the business?" Carol said.

"Yup, we'll get forty cents for you, if Randall thinks you're newsworthy," Noah said. "Maybe seventy-five, if you're Colvin's niece—Pokey, back her chair around while she fixes her hair. Mrs. Porter, would you sit yonder? Pink, toss me that cord. An' say, Asey, we'll take a shot of you, too. You—"

"Why?" Asey said. "I ain't done nothin', Noah."

"You're back after a trip," Noah said, "an' you're always good for fifty cents—now—"

Ten minutes later, Noah zipped up the knapsack and slung it over his shoulder.

"There," he said. "That was swell. Give Miss Garth one

of our cards, Pokey. If you got a dog, we do fine dogs."
He glanced sideways at Betsey. The Porters owned any
number of dogs. "Say, Asey, will you have room for us
goin' home? That old goon Bert, he's back again. He's—"

"He's come back three times," Pokey said. "We been
watching the car lights. We thought, Asey, maybe you'd
take our cameras and stuff, and we'd walk through the
hollow—"

"The Pilgrim Camera Club," Asey explained to Betsey,
"is wanted by the law. So Bert's there, huh?"

"Yup, he's there—geeps, isn't he dumb?" Noah said.
"Up on that hill, in the rain. Whyn't he come here, if he
thinks we're here?"

"What d'you say," Asey suggested briskly, "if we fox
the old goon? We'll stow you three inside the rumble, an'
Miss Garth an' Mrs. Porter can ride in front, an'—" he
paused, "we'll take the other road—"

Betsey's eyes narrowed. Saddled with three twelve-year-
olds and two women, Asey was going to retreat from whoever was waiting on the hill. It wasn't Bert Blossom, she
felt sure. Asey would never bother to change his route for
that stupid lump.

"Asey, you mean the hollow road?" she asked. "Oh, you
do. You're not forgetting that my beach wagon is mired
there, are you?"

"The Porter car," Asey began, "goes through mud
like—"

"Yes," Betsey said. "But it happens to be the Porter
beach wagon that's stuck. So what?"

"But I," Asey said, "got the new Porter engine in my

old car. I been road testin' for the last month—didn't Bill tell you? Come on—"

The boys and Carol kept up a steady stream of conversation as they walked out to the car and packed themselves in. Betsey was silent, until Asey started down the drive.

"There's an old custom," she said, "called putting on headlights, or don't you hold with such new-fangled things?"

"It's somethin' I didn't want to break to you," Asey told her lightly, "but I got a custom older than that. They call it faulty ignition."

"Asey Mayo!" Betsey was genuinely scared. "You can't drive the hollow road without lights! Not with this rain, and that mud! You can't do it—think of the bridge! Asey, you simply—you—you can't!"

The car swung past the driveway gates and turned up the shore lane toward the hollow and away from Cannon Hill.

"Don't grab the reins, Betsey," Asey said. "I drove the first Porter over these roads—you know, Carol, I sold your father one of 'em."

"The electric buggy? That one? I remember the pictures—"

"That one," Asey said, "with all the electric storage bat'ries. He had one of the first gasoline Porters, too."

Casually, he chatted about the first gasoline Porters.

"There now," he said at last, "you can let out your breath, Bets. We're over the bridge, an' way past your beach wagon. Yes, it was fun drivin' then, back in 1900 an' before. I once spent forty-seven hours in one stretch, drivin' from where we just started at the house, to about here. I said then, I'd never really forget this road. It got sort of etched on my mind, as you might say—"

"What'd you do after the forty-seven hours?" Carol asked.

Asey grinned. "We invented a new engine." He leaned forward. "An' some things is still good about it—well, well, what do you know about that?"

"Why, the lights—the headlights! They've come back!" Carol said. "What happened?"

Asey ignored Betsey's derisive snort. "We must of bumped, or hit somethin' just right. Well, well!"

A few minutes later he drew up in front of the Inn.

"There you are," he said. "Hustle in before you get any wetter—oh, Betsey. Just a sec. Just wait a second—"

"Yes?" Betsey said. "What is it, old show-off?"

"Just for fun, stick close to her, will you?"

"Just for fun," Betsey said. "Also, just so that I don't follow you to see what's up. What *is* going on? Who's down at the hill? What's all this about?"

"I don't know," Asey said, "but I don't like it. Stay here till I get you tomorrow, will you? Promise? If people are wanderin' around the beach by your house, you might as well let 'em wander in peace—"

"Asey, what are you going to *do*? What—oh, I'll promise! Good night. And," she added, "have fun with your annulet, or ring, won't you?"

Asey stared at her.

"Mayo, the wool-puller," Betsey said with some satisfaction. "I've just come to, and thought of the things Bill's let slip, and why I didn't remember you in uniform. And why Terry Warner was at the factory. So you peeled potatoes in a galley, did you? My, my. Well, well!"

She ran up the path to the Inn, and Asey took the Pilgrim Camera Club home at a pace which thrilled them.

He cut short their profuse thanks.

"Have you," he asked, "got a gadget—a lens where you take a picture here, an' the person six houses down appears in a closeup?"

"Telephoto," said the three in unison.

"My pig of a brother Ralph's got one," Pokey said. "A Zeiss that cost—"

"But he won't let us have it," Pink said. "The old pinhead—"

"What brother Ralph?" Asey said. "I seen your sisters, but I never heard of him."

"Oh, he used to be an interne, and now he's a doctor," Pink said wearily, as though Ralph had progressed from bad to worse. "He's a pig. He won't let us touch his old camera—"

"Is he home?" Asey demanded. "Get him, please. I want to talk with him—"

Ralph Budd, a pleasant young man with shell rimmed glasses, came hurrying out to the car.

"I've been trying to get you," he said as he shook hands with Asey. "Scram, you brats. I've been—look, I want to talk with Asey Mayo—"

"He wants to ask you about your telephoto lens, pig," Pink said. "He—"

"If you want supper, scat!" Dr. Budd got in beside Asey. "Beat it. Mother's clearing away—"

"Butch is clearing away? But Butch said she'd wait!"

"Butch didn't," Dr. Budd said. "So scat. Look, Asey—I mean, Mr. Mayo—"

"Asey'll do."

"Thanks. I feel as if I knew you, anyway. Look, Asey, I've called and called your house—you know, I'm taking over Cummings's practice while he's away on his vacation, and he said if I got puzzled about anything, to get you. And the damnedest thing has happened at Colvin's just now. Hector Colvin's. He's away, but he's let his house—"

"To this exotic blonde," Asey said, "an' a lot of servants in green shirts with curved daggers. I know. I know it by heart."

"Well, I got a call to go there about an hour and a half ago," Budd said. "Someone had been shot, they said, and would I hurry—hurry—hurry. So I did."

"An' what happened?"

"Nothing."

Asey stared at him.

"Just that. Nothing," Budd said. "The servant that answered the bell asked what I wanted, and I told him I was the doctor, which seemed to baffle him. I told him again, and then I said 'Doktor,' and then I said 'Docteur' and then I yelled it several times. He said he understood, I was the doctor, and perhaps I had the wrong house. I said, someone called me from Colvin's, and he said, oh, no."

"No," Asey remarked, thinking of Betsey's interview, "is

a word they favor in that household. No shilly-shallyin', just 'no.' Did you go into the matter with green shirt?"

"I insisted on seeing the head of the house, or whoever was in charge, and green shirt finally produced a tall man in a green coat. He said, everyone there was in the best of health, he was awfully sorry I'd made a mistake, doubtless some other Colvin was probably waiting for me, and perhaps I'd excuse him. And green shirt shut the door. I should have raised a rumpus, of course, but I felt so foolish. And then when I got home, mother and I talked it over and decided to ask you what to do. Because that call was genuine enough!"

"You're sure it come from Colvin's house?"

"Yes, I checked with the operator. She knew, because they'd asked for the nearest doctor, and she called me. What do we do?"

Asey shook his head. "I don't know. A person has a perfect right to change his mind about gettin' a doctor. Maybe they got another, an' didn't want to pay you—Cummings has had that happen. P'raps it was just a mixup, with a lot of excitable foreigners like those servants—"

"The servants I saw weren't excitable," Budd said. "They had all the chill composure of a block of ice. Asey, people change their minds about calling doctors for nose bleeds and stomach aches, but not about gun shot wounds. Unless—look, this is fishy, and you know it. We ought to do something!"

"We ought," Asey agreed, "but I don't know what, any more'n I knew what to do a little while ago, when a girl saw a hat shot off the head of a man on the beach. It was my hat, an' someone else's head. Look, when you called my house, didn't my cousin tell you where I'd gone to?"

"Your cousin? Why, no one answered, Asey."

"How many times did you call?" Asey asked sharply.

"Six or eight. Then I told the operator to ring you every few minutes until she got you. But—"

"Are you busy right now?" Asey demanded. "No? Then you run get your coat, an' tell 'em you'll be with me if anyone wants you. An' p'raps you better bring your bag—"

"Right." Budd got out of the car. "Oh, Pink said you wanted my telephoto lens—do you?"

"No," Asey said, "not now, I don't think this is goin' to be as long distance as I sort of felt, at first. D'you mind hustlin'?"

As the roadster tore through the rain on the road to Wellfleet, young Dr. Budd looked at the speedometer and then at Asey. Dr. Cummings had warned him what to expect, and once again young Dr. Budd admitted to himself that Cummings was a fine diagnostician. Driving with Asey was all that Cummings had predicted, and then some.

"I gather," he said, "that you've got something weighing heavily on your mind?"

"Three hundred pounds," Asey said.

"Three—what?"

"Jennie Mayo, my cousin's wife," Asey said, "weighs about that. An' right now, every last ounce is weighin' on my mind. It ought to of weighed b'fore, when I seen that hat with the hole. I guessed Warner, but—you see," his foot pressed down on the accelerator, "Jennie was cleanin' my house today. She also aimed to get my supper. She was bakin' beans, an' she had hot biscuits an' an Indian puddin' in view. An' she also murmured somethin' about apple fritters—"

"I don't know that you'll need me right away," Budd said judicially, "but before the night is over, maybe—"

"That side of it don't matter," Asey said. "What does matter is that Jennie's at my house, involved with food she'd never leave. An' no phone ever rang within a mile of her that she didn't answer. An' she didn't."

They found the reason why when they looked in the hall closet.

3. WHILE Asey cut the

clothes line which trussed Jennie Mayo's ankles and wrists, Dr. Budd removed the twisted calico apron that served as a gag, got a glass of water and presented Jennie with a red pill, which she swallowed absent-mindedly.

"Can you move?" Budd asked. "Say, you're a lucky woman! Most people couldn't, after being jammed into that space—can you really move your legs?"

Asey silently gave the doctor credit for the suggestion that inspired Jennie to ease herself up from the closet floor. He had been wondering how the two of them could pry her out.

"Swell!" Budd went on. "Sit here, now, and taste my thermometer and get your breath." He felt her pulse. "Dr. Cummings said there was never a dull moment around Asey Mayo, and Cummings seems to be right. Let me rub that wrist—they tied you very considerately, didn't they? When I was on the ambulance, we had two gangsters that'd been bound with wire, and it certainly was horrid. How," he removed the thermometer, "do you feel?"

Asey braced himself for the indignant tirade he fully expected to pour forth from Jennie's mouth.

But Jennie was apparently taking this experience in her stride.

"Just like old times," she said, "as I told Mr. Warner—they didn't catch him, did they?"

"Warner!" Asey said. "So he's been here—when?"

"This afternoon. Mr. Warner," Jennie said reminiscently, "was always so fond of my apple fritters, he was real glad when I said we'd have 'em for supper. He was dripping wet, an' I thought he'd better change, an'—he didn't want to, though. He said he wanted to talk to you before people caught up with him. Just like the last time he was here, remember, Asey? Durin' the war, when Cap'n Porter's tank plans got stolen, an' you an' Mr. Warner—"

"Who was tryin' to catch him?" Asey interrupted. "Who come after him?"

"I don't know. I said I'd watch out while he got into some dry clothes, an' I showed him your closet an' things, an' then I come down into the kitchen. An' not five minutes later, they came—"

"Who came?" Asey demanded. "Who?"

"Why, I don't know, Asey!" Jennie said. "Land's sakes, how could I tell who come up behind me so quick? Somebody stuck a dish towel over my mouth so's I wouldn't make any noise, but I fooled 'em! I had that skillet in my hand, an' I flipped the hot butter over my shoulder, an' one man yelled like anything. Then I threw the skillet, an' it banged, so I knew Mr. Warner'd catch on."

"Jennie, you old sport!" Asey said admiringly. "How'd they get you into the closet?"

"They made me walk," Jennie said, "an' I can tell you, whoever it was has got some sore legs—my, how I kicked! I give 'em a good tussle, so Mr. Warner could get away.

Wasn't it lucky I hadn't put the biscuits in! An' the oven still on low! An'—there's that phone ringin'—it's been ringin' an' ringin', an' I near went crazy, wonderin' who it was!"

Asey answered, and nodded to Budd as he replaced the receiver.

"Your call for me," he said. "Jennie, I'm terrible sorry this happened—"

"Sorry?" Jennie said. "Why? It was real excitin'. Just like old times, only I wish you'd told me that you an' Mr. Warner was doing things again, together. Remember when Syl used to take the motor boat out the harbor, to get you off that torpedo boat? An' how I used to sit on the wharf with the searchlight? I used to like that a lot more than makin' bandages for the Red Cross."

Dr. Budd gulped.

"Yes," Jennie said. "Yes, indeed. I told Syl only the other day, I said, they make all this fuss over Asey an' his murder case detectin', but it don't hold a candle to what he used to do in the war that no one knew about. This is just talk, but that was excitin'. Oh, I think they took their boots off, Asey. Those men, I mean. They must have been in their stockin' feet, because I didn't hear a thing. Is the kitchen floor muddy?"

"No," Asey said. "I noticed that—"

"Must have sneaked in through the shed," Jennie got up. "Those rolls got to be seen to—"

Muttering things about the oven, she bustled out to the kitchen.

Dr. Budd sat down heavily in the chair she had vacated.

"And I," he said, "gave her a little red pill. What a woman! Look, Asey, I've got a pretty good bird's eye view of this, but it's not very coherent."

Asey looked at him a moment.

"It ain't," he said, "a very public view, but I might as well straighten it out. You see, in Berlin just before the war, I met a man named Terence Warner. His official job was office boy to his uncle, who was a senator an' the head of a lot of committees an' stuff. Somehow I got to be an assistant office boy, an' we had a lot of fun. Later on, when this country stopped bein' neutral, we really enjoyed ourselves."

"So," Budd said, "I gathered. Cousin Jennie liked it too. Go on."

"I ain't heard from Warner for years," Asey said. "Not till this afternoon, in a left handed way through Betsey Porter. I don't know what's goin' on. But Warner's been here to see me, an' got chased off, an' I sort of suspect that someone shot my hat off his head on the beach."

"I see. You don't think that your friend Mr. Warner might just possibly be my gun shot wound, do you?"

"If," Asey said, "any of the folks who wanted to shoot Warner ever hit him, there wouldn't be any need to call in a doctor. That's one statement I can make without knowin' any more'n I do. If he's involved with your gun shot wound, it's more likely he was on the shootin' end."

"Would this Warner be connected with the government, or something?" Budd asked.

Asey shook his head. "He don't use the proper methods. Sometimes, though, when people don't want proper meth-

ods used, they—somehow, I sort of feel it would be nice
if we had a reason for visitin' the tenants up to Hector
Colvin's. We—"

"Good evening," Budd said, "we are the Fuller Brush
men—and by the way, how're you fixed for gun shot
wounds tonight? Something that we can do for your radio,
maybe?"

Asey grinned. "It's late for a plumbin' inspector to call,
but we can always play with the electricity an' then mend
it. The storm's a nice excuse."

"If you can find an excuse that'll get by green shirt,"
Budd said, "you'll be doing something—look, about this
man Warner. He's all right—well, I mean, of course he's
a friend of yours and all. But are you sure that he's engaged in—uh—"

"Legitimate enterprise?" Asey said. "I wouldn't know.
He don't do things legitimate, like, but I think you can
sort of take it for granted that he's on the right side—"

The phone rang, and Asey picked up the receiver.

"What?" he said blankly. "Who, Pink? You say that
Butch wants the pig—"

"He means," Budd said, "in his picturesque way, that
mother wants to talk with me. I—all right, brat, let me
speak with her."

He listened for a minute or two, said "Okay," and turned
to Asey as he hung up.

"Tie that one!" he said. "Asey, there's just been another
call from Colvin's! Mother told 'em to call me here. She
thought you better get in on it. When they ring, you answer and see what's up—there, there they are!"

Asey reached for the telephone.

"This is Asey Mayo speaking," he said, and Budd noticed that his voice was crisp, without any trace of his Cape accent. "What? Yes. I'll take a message for the doctor. He is busy."

"Man or woman?" Budd whispered.

"Man," Asey said. "He's gettin' someone else—yes? Yes, I'll take the message. Will Dr. Budd come as soon as he conveniently can to Mr. Hector Colvin's house. Yes. Who is this calling, please? Thank you. I'll tell him."

"Who?" Budd asked.

"A Mrs. Monfort," Asey said, "an' she didn't sound like any exotic blonde to me! She sounded like a forceful woman who was used to givin' orders an' havin' 'em minded—" he cranked the bell on the telephone box. "Hey, Nellie— would you know if that call came from Colvin's? Sure? Okay. Thanks."

"Genuine?" Budd asked.

"Seems to be," Asey said. "Wait'll I put on a dry coat, an' we'll get goin'—Jennie, can you bear the thought of stayin' here alone?"

Jennie assured him she wouldn't mind a bit, and besides, her husband would be along shortly.

"An' can I tell Syl about everything? He'll be real glad Mr. Warner's back. An' say, Asey, I'm awful dumb, I just remembered about those foreigners at Colvin's. There's—"

"A lot of servants in green shirts, a blonde woman, an' so forth an' so on," Asey said. "Yup, we're goin' to call on 'em right now—"

"Oh, dear, you're wearin' that gun!" Jennie pointed accusingly to a shoulder holster, which Budd hadn't noticed. "Now, you be careful, Asey, an' don't hurt those foreigners— I'll keep supper for you."

Something had happened to the Cape, Dr. Budd thought as he followed Asey through the puddles to the car. It didn't seem like the Cape, it didn't look like the Cape, it—

"S'matter?" Asey asked as they started off.

"I seem to feel," Budd said, "that footlights ought to go on. Why, this afternoon I lanced a boil and looked in on a cold and some lumbago, and we were going to have beans for supper. And now we're setting out—why, it's fantastic! Things like this didn't even happen at the City Memorial Hospital, and everything happens at the City Memorial Hospital! And Asey, how are you going to get in? Are you my assistant, or what?"

"I forgot to tell you," Asey said. "You got a sprained left wrist. Make yourself a sling right away, will you? So I have to drive an' carry your bag. You better remember to wince when you forget, an' try to use the arm, an' if you could look pale, that might help. An' stop lookin' so awful eager—"

"But aren't you at all curious to find out what's happening?" Budd demanded.

"I certainly am," Asey said. "That's just why we can't seem to be. Hustle with your sling."

Ten minutes later he was pushing the bell of Hector Colvin's massive oaken door.

"Curtain," Budd murmured. "Lights—aha!"

A green shirted servant opened the door and stared impassively at them.

"Dr. Budd." Ralph announced himself and started over the threshold.

Unobtrusively, the servant blocked his way.

"I am Dr. Budd!" Ralph said sharply. "Mrs. Monfort sent for me."

"I have no orders, sir, to—"

"Go get them, then! Hurry, please. My arm is injured, and I can't be kept waiting in this rain!"

"No doctor has been called, sir," the man said firmly, and closed the door.

Quietly, but with a certain fluency, Ralph Budd told the door what he thought of Hector Colvin's tenants, their habits and their ancestry.

"And oh boy," he concluded hotly, "I hope that one of these fine days one of you guys needs me, and needs me bad! That's what I hope!"

Asey grinned.

"Come 'long," he said. "We—"

"Leave this place? Listen, Asey, this is the second time I've been made a fool of—"

"I know, but there's lots of ways to kill this cat. I think first we'll get Bert Blossom. You an' your mother an' I can all swear that you been called here urgent, Nellie can swear the call came from here, an' Bert's got somethin' to work on. 'Course, I don't know as there's a law to cover this, but if you wave your arms in the air an' talk loud enough about the basic statutes of the Com'nwealth of Mass'chusetts, almost anythin' sounds legal. An' forceful. Come on—"

As he started the roadster, the oaken door opened, and two men ran out into the rain.

"Dr. Budd—"

Asey ignored them.

"Doctor! Doctor Budd—wait! Stop!"

Asey made them follow the car all the way to the end of the drive before he stopped and let them catch up.

"What is it?" he said. "What do you want? Don't you know any better than to throw things at a car? What d'you mean?"

"We wanted you to stop! Dr. Budd—"

"Well?"

"We want you—"

"Why?" Ralph Budd took his cue from Asey. "What do you want me for?"

"There has been a mistake. Mrs. Monfort wants you—"

"Is that so?" Ralph said. "Mrs. Monfort wants me, does she? Well, I've been here twice, and both times I've been sent away—"

"But we'd been told—we didn't know—please, will you come back? Mrs. Monfort herself wants you!"

"No," Ralph said. "No."

That simple negative gave him a great deal of pleasure.

"But Mrs. Monfort—"

"If she wants a doctor, let her get someone else. As a matter of fact, what with illnesses and vacations and a medical convention, your nearest bet is fifty miles away, and I hope you have fun finding him. Drive on, Asey!"

Before Ralph and Asey consented to return, the two

green shirted servants were soaked to the skin, and the short one seemed very nearly on the verge of tears.

Inside Hector Colvin's house, they were ushered with great ceremony to the long drawing room, whose sole occupant was a woman seated in an arm chair by the fire. Both men knew, even before she spoke, that she was unquestionably the woman who had summoned the doctor the second time.

She was well over sixty, Asey thought, and once she must have been very beautiful. Her hair was snow white, her gown was black velvet, and her eyes were blue and snapping.

Curled on a hassock at her feet was a sleek Siamese cat, who looked up, sniffed disdainfully at the intruders, and went back to sleep.

"Dr. Budd, I am Mrs. Monfort."

Ralph bowed, rather as Pink had bowed earlier in the evening.

"This is Asey Mayo," he said.

"Ah, yes, I spoke with him. How fortunate that you— Dr. Budd, I'm very sorry to find that you've had such a trying series of experiences here. I assure you that the situation will be—er—dealt with."

Ralph suddenly felt very sorry for the green shirted men who were to be dealt with.

"I'm sure," he said, "it was a mistake—"

"Yes," Mrs. Monfort agreed, "it was. One of the men was cleaning out Mr. Colvin's gun room, and of course he chose to fool with the only weapon there that was loaded. It was only a flesh wound, but of course I ordered a doctor. It now appears that the man was unwilling to see a doctor, and my order was countermanded. I understand that you were very nearly sent away again. I'm very sorry that this happened."

"Then," Ralph said hesitantly, "you don't want me to see this man?"

"Yes. Oh, yes. Later. But there is something else which has been tardily brought to my attention—"

Asey kept trying to place her accent. She was an American, but she talked a little like Betsey Porter's aunt from Boston, and a little like Bill's English cousin. But she was more American than anything else.

"So," she continued, "perhaps you will come with me—"

"Of course," Ralph said. Under his breath, as Mrs. Monfort got up, he whispered to Asey, "The blonde—where is she?"

"I think she's been spanked," Asey whispered back, "an' sent to bed—"

They followed Mrs. Monfort down the long hall to the dining room. At the French door, another green shirted man waited with a wrap for her.

"This way," Mrs. Monfort said, and stepped out on the covered terrace.

They followed her past the guest house, past the greenhouse, past the swimming pool.

"What an outfit!" Ralph Budd murmured in Asey's ear. "I never knew—whee!"

Two more men appeared with umbrellas. In silence they walked along a wet gravel path to a cottage beyond the tennis courts.

"Here," Mrs. Monfort said, "if you please. Open the door, Ernst."

In the living room of the cottage, Ralph Budd nearly screamed at the pressure of Asey's fingers on his forearm.

Sitting on the couch, with the green coated Johann towering behind them, were Betsey Porter and Carol Garth.

On the floor in front of them lay the body of a woman.

"The blonde." Ralph Budd didn't realize that he had spoken out loud.

"No." Carol Garth's face was grey, and her voice was thin and taut, like a stretched wire. "That isn't the—it isn't the exotic blonde. That is—my mother. Vivian. She's—been killed."

$4.$"THAT is why I thought it was so fortunate, Dr. Budd," Mrs. Monfort said smoothly as he knelt down on the floor, "so fortunate that you should have brought Mr. Mayo with you. I understand from Mrs. Porter and Miss Garth that they know Mr. Mayo, and that he rather specializes in murders. How things work out, do they not?"

Betsey Porter turned brick red.

"You certainly can insinuate things!" she said angrily. "Just because we happened to—to find—"

"I believe that you said—"

"What I said," Betsey raised her voice, "when that brute Johann jumped on us, just after we found—found Vivian, all I said was, for the love of heaven to send for Asey Mayo! And you make it sound as though we were all in cahoots—"

"I know them," Asey interrupted quietly.

"And I'm sure," Mrs. Monfort said, "that is very fortunate for them, considering this very unfortunate occurrence. Now, if you'll be good enough to tell me what steps to take, whom to summon, what—"

"Asey can take charge!" Betsey was too excited to pay any attention to the warning in Asey's eyes. "He's got to take charge—he must!"

"I'm sure you would like him to take charge," Mrs. Monfort returned. "But perhaps, Mrs. Porter, it might be best to notify the proper authorities at once. Well, Dr. Budd?" she added as he got to his feet.

"She is dead," he told her. "Johann, that blanket from the couch, please. I'll cover—yes, Mrs. Monfort, she is dead."

"And how did she meet her death?"

Asey drew in his breath sharply as the reasons for Mrs. Monfort's manner suddenly became apparent to him.

At a table in the next room sat a green shirted man, busily taking notes on the conversation.

Whatever casual statement Budd might make, whatever Betsey or Carol might say in their worked-up state, all those random utterances would go down in the notebook. And unless Asey was greatly mistaken, Mrs. Monfort would see to it that the words came back later like boomerangs.

Providentially, as far as Mrs. Monfort was concerned, Betsey and Carol had stumbled into this thing. Now that they were involved, the lady was going to imbed them if she could.

"I said, how did she meet her death?"

"I think," Budd said, "that you would not want me, Mrs. Monfort, to offer any snap judgment under such serious circumstances. Now Sorenson, the medical examiner, is ill. I know because I've taken his place twice during the last week, and I'll phone him for instructions. I'll also notify the police—"

"The local police, of course. The village constable," Mrs. Monfort said.

She seemed, Asey thought, to relish the idea of a local

constable. Someone whom she could confront in her regal manner, someone who would be sufficiently impressed by her to arrest Betscy and Carol on the spot.

"Yes, and the state police, too."

"Really?" Mrs. Monfort was a little taken aback.

"Yes, indeed. A remarkably efficient group," Budd said. "And of course I'll also report to them this shooting accident in your household."

"Will that be quite necessary? I do not see how that concerns the police—"

"Considering this unfortunate incident," Budd used her own phrase, "I think so. I'll phone now—and you'll have all your men, all your household, ready to aid the police when they arrive? That will be—"

"Do we have to stay here?" Carol Garth's voice was still high and tense. "Do we have to stay here any longer? I— I don't think I can bear—"

Asey nodded ever so slightly.

"I'm afraid so, until I return," Budd said promptly. "There are things I'll want to know about—Asey, perhaps you'll stay with Mrs. Monfort's men, too. You're going back to the house, Mrs. Monfort?"

The first skirmish, Asey decided, was more or less of a draw.

Budd hadn't been tricked into saying anything, he had met Mrs. Monfort's insinuations with more insinuations, and he'd caught on that it was better for the girls to stay there, with Asey, than to allow Johann or any of the green shirted men to be left in charge of the cottage. And the body.

Of course Vivian Garth had been killed. There was no

doubt about it. The thin braided leather belt beside her on the floor, the marks on her throat—she had been garrotted. And—

"Asey!" Betsey burst out. "What—what have we got into? What'll we do? You—"

"Your name is Johann?" Asey asked the tall man. "What a lot of you there seems to be around this house. Everywhere I look, there's another green blouse. All those in the house, those out on the porch, an' then that feller in the next room, writin' down things in his notebook— D'you," he glared at Betsey as she tried to interrupt, "d'you suppose, Johann, he'd give me a page to jot down a few items on? Now, that's real nice of you, yes, sir!"

Johann's lips were tightly compressed when he presented Asey with a sheet of paper.

"You don't mind," Asey inquired blandly, "if I take notes on this too?"

"No!" Johann snapped.

"Your favorite word," Asey said. "Well, if you don't really mind, then I'll get to work. Notes," he went on hastily, trying to stare Betsey into silence, "are always such a help. Afterwards. Like in court. You much interested in courts?"

"No!"

"Too bad," Asey said. "We got some real interestin' laws in this state. They's a law in Pochet says you can't own or possess a dog more'n eighteen inches tall. I don't know why. Maybe you're more interested in the laws of your country— by the way, what did you say your country was?"

"I did not say!"

"Well, now, so you didn't," Asey said, unruffled. "So you didn't. You interested in goats, Johann?"

"What?"

"I was thinkin' of a law about goats," Asey said. "It's unlawful to call a person a goat, or to represent 'em as such, in East Weesit—"

"I am not interested in goats!" Johann said.

"No?" Asey said. "I am. I always try to see that the laws about goats is upheld, particularly the ones about representin' people as such."

Light finally dawned in Betsey Porter's eyes. And, Asey thought wearily, just about time, too. Carol Garth didn't understand what he was driving at, but that didn't matter so much. She was still too broken up to do any talking, and it was what the girls might say that was so important.

With great care, Asey constructed a bird cage out of the sheet of paper, and gave himself up to the task of getting Johann into a fine, glowing rage.

By the time that Ralph Budd returned to the cottage, Johann was so annoyed with Asey that he was almost growling.

"I phoned Bert Blossom," Budd said. "And Sorenson said for me to carry on, Asey. I got Talbot, and Davis. By dumb luck, Talbot was at the barracks. They're on their way over. Shall we leave things till they get here?"

Talbot, the state police lieutenant, greeted Asey and Budd, and then gaped at Betsey Porter on the couch.

"You?" he said. "Dr. Budd said something about a Mrs. Porter, but I never thought of you—what are *you* doing here?"

"I'm Exhibit A," Betsey said. "Oh, dear heaven, can I talk now? If I can't, I'll scream this cottage down! Let me talk, and let me get Carol out of here, please!"

Talbot looked inquiringly at Asey.

"What with one thing an' another," Asey explained, "we waited for you. I don't know what's happened, myself. Go on an' talk, Betsey—only first—" he nodded toward the green shirted servants and jerked a thumb toward the house.

"I see," Talbot said. "Okay. Report to Davis at the house, you men. He wants you. All of you. I'll be up presently— yes, all of you—"

Johann tried to argue the point, but Talbot sent him away with the rest.

"Now," he said, "what is this? Who are all these fellows? Who's the woman at the house? Who's that?" he pointed to the blanket covered figure. "What are you doing here, Mrs. Porter?"

"It's all my fault," Betsey said. "All my—"

"That," Asey said, "is not the way to tell your story. Can't you understand, Betsey? Can't you grasp this?"

"It's *my* fault," Carol said. "I wanted to as much as you did, Bets. You wouldn't have done it if I hadn't egged you on—"

"No," Betsey said. "You wouldn't have if I hadn't egged you. And it was so dull, and all that rain, and it seemed like something to *do,* and so we came, and—well, here we are!"

"An' if you two had said anythin' like that," Asey informed her, "while Mrs. Monfort's green shirt was in the next room writin' things down, then— Talbot, I give up.

The woman there on the floor is Miss Garth's mother, Vivian—what is her name now, Carol?"

"I don't know," Carol said. "This one was a Spaniard. He was Spanish. She—oh—I—"

She burst into tears, and Betsey, instead of trying to comfort her, started weeping wildly herself.

Talbot looked at Asey. "Who's been killed?" he asked. "And who's this Mrs. Monfort? And these green—oh, this'll never get us anywhere! Asey, do something about Mrs. Porter and the other—take 'em into some other room here—"

"No!" Carol sobbed. "No, no, no, no! Not in this house! I can't stand it, oh, I can't stand it! I've got to get away from here!"

"Take 'em up to the big house, then, Asey," Talbot said. "And I'll start—"

"Up to that house, and face that woman again?" Betsey demanded. "That woman who thinks we killed Vivian? I guess not! I guess—"

"What's the building up the path?" Talbot asked. "Greenhouse? Asey, you take 'em there and quiet 'em down, while I start getting things sorted out—"

After a quarter of an hour of utter confusion, Asey found himself alone with the two girls in the unused greenhouse.

The rain beat heavily against the glass roof, and trickled noisily down the east side. At intervals, Carol's shoulders shook in silent sobs. At intervals, Betsey wiped her eyes.

"This," Asey said, "is what I call an awful damp gatherin'. Now, you two, you've got to rally round an' pull yourselves together. You got to."

"For heaven's sakes, Asey!" Betsey said. "Must you be so cold-blooded? After all, it was Carol's mother!"

"I dud—didn't know her," Carol said, "but I feel just as bad—"

"I know you do," Asey said, "an' I'm sorry. I know you're both upset, an' I know Carol feels bad, an' I know you feel bad too, Betsey. But time is short, an' I got to get this into your heads. No matter how much or how little you two girls had to do with this, Mrs. Monfort is goin' to make you the goats. Do you understand that?"

"I should think so!" Betsey said. "You've done everything but sky-write it. But what of it? Why get so excited about Mrs. Monfort and what she thinks she can do?"

"I don't know what she *can* do," Asey said, "but I know what she intends to do, an' it's my opinion that with her, that amounts to the same thing. Now, you two pull yourselves together an' listen—"

"Asey—"

"Listen to me. Vivian Garth is killed here. Mrs. Monfort is not goin' to let that fact disturb either her or her household, or whatever she has on her mind. You two popped in on this. She's goin' to toss it off on you. So, Betsey, no matter how bad you feel, don't you an' Carol start any more speeches by sayin', 'This is my fault,' or 'Oh, no, I did it.' Not unless you want to feel a whole lot worse than you feel now. Because if at some later date, Mrs. Monfort springs her green shirts on you, all testifyin' with perfect truth that you did say such things—well, it's not goin' to be any fun for you. I'm sorry about Vivian, an' I'm sorry for Carol. But mostly, just now, I'm worryin' about you."

Betsey gave Carol a cigarette and lighted one for herself.

"But all we did, Asey," she said, "was to—well, we just came here at the wrong time, that's all! You see, after you left us, we got to chatting, and decided that for a lark we'd come here and get the things Carol wanted out of the cottage. After all, the cottage belongs to her and Lewis, and the things are theirs!"

"If you were the Pilgrim Camera Club," Asey said, "I could excuse you. Did it occur to either of you what might happen if you were caught?"

"Why, what could be done?" Betsey said. "It's Carol's house. We had a key. We weren't breaking or entering, or anything like that. Anyway, we climbed the wall, and came here, and went in the back way. The lights were off, but Carol thought she knew where the switch was, but she couldn't find it."

"It should have been in the entry off the kitchen, it always used to be," Carol said. "But it wasn't, so we decided to get along with the flash. And in the living room, I—I tripped—"

"We both fell," Betsey said. "Over—over Vivian. Only of course we didn't know then, we thought it was the blonde woman from the house. And of course we didn't know she was—was dead. We ran back to the kitchen and found the switch box, finally, and put on the lights, and came back, and then we both recognized Vivian, and we were frantic. We didn't know what on earth to do. And while we were trying to think, that tall brute of a Johann came in and grabbed us—my shoulder's going to be black and blue for months, and then he blew a whistle, and it was just like

Robin Hood. The place was filled with green coated figures in the twinkling of an eye. Only," Betsey added wryly, "you can't call this bunch merry men!"

"Just exactly what," Asey said, "did you an' Carol plan to get here?"

Betsey hesitated.

"A watch chain," Carol said. "Father's watch chain. And a little blue locket, shaped like a heart. Father gave it to me. And a teddy bear—the last time I was in the cottage, Asey, was the day that mother ran away with Bruce Munro, and father killed himself that night. And that same night, Lewis and I were taken away, and things were shut up. Nothing's ever been changed in the cottage. Uncle's had it cleaned and repaired and all, but things haven't been touched. I'm telling you this, because I'm almost crying more because— oh, how can I say it, Betsey?"

"I know what you mean," Asey said. "Goin' back to the cottage after all these years made you think of things as they used to be. Carol, that was all you wanted, just little things like that?"

"Yes. Vivian had written Lewis for things that were in the wall safe up in her bedroom, but we weren't going to touch anything there. That is, Bets and I. They're not valuable things—naturally, Vivian wouldn't have left valuable things, and naturally they wouldn't have been left there all these years if they had been valuable."

"Of course they wouldn't," Betsey said, as Asey made no comment. "Oh, go on and say what's on your mind, man! Motive, robbery. That's what the Monfort said when she majestically arrived on the scene, looking like the 'Ile de

France' with all the tugs around her. In a trice, she diagnosed the situation as robbery with violence, murder with theft, and all the variations. Then someone dashed in and salaamed and announced that Dr. Budd had come—why'd she call him, Asey, was someone sick?"

"I wish," Asey said, "I knew. What did she say?"

"Said to send him off. Like the Queen of Hearts saying 'Off with his head.' Then she sort of purred and changed her mind, and said to bring him in. I asked her if she'd get you, and she just smiled grimly and started ordering the servants about—a fine staff general was lost to the world in Monfort."

"What orders did she give?" Asey demanded.

"She spoke French," Betsey said, "and I must say, French Eleven never prepared me for anything like that. It could have been Sanskrit for all I understood. How about you, Carol, did you get any of it?"

"I had a German governess," Carol said. "All the French I know is about the cabbage of my aunt. If I order lamb in a French restaurant, I get onions. I think, though, that she mentioned Uncle Hector once or twice, and if arms are the same thing in French as in English, they had a lot of talk about arms. I didn't understand that—"

"I remember that part," Betsey said. "I got 'armory,' too —you don't suppose she has any designs on the county arsenal, do you?"

"I think," Asey said, "that I'll shortly take a look at Hector Colvin's gun room—oh—"

Ralph Budd came in.

"Yes, they're here," he said in answer to Asey's question. "The place is overrun with police, I never saw so many. What are they doing? Principally they're being told by Mrs. Monfort about Mrs. Porter and Miss Garth. They—"

"Have they found out anything about Mrs. Monfort?" Asey asked.

"She's telling them," Budd said, "what she thinks of things. Mrs. Garth—Vivian—she was garrotted, Asey, with that belt that was beside her. There's a perfect mark of the braided leather on her throat. I've never actually seen a garrotting case before, but I should say that this was done by someone who knew how."

"When did it happen?" Asey asked.

"Oh, I can't tell you exactly. Three hours ago, more or less."

Asey looked at his watch. "That would make it around seven this evening?"

"After seven, probably. At six-thirty, Bert Blossom helped her fix the blade of her windshield wiper on her car, just out of town on the main road. He's sure about the time, because he'd just turned his car radio on to some program he always listens to. Look, she told Bert that her name was Colvin—"

"It was, originally," Carol said. "She is Hector Colvin's sister, you know."

"And she said," Budd continued, "that she was on her way to visit Mrs. Porter—"

"Why, she never was!" Betsey said. "I don't know her! I haven't seen her since I was a child, except in the roto-gravure!"

"That's what she told Bert Blossom, anyway. And, Asey, I saw Mrs. Monfort's man with the gun shot wound. It's not what I'd describe as a scratch, but it's nothing serious. He'll be all right in a day or so."

"Just a nice clean hole in the right shoulder, huh?" Asey asked.

"How did you know? Have you seen him?"

"No," Asey said. "Would it have been a thirty-eight or a forty-five?"

"There wasn't any bullet, of course, but I'd say it was something larger than a twenty-two," Budd said. "How do you know so much about it?"

"He's master-minding," Betsey said. "Just master-minding."

"Nope," Asey said, "I just think I know the habits of the man I think shot him. Now, I'll go take a look at this gun room, an' see what Mrs. Monfort's boys decided to—"

"Wait," Budd said. "Has Talbot been here? Have you talked with Talbot yet?"

"No, but he can see me later, after I've been shown what got stuck among Hector Colvin's antique pistols to prove that the shootin' was an accident in the house—"

"Wait, Asey, please! You—then you don't know that—" Budd hesitated.

"Know what?" Asey put on his cap and buttoned his coat.

"Well, it's—but he can tell—look, maybe if you came outside and talked—" Budd was confused to the point of incoherence. "Come out on the steps—"

"Talbot said he'd come after Betsey an' Carol an' me," Asey said, "after he'd done some sortin' an' ironin' out. If—"

"Please!" Budd said.

Asey rather unwillingly allowed himself to be yanked outside the door.

"It's the belt," Budd said. "I mean, the one that was used to—that one on the floor. The one that was used to garrotte her—"

"It was her own belt, wasn't it?" Asey said. "It matched the lacin' at the front of her dress, an' the lacin' in the sleeves."

"Well, I thought it was hers, too," Budd said unhappily.

"Whose is it?"

"Well, it seemed to match her dress and all," Budd said. "But it—here comes Talbot. Talbot, you tell him about the belt."

Talbot looked as worried as Budd sounded.

"In all my life," he said, "I never coped with such a mess. I don't know what language those fellows in the green shirts speak, but we can't—and Asey, will you look at this belt?"

Asey looked at it, and at the small circular buckle with its two initials.

"See?" Budd said. "That's Mrs. Porter's belt."

$5.$ ASEY marched straight into into the greenhouse and confronted Betsey.

"Is this your belt?"

"Why," Betsey's hand groped around her waist, "why, yes—"

"What time did you leave the Inn?"

Betsey lighted a cigarette. She did not seem to notice that she already had two cigarettes, freshly lighted, beside her in the tin can lid which was serving as an ash tray.

"We left very soon after you deposited us at the Inn, Asey. Before seven. Mrs. Hoyt serves her out of season dinners on the dot of six, whether you're there or not, and the leftovers didn't appeal to us, though Lewis said it was good —Asey, you'd better call Lewis."

"I will. You left b'fore seven, without your dinner. Why did you come then?"

"It just seemed the ideal time," Betsey told him. "We figured that everyone here would be busy with dinner, and all. We thought that afterwards, we'd drive over to Orleans and get something to eat there, at that place by the cross-roads."

"Were you wearing this belt when you came?" Asey dangled it before her.

"Yes. Asey, you're like a district attorney in a movie! If

you start waggling your finger at me, I shall lose my temper entirely."

"You were wearing this belt!"

"Yes, heavens, yes! I put on dry clothes before we came, these slacks and this old sweater, and that gilt braided belt over the sweater. I don't know why. It belongs to my green dress—Vivian had one on just like it. Was hers black or blue?"

"Black," Carol said. "I've got one like it in brown."

"So've I," Betsey said. "Brown wool with a plain sort of pigskin belt and lacing. Anyway, Vivian's black one had the same trim as my green one—it's a sort of standard uniform, that model. One of those Bickum and Chase things that you could get in any Bickum and Chase store in half a dozen cities. You—"

"When'd you lose the belt off?"

"I don't know. It doesn't matter, does it? Just because it happens to be like the one from Vivian's dress, the one that was on the floor."

"This is the one that was on the floor," Asey told her.

"What nonsense! It isn't. It can't be."

"It is," Talbot said. "It's the belt that killed her."

"Faced—no, confronted is the proper word, isn't it? Well, confronted with this bit or shred of damning evidence," Betsey said acidly, "Mrs. Porter expressed herself in a brief but comprehensive monosyllable. Pooh, said Mrs. Porter."

"Those men—" Carol began.

"Of course it was those men," Betsey said. "My coat was open, and Johann or one of the lads saw that my belt was like the one on the floor, and did some handing that was quicker than the eye. Or else they found it out in the kitchen or somewhere, and stuck it there—"

Her sentence stopped in mid-air as Asey's blue eyes fixed themselves on her.

There was something about that piercing look that made people feel Asey had somehow penetrated their heads, and was strolling around intimately inside their thoughts.

"Well," Betsey said, "how else did the belt get there?"

Asey turned and looked at Carol.

She made a tremendous effort, but after a few seconds her glance wavered.

"It won't work, Bets," Carol said. "She followed me into the cottage, Asey. I went in alone, and I was there for— oh, I don't know how long before she came in after me. And that belt—"

"Darling," Betsey said easily, "I hate like hell to call you a liar, but a ranker fable was never told!"

"It's no lie and you know it isn't!" Carol retorted. "You thought you could pull me out of this by dragging yourself in, but I'm not going to have you play human sacrifice for me. That belt—"

"Caro, I never heard such magnificent fabrication—"

"You know it's the gospel truth—"

Talbot looked at Asey as the two girls, without raising their voices, began a fluent and dogged dispute. He tried once or twice to interrupt, but they didn't pay a whit of attention to him.

Talbot sighed. If Betsey Porter wasn't Betsey Porter, and if the Garth girl wasn't Hector Colvin's relation, he'd soon get the story out of them. But he'd seen Betsey Porter before, and he knew just how far he'd get if he took a high hand. He had more than a suspicion that Betsey Porter knew it, too.

"Get one of your men," Asey said. "Get—there's Finlay outside there. Call him in. Now get some paper an' pencils. Finlay, you see these two women? They're going to do a little writin' for me. Hear that, you two? Each of you write down your story of your comin' here, an' your own particular version of that belt. Understand? Finlay, if either of 'em talks, or tries to carry on in sign language, you got my permission to spank 'em."

Finlay looked at Betsey Porter, and raised his eyebrows.

"If she opens her mouth," Asey said, "smack it. I'm so ashamed of her, I could wallop her— I mean it, Finlay. If they get fresh, treat 'em like the kids they're actin' like. Come on, Talbot!"

With Dr. Budd following, Asey and Talbot started up the terrace to the house.

"Well," Talbot said, "it *is* her belt, all right, and it's *the* belt, too. There are the marks of the braided leather on her throat. And Bert Blossom said Mrs. Garth—Colvin—what *is* her name? I haven't even been able to find that out, yet!"

"Call her Vivian," Asey said.

"Well, Vivian told him she was going to visit Mrs. Porter. There you are. What do you make of it?"

"I thought," Asey said, "them two girls just happened to land into this. Now I'm not so sure that Carol didn't go in first, or Betsey lent her the belt, or what."

"What are they trying to cover up?" Talbot demanded. "Don't they understand yet the spot they're in? This Mrs. Monfort says one of her men saw them go in the cottage, and heard a woman scream, and he went off and got some other servants, and that's what they found. Those two and Vivian. Can't you make 'em understand their position? I don't see, Asey, why they don't get it."

"It's just possible," Asey said, "that they do."

"Then why—"

"Betsey's brain," Asey said, "works a lot quicker than you think. It gets to things quicker than you'd believe possible. Only trouble is, the steps in between ain't always as clear to the male mind as they might be."

"The Pilgrim Camera Club," Ralph Budd observed as they paused at the end of the terrace, "is a little the same way. D'you mean, Asey, you think those two have decided to confuse things to a point where no one can tell what's what, anyway?"

"They made a good beginnin', ain't they?" Asey said. "Well, let's go in—oho, there's a green shirt, skittlin' off to tell Mrs. M. that we're comin'. First I want to call Lewis Garth, an' then let's take a look at the gun room. An', Talbot, I wish you'd try to make Mrs. Monfort pin herself down on who she is, an' what she's doin' here, an' where all her outfit was, around the time that Vivian was killed."

"Perhaps," Talbot said bitterly, "you think I haven't tried?"

The gun room was a bleak east room on the second floor, and it had been dismantled, Asey thought, very quickly indeed. He said as much, and Ralph wanted to know why.

"It looks to me," he continued, "like a pretty thorough job. All those cases packed, and the curtains down, and the rugs up—"

"Uh-huh," Asey said, "but the guns that ain't been put in cases have all got laid on today's evenin' paper."

"What're those things?" Ralph pointed to a glass topped case.

"Four-barrel revolvin'-flintlock pistols," Asey said. "I'd like to see Colvin's face if he caught sight of those items laid around so casual. Look, you go out into the hall, an' bring in that green bloused feller that's hoverin' so handy an' purposeful out there. Seems a shame to make him fidget any longer."

The green bloused man bowed deferentially.

"Where's the gun," Asey asked, "that went off an' wounded someone?"

"Here, sir."

The man swung around and whisked a gun from behind a pile of cases.

Asey grinned at the nickel-plated little .22 that sat forlornly on the gleaming silver tray.

"That? That mangy little thing? So that was what got accidentally fired. An' how nice of you to go an' clean it up so nice! Talbot, how much money would you pay for a weapon like that?"

"I wouldn't," Talbot said promptly.

"Neither would I," Asey said. "It ain't hardly what you'd call a modern weapon, an' I can't imagine why anyone'd want it around the house. A bean blower'd do about as much good in the line of defense. If Hector Colvin— I s'pose it's Hector Colvin's, ain't it?"

"Oh, yes, sir," the green shirted man said. "It was here—"

"Uh-huh. Well, if Hector gave over a dollar forty-nine cash for it, he got stung. Amazin', when you stop to think, Ralph, that them pistols you asked about cost seven or eight hundred. But of course, you couldn't get ammunition off-hand for any of the antiques. An' I s'pose you got lots of cartridges for the .22?"

"I'll show you," the man said uncomfortably, "the box—"

"Don't bother. You," Asey pointed a finger at him and the man jumped, "you seem to have quite a burn on your neck, feller."

"Sir?"

"A burn," Asey said. "A sear, as you might say. A place where you come in contact with somethin' hot—oh, Mrs. Monfort—"

She was breathing heavily, as though she had been hurrying.

"That's quite a burn your man's got," Asey went on conversationally.

"Oh, that. Yes. Our hot water system broke down," she said. "Alex got burned while attempting to repair it. The plumbers had gone. The pipe—what did it do, Alex? It broke, didn't it?"

"Yes, madam." Alex was clearly relieved to have someone to fall back on.

"I see it lamed him a bit, too," Asey said blandly.

"That was the wood," Mrs. Monfort returned with equal blandness. "The fireplace wood was insecurely piled in the cellar. Wasn't that it, Alex?"

"Yes, madam. Carl and I—"

"Were getting wood, and the logs fell. This house," Mrs. Monfort said, "has not been lived in for some time, you know. Things have been disgracefully neglected, or attended to in the most slovenly manner."

While she enumerated the examples of neglect, Talbot nodded and looked sympathetic, and Asey wandered around and looked at the guns.

He had found out what he wanted to find, and a little more besides.

The little twenty-two had been planted among the collectors' items, of course. Hector Colvin had never owned anything like that. And even if he had, that little gun would never have gone off and wounded anyone.

It was Warner, he felt sure, who had shot at that servant, after the hat shooting episode that Carol Garth had witnessed on the beach. It couldn't have been anyone else but Warner.

And Alex and Carl were the fellows who had jumped Jennie, back at his house. Jennie's hot butter had left its mark on Alex's neck, and her kicks had been just as forceful as she said.

No matter how you looked at it, it all boiled down to the fact that Mrs. Monfort, or something to do with her or her household, was the reason for Warner's coming. And their relationship had progressed to an extent where they potted at each other.

"I certainly do hope," Mrs. Monfort said, "that we have no more accidents."

"I hope not," Talbot said politely. "Now, there are several points I should like to clear up. You—er—is there any particular reason for your being here in town?"

Mrs. Monfort stared at him.

"Is there any particular reason," she said, "why I should not be here in town?"

"I mean," Talbot said hastily, "you're a friend of Mr. Colvin's, perhaps?"

"I'm sure," Mrs. Monfort returned, "that even if you do not know Mr. Colvin, you have at least heard enough about him to gather that he would hardly let his house to anyone who was not recommended."

Talbot was stumped.

"And—er—your companion?" he asked weakly.

"Kublai Khan? Khan has just been given her milk and put to bed."

Asey came to the rescue.

"I don't think Mr. Talbot refers to your cat," he said. "He means the woman who saw Mrs. Porter this afternoon. A blonde woman."

"Oh, yes. Eda. Eda has gone away for a few days."

"When did she leave?" Talbot asked quickly.

"What time was it, Alex?" Mrs. Monfort said.

Alex did not quite know, he said. He had not been present.

"I'm sure that it's not important," Mrs. Monfort dismissed the subject. "Now, if you'll excuse me, I shall retire. I shall be glad to assist any of you, of course. Don't hesitate to wake me if you really want to. Good night."

A brief smile flicked over Alex's face as he turned and followed Mrs. Monfort out of the gun room and down the hall.

"If he'd laughed outright," Asey said, "I don't think I'd of blamed him a bit. So we can wake her if we really want to, huh?"

"Personally," Ralph Budd said, "I'd as soon wake a basket of starving rattlesnakes with my bare hands. She's just awfully sorry about Vivian, isn't she? Just too, too moved about it all. What do you want to bet that she sleeps like a log?"

"Why didn't you pin her down, Talbot?" Asey asked.

Talbot glared at him. "I don't think you got so damn far with her, yourself!" he said. "My God, these self-willed women, I never met so many in my life. Now I suppose we've got to tackle Mrs. Porter and the Garth girl—aren't there any men mixed up in this?"

"The servants," Asey said, "for all you know."

"Me no spika da Eng," Talbot said, "or words to that effect. Well, let's get to the greenhouse—"

They found Finlay pacing restlessly back and forth.

He pointed silently to the notebook pages which still lay, untouched, where Asey had left them.

"I think it's a sit-down," Finlay said. "They just sit there and smoke. After you left, they looked at each other and nodded, and then they just sat and smoked."

Betsey looked expectantly at Asey, but instead of speaking to her or Carol, he took Talbot's elbow and went outdoors.

"All right," Talbot said, "now you tell me how to pin these two down. What's the matter with 'em? What'll I *do* with 'em? I can't put 'em in jail, there isn't any handy. If we leave 'em together, they'll cook up something. What'll we do?"

"We ain't goin' to do much of anythin'," Asey said, "until we get the truth out of them. You find some handcuffs, an' we'll see how far they're willin' to carry this business—"

Betsey and Carol eyed the handcuffs with the greatest interest.

"Bracelets. Gyves," Betsey said. "I know, we're going to jail. Do they still pick oakum in the ladies' section, or is that where they make the auto-license plates?"

"I wouldn't know," Asey said, "but you'll soon have every op'tunity of findin' out. Good night. D'you want me to— oh, well, the r'porters'll get hold of Bill sooner or later, prob'ly easier than I can. He's out road-testin' this week. So long."

He strode out the door.

Betsey caught up with him in front of the swimming pool.

"I should have known better," she said contritely, "than to try bluffing you. Come on back, Asey, I had the belt on, but I don't know where I lost it. It might have come off anywhere from the car to the cottage, or in the cottage, or getting over the wall."

"You didn't lend it to Carol?"

"No, she just said that because I'd said that I went into the cottage at the same time she did. That was just her contribution. Actually, she did go in first. But I'll swear she didn't have the belt, Asey. Johann or someone planted it there later. Please come back, Asey. That's absolutely the whole story, that's all, truly!"

Asey did not for one moment think that it was the whole story. But if Betsey had made up her mind that was all the story she intended to tell, there was nothing to be gained from pursuing the matter any further. The time would come, he thought to himself as he followed her back to the greenhouse, when he would find out the rest.

"I certainly am glad you've finally got to believing me," Betsey said in evident relief. "We simply didn't have a thing to do with Vivian Garth, on my word of honor we didn't. I'll admit that perhaps we haven't acted very well—"

"That's one of the finest understatements I ever listened to," Asey said.

"Well, you've got to admit, there's been every reason for us to be a bit upset, and to act strangely—old Monfort's insinuations just scared us to pulp. By the way, where is that wench? I wouldn't put it beyond her to have gone to bed."

"She has," Asey said.

"I can see her," Betsey held out the collar of her trench coat to let the rain run off, "sitting back among little pink satin pillows, her feet all warm and comfy in Jaeger or something. And a nice hot toddy in one hand, and Blackstone in the other. Come tomorrow, she'll probably have me condemned."

"Tomorrow's Sunday," Asey pointed out. "She'll have to wait till Monday mornin' really to get any dirty work done.

Betsey, didn't anyone see you come here, don't anyone know what time you landed here, exactly?"

"I don't think we met a soul on the way over," she said, "except that drunk on a bicycle. He decided abruptly to stop me, and I nearly stopped him permanently. But we were just ships passing in the night—what's to become of us, Carol and me?"

"I'll talk with Talbot about that. It's lucky for you, Betsey Porter, that he knows Bill an' me!"

Lewis Garth arrived before Asey finished his talk with Talbot. He was about twenty-five, tall and very light, and he somehow looked as though he should have an oar over his shoulder or a football in his hand.

He listened to the story from the girls.

"Poor mother," he said, "she's not had a very happy life, has she—oh, Caro, why didn't you tell me that you were coming here?"

"You told us not to disturb you, you were finishing a book—"

"I know, but—why, I'd half a mind to sneak over here myself. I would have, if my car'd been fixed. I nearly set out to swipe yours, Caro. It galled me, that blonde not letting us in our own house! Look, how did mother get here? And when? I thought she was in Spain—and oh, Caro, think of Hector!"

Carol shivered. "Isn't there enough without thinking of him! Mercifully, he's in Monte Carlo, and it'll take him some time to get back in the yacht, even if he decides to come. Considering what he thought of mother, I doubt if he does."

"Yes," Lewis said, "but it all happened here. And you know what that man can do with cables, and phones, and his lawyers!"

"You see," Carol said to Asey, "once you've lived under Hector's thumb, you know what to expect. Well, what do you do with us? And Lewis, you'd better find out what should be done about—about Vivian. Call Mr. Ogilvy. He was always more sympathetic about her than anyone else at Hector's office. Call him and find out—"

Two hours later, Asey crept down the back stairs of his house to the kitchen.

"There!" he said to Jennie, and her husband Syl, who were sitting at the pine table. "Lewis is finally done with his telephonin', an' the girls are in bed. You do just what I told you. There's cops out back an' front. If Warner comes, find out what in tarnation is goin' on—no, don't ask me any more questions, for the love of goodness! I'm goin' out—"

The long roadster slid silently down the driveway and over the road toward Pochet.

Asey clamped his teeth down on his pipe and tried to figure things out.

The whole thing, he decided, was a little worse than the shambles of the Porters' renovation. There were a lot of things going on, but they seemed not to bear the slightest relation to one another.

Warner probably had something to do with Mrs. Monfort. Mrs. Monfort's men didn't like Warner. They shot at each other. That was one item.

If Mrs. Monfort was in Hector Colvin's house, she probably had something to do with Hector Colvin. Hector Colvin was abroad.

From there on, Asey thought, you could practically write your own ticket. Hector hated his sister Vivian, who was supposed to be in Spain. But Vivian was strangled in the Garth cottage on Hector's estate. That brought you to Betsey and Carol, and the thought of all their complications made Asey sigh deeply. The only fact that emerged with any degree of definiteness was that Mrs. Monfort was going to involve the girls as much as she could, and she had what amounted to every reason for doing so.

And then there was the blonde who had disappeared. Why had she started out by holding the center of the stage, only to be shoved into the wings at this point? Everyone had spoken of the blonde. Everyone had noticed her. But now it was Mrs. Monfort who appeared as the ruling power in the household.

"I'm a fool," Asey told himself. "A fool!"

That was just exactly what the blonde was there for, to hold the spotlight. She was like the magician's patter, something to distract you while the rabbits turned into an American flag wrapped around a puppy. While the blonde paraded for the edification of the natives, Mrs. Monfort quietly went around about her business, whatever business it was that had brought her here. But now that Vivian had been murdered, Mrs. Monfort had been forced to take charge and come out into the open.

And the exotic blonde—wherever she'd gone, she was going to be produced, Asey thought. There wasn't any reason why she might not have killed Vivian, herself.

Without quite knowing why he did so, Asey drove past the Colvin estate and pulled up beyond the boundary wall, by the side of the road. After he had brooded over things, he'd go in and mosey around.

He wondered, as he lighted his pipe, why Vivian had turned up. She had called herself Colvin, and told Bert Blossom that she was going to visit Mrs. Porter. Both facts bothered Talbot, but to Asey they seemed natural enough. There was no simpler or quicker method of identifying herself as belonging to the elect. But why Vivian had come, and why the Garths were there—that business of collecting childhood trinkets seemed just a little too precious.

One of the police cars swung down the Colvin drive.

Talbot, Asey decided. Talbot had a day in court ahead of him on Monday, and a trip to Boston that night. Someone was staging one of those sporadic racket clean-ups, and even Talbot didn't know what had become of half his men. He had been beefing about it all.

The car swung back. Asey smiled, and wondered how blue the air was. Talbot always forgot things, and he always swore in exactly the same words when he went back to get things.

But the car did not turn up the Colvin drive.

Instead it passed the entrance and slowly picked up speed. By the time it passed Asey, it was roaring along.

Asey's hand went to the starter button.

That car, he knew, was a Porter. The police did not have Porters.

But Mrs. Monfort had one in the garage.

6.

A PORTER limousine, in Hector Colvin's garage. The three confiscated bicycles of the Pilgrim Camera Club had been lined up alongside all its gleaming elegance.

Without turning on his lights, Asey cut his roadster back on the road and slowly started after.

So now Mrs. Monfort was taking a surreptitious spin in her shiny car, was she?

Grinning, Asey settled himself behind the wheel.

At a crossroads some twenty yards ahead, he snapped on his headlights, but he made no attempt to close up the distance between him and the car ahead. He had no desire to catch Mrs. Monfort. He wanted to know where she was going, and what she was doing. His only task was to keep the tail lights of the Porter in sight.

It was stupid of him not to have gathered that something like this was going to take place. She had squelched Talbot so completely, she had made such a gesture of retiring, she had so effectively prevented any chance of being disturbed. Her acrid invitation to waken her if they really wanted to was enough to keep them away. Of course she had planned it all.

"Game to Mrs. Monfort." Asey gave the devil her due.

Alex's smile alone should have warned him.

He slowed down. He was getting too near. The road was getting worse, too.

Asey wished that Dr. Cummings, or Betsey, or any of those people who always accused him of driving at such a furious pace—he wished, violently, that they could see him padding along after Mrs. Monfort at twenty miles an hour!

Yes, this trip had been scheduled, and Mrs. Monfort wasn't going to let anything like a murder prevent her from carrying out her plans. She had simply waited for some of the confusion to die down, waited until enough police cars had come and gone so that the departure of a car was nothing for anyone to get excited about. No one expected her to leave, so no one had been watching for her. With all the rain, no one had bothered to set a guard at the gates. And Talbot, Asey remembered, had commandeered one of the cars in the garage, a beach wagon. There was a car shortage, and the limousine's use wouldn't have attracted attention. Probably no one even noticed.

The car ahead swerved sharply, and then proceeded at an even slower pace.

"Thanks," Asey said, and in turn swerved around a steam roller, abandoned in the center of the road, whose lanterns had not apparently survived the rain.

It was not a roller, he decided as he shifted, but a cutter, one of those spiked things for tearing up road surfaces. What was left of the road ahead looked more like the proving ground of the Porter plant.

The drizzle suddenly turned into a pelting rain again, just as Asey discovered that the space beyond the left rut was a four foot drop into the swamp.

He came to a dead stop and waited for the limousine to get along. Mrs. Monfort's driver, whichever one of the green shirts it was, had obviously not spent any time on proving grounds.

"Come, come," Asey said impatiently. "Get a wiggle on, you! Get on with it! What you so scared of? By golly, for two cents I'd give you a push!"

Chasing a car that barely crawled was something quite new, and not particularly appealing to him.

Forty minutes passed before the torn-up strip was negotiated.

And the strip was not three miles long.

"Now, you snail," Asey spoke with a deadly calm, "get along! You got lovely tar under you. Maybe it was laid in the spring of nineteen-ten, maybe it feels like you was drivin' on a buttered banana peel, maybe it's got a crown— well, it's about time, brother!"

The car jumped ahead, but Asey again made no attempt to follow it closely. If he knew Mrs. Monfort's driver— and after that crawl, he felt that they were old, old friends —the fellow wouldn't tackle any of the side roads. He could hardly know about them, and besides, such a timid soul wouldn't want to. That left only one possible destination, the bay side of Weesit.

The limousine continued to pick up speed.

Then, suddenly, the brake lights of the car ahead flashed on, and as suddenly, all the lights went out.

Asey's foot jammed down on the accelerator just as a man jumped into the road before him.

"You couldn't," he told Bill Porter later, "beat the brakes

on that car. You never will. That roadster stood up on its hind legs an' clawed the air. An' then it wobbled a little to the right, an' then it wobbled a little to the left, an' then it pawed the rain, an' then it really got into action an' did the Big Apple from start to finish. With two new steps. Did it stop? Oh, yes. It stopped not two feet from where it started to stop. But we'd veered off a bit to starboard, like. About twelve feet off, in a sort of sink hole."

Asey removed the pipe stem from his mouth and wondered where the bowl had landed.

He found it and tossed it out the window, narrowly missing the man who approached.

"Have you," the man inquired politely, "seen an elephant?"

"Have I what?" Asey paused between each word.

"Have you seen an elephant?"

Asey leaned back against the car seat.

"Have you seen—"

"I know," Asey said. "I heard you. I heard you very distinctly. You asked me if I'd seen an elephant."

"Have you?"

"An' I," Asey said, "am countin' to five hundred by fives before I answer you."

The man waited.

"There," Asey said. "I don't honestly think it's done much good. Look, let's get this straight. You see my car comin', an' you march—you leap—you dash out in front of it. Directly in front of it. You—"

"You stopped very quickly, didn't you?" the man said. "You must have good brakes."

Asey's fingers drummed against the wheel of the car.

"Are you counting again?" the man inquired.

"You stopped me," Asey said, "an'—do I understand, mister, that your purpose in stoppin' me was to ask me if I've seen an elephant? Think, now, before you answer. Did you stop me to ask if I'd seen an elephant?"

"Yes, I tried to get to the road in time to stop that car ahead, but they were going too fast."

"That car ahead," Asey remarked. "That car that is now—well, I suppose that the Almighty is the only one who could tell where it's gone now. Durin' the process of pausin' for you, I sort of lost track of that car."

"Oh, it went right along," the man said. "It stopped, but it went along again."

"I bet it did," Asey said. "I just bet it did. Game, to Mrs. Monfort."

He leaned forward and pulled a flashlight from its clamp behind the dash.

"You don't," he snapped it on and considered the man, "you don't look like Fate, do you? You know, you don't even look drunk!"

The man was hurt by the suggestion.

"I don't drink," he said with dignity. "I signed the pledge when I was ten and a half, and I always keep my pledges."

"If I'd known that," Asey observed, "I shouldn't have counted so hard. Then it's just a whim of yours, like, prancin' in front of cars an' askin' people if they've seen elephants?"

"Just one elephant," the man corrected him.

"Just one ittle bitty elephant," Asey said. "Just—"

"He's not as small as that," the man said. "I mean, he's small, yes. But not—"

"Not as small as ittle bitty," Asey said. "I see. Do I begin to gather that you've lost one small elephant?"

"Yes. Aren't you going to get out of the car?"

"Why?" Asey asked.

"To see if it's hurt—you're really on quite an angle there. That's a ditch you're in."

"I guessed that," Asey told him. "Right off the bat I said to myself, 'Mayo, you're in a ditch, you are.'"

"But shouldn't you see if your car is damaged?"

"I know this car," Asey said, "an' it ain't damaged. It's stuck. But I don't know the ditch."

"Then shouldn't you get out?"

"I might," Asey said, "I might get out an' get all damp, but I think I'll sit right here an' wait for daylight or another car, whichever comes first."

The man waited, apparently digesting Asey's words.

"Then," he said, "if you're going to wait here, should you mind if I sat inside with you?"

"Haven't you caused me enough grief?" Asey had no desire to while away the rest of the night with this lunatic, even though he was a polite and harmless appearing lunatic. "Haven't you—don't you think you'd best go find other cars to stop?"

"There aren't very many cars out tonight," the man said with perfect candor. "And I've lost my vehicle."

"You mean, the elephant?"

"No, my bicycle. It wasn't my bicycle, either. I borrowed it. You know, it's really very wet out here."

"Oh, come in!" Asey said wearily. "Slosh around to the other door an' get inside!"

After all, the man was shivering cold, and wet to the skin.

He snapped on his flashlight and found a blanket, which the man accepted gratefully.

"You're a Cape Codder, aren't you? A real native?"

Asey admitted that he was.

"I guessed it by the way you talk," the man said with a certain quiet pride. "No g's, and all that. The Cape is not a very hospitable spot, is it?"

"If," Asey said, "you been goin' around stoppin' people, askin' 'em if they've seen an elephant, I think I can understand how you might get that impression. Look, what about this elephant, this small elephant of yours, anyway?"

"It's not *my* elephant—"

"Oh, I see. Borrowed, like your bicycle, huh?"

"It's Mr. Romano's elephant. It belongs to Mr. Romano's show. Not," the man added critically, "a very good show. Mr. Romano sells vanilla and flavorings and hair tonic and regulators. It's not real vanilla. It's tonka bean. I don't know about the rest. I never tasted them."

Asey leaned back and laughed until the tears rolled down his cheeks.

"Romano," he said at last, "he—oh, golly, tonka bean! Romano has a medicine show, is that it? An' you really lost an elephant that belongs to the show?"

"Yes. I don't think Mr. Romano really cared. I think he

was glad. It cost so much to feed. And elephants don't seem to have the appeal they had when I was a boy. I think it's the moving pictures. People are used to elephants. People are used to so many things nowadays, don't you think?" the man added. The blanket, it seemed, was thawing him into a philosophical frame of mind. "They really are. As I said to Mr. Romano last week, I wonder if perhaps people don't know too much."

Asey chuckled. "I gather," he said, "that business ain't been so good. When'd you lose the elephant?"

"He was gone yesterday morning. I think he left during the night. He doesn't like the rain much. Of course I offered to help find him, and Mr. Romano lent me his son's bicycle—his son does a bicycle act, and it's rather a strange bicycle, it comes apart. That's why I lost it. The last time it came apart, I couldn't find it."

Asey howled.

"So you went off yest'day mornin'," he said, "on a collapsible bicycle, to find an elephant. My, my! What's your part with this outfit, do you take care of the beast?"

"Mr. Romano's son does that. I make the vanilla and the flavorings, and all."

"But you never tasted 'em. I see. Did Mr. Romano's son hunt, too?"

"I think so," the man said cautiously. "Mr. Romano told me to hunt, and if I couldn't find him by Sunday, to give it up and come back."

"Oh, he did, did he?" Asey said. "It wouldn't be possible that Mr. Romano owed you money, would it?"

"He owed me three weeks," the man said. "So I thought,

just to be on the safe side, I'd better take it before I left. Of course, Mr. Romano is a very honest man, and his son is very honest, but I never entirely trusted his wife. I'm very glad now that I took the money, because a man told me this evening that Mr. Romano *had* gone."

"Mister," Asey said, "I—what is your name?"

"I'm afraid it's not a very unusual name. It's Smith. Leopold Smith."

"Mister Smith," Asey said, "I've cruelly misjudged you. But now that Romano's departed, what's goin' to happen to you an' the elephant?"

"I think I'll go to Schenectady," Smith said. "There's a man in Schenectady who can always use me. He makes hair tonics. Of course I would like to find Frederick before I go. That's the elephant's name, Frederick. But I'm not quite sure what I could do with Frederick if I did find him. Perhaps you could see to it that he gets a good home, when he's found?"

"There's always my spare bedroom," Asey said.

"You joke a lot, don't you?" Smith said. "I thought as much when you turned on the flashlight and said I didn't look like Fate. But many a true word is spoken in jest, I suppose. Perhaps if I hadn't stopped you, you might have had an accident and been killed. Perhaps that car ahead was waiting for you, to rob you or something. I don't suppose we can ever tell what form Fate will appear in, can we?"

Asey, looking outside at the mud and the rain and the side of the ditch, agreed.

"Leopold F. Smith," he said. "F for Fate."

The truth of that particular jest first dawned on Asey

hours later, long after Leopold Smith had gone his literal way on a milk truck.

"Harry," Asey said to Noah Snow's father, who had just finished extracting the roadster from the mud hole, "I'm pained to tell you that the garage'll have to send a bill. I got wallet trouble."

"Forgot it, huh? Well, don't lose any sleep—"

"No, I didn't forget it," Asey said. "Believe it or not, Harry, it got removed by a gent name of Smith. Go on an' laugh."

"I am," Snow said. "From you, of all people! By a man named Smith!"

"He'd lost an elephant, if that makes it any funnier," Asey said. "Named Frederick. Harry, I don't mind the wallet so much, but Frederick's goin' to haunt me for some time to come."

"That the elephant you got over to your house?" Snow inquired.

"What!"

"Why, yes. The twins called Noah around six this morning about it. I guess the doctor'd told them. They set right out with their cameras—"

"You're makin' it up!"

"Oh, no," Harry said. "I thought you knew—but of course, you been here all night. Heard of this mess up at Hector Colvin's, I s'pose."

Asey said that the mess had come to his attention.

"I thought it probably had. She's all right, Asey," Snow referred to the car, "but it's just as well you didn't try to work her out of that muck by yourself. Yes, I guessed you'd probably know about Vivian Garth. I wonder who's goin' to break the news to Colvin, or have they? There's a job I wouldn't relish."

"Thank the Lord," Asey said, "Colvin's over the seas an' far away. I hate to contemplate what this affair'd turn into if Hector was here in person— Harry, I don't like that look on your face. There's a leer about it."

"Colvin's here," Snow said. "His yacht anchored off Weesit last evening—"

7. ASEY had hoped, as he wearily turned the roadster toward home, that both items of Snow's information would turn out to be completely and definitely wrong. To be sure, Snow had a reputation for veracity, but it didn't seem quite fair at this point to have both Hector Colvin and an elephant wafted simultaneously into all the mess there was already.

But at the South Pochet crossroads, thumbing for a ride, stood a sailor with 'Dorinda' in small red letters on his jersey. In town he caught sight of a steward.

Asey sighed.

Hector Colvin had returned, all right, and something told him that the elephant would probably be there, too.

And it was, chained to an elm in the yard by the side of his house.

The thin drizzle hampered his first view of it, but Asey could see that it was not a large elephant. He had seen larger elephants. On the other hand, Leopold Smith had accurately rejected "ittle bitty" as the ideal adjectives to apply to its size.

Around the beast were grouped the Pilgrim Camera Club, his cousin Syl Mayo, a state trooper, and any number of neighbors.

Asey sighed again, and got out of the car. At least this was a problem you could see, and cope with.

Betsey Porter and Jennie Mayo came out of the house and hurried over to him.

"That splendid elephant!" Betsey said. "Where did you get it, Asey? How did it know where to come?"

"Did it?" Asey asked.

"Why, it just loped up to the front door about four this morning, nearly scared us all to bits! And then it bumbled over here to the field, as though he liked the field, and we didn't know quite what to do, until the milk man brought the note—"

"What note?"

Jennie gave him a crumpled milk order blank, and Asey turned it over and read the writing on the back.

"Dear Mr. Mayo, I understand from the milk truck driver that Frederick is already at your house. I am sure you will like him. Mr. Romano always said Frederick saw the funny side too. If you plough, you could use Frederick. Sincerely yrs, Leopold Smith. P.S. If I had more room, I would make you out a bill of sale."

Asey thrust the paper into his pocket.

"Isn't he a dear?" Betsey said enthusiastically. "He's the dearest beast—listen, he's talking, Asey. I think he's hungry. He's already drunk about a million gallons of water that the boys have fetched for him—"

"Thirty-two," Pink said. "The elephants at the circus drank more."

"What are you going to do with him, Asey?" Betsey demanded. "Can I have him for the church fair and the club bazaar, later?"

A sudden gleam appeared in Asey's eyes.

"Lend Frederick for a lot of folks to goggle at?" he said. "I guess not!"

"Is his name Frederick? Oh, I wish I had him!" Betsey said. "I've always loved elephants!"

"What would you feed it?" Asey asked.

"Oh, peanuts, of course. And shoots."

"An' what?"

"Shoots," Betsey said, vaguely waving a hand. "Tender shoots of something. Oh, I wish I had him, Asey. You know last year we had those darling long-haired kittens, and it was perfectly wonderful. All summer long, our guests just sat and played with the kittens. I didn't have to entertain people at all. They just sat on the floor and dragged pieces of string, and threw balls."

"D'you think," Asey said, "your guests'll throw ping-pong balls to the elephant?"

"No, but you know what I mean. What are you writing so busily?"

"Got a dollar?" Asey asked.

Betsey fished in the pocket of her coat. "Here. What for? What's that paper?"

"Take it," Asey put it into her hand. "There! That's a bill of sale, Betsey. For the sum of one dollar an' other considerations an' whatnot, you're the owner of an elephant name of Frederick. Please to feed your elephant, Mrs. Porter, an' get him out of range of my garden. If he's there in an hour, I'll sue you for damages, an' the Porter comp'ny can't afford a damage suit."

Betsey look at him.

"What—what do I feed him?" she said.

"Well, I'd begin with a couple bales of hay, an' seein' he's had to forage for a day or so, I think I'd let him top off with some carrots. Couple bushels ought to do, I think."

Betsey grinned, and Asey grinned back.

"If you meant to get back at me for the way I acted last night," she said, "you have. We'll call it quits, Asey. Hey, Pink. Does the Pilgrim Camera Club want to go on the Porter payroll? Fine, you're on it!"

Before going into the house, Asey walked over and took a closer look at the elephant.

"Kind of beady-eyed," his cousin Syl remarked.

Asey nodded. Frederick might have a great sense of humor but it was not very apparent.

"Fighter, too," Syl said. "They cut his tusk off, see? Looks like they'd banded it, too, to keep from splittin'."

"I think," Asey said, "I'm goin' to like Frederick better in his new home, an' he'll loom higher in my estimation the sooner he gets to Bill Porter's."

"Bill Porter," Syl said, "won't thank you none."

Asey chuckled and went indoors. He washed his hands of Frederick. Betsey could do all the explaining about him from now on.

Talbot came as Asey began breakfast after changing his clothes.

"I know," Asey said. "Hector's here. You hoped a man would come into this case, an' didn't you get one!"

Talbot poured himself a cup of coffee before he answered.

"There is this advantage," he said. "The reporters are swarming around him. Vivian, Mrs. Monfort, me and my men, we might as well be two other places. That suits me very well. It's the only thing that does."

"Who told Hector?"

"He seemed to be in full possession of the facts," Talbot said, "when he barged in a little while ago. He was really too busy asking me questions for me to find out much from him."

Asey grinned. "An' what's Hector's impression of things?"

"He's said quite a lot," Talbot told him. "He considers the police quite bright, ordinarily, but in this case, we have achieved heights of stupidity which he personally would not have believed possible, unless he had seen them with his own two eyes. I quote."

"What's Hector want done?"

"He wants us to catch Vivian Garth's murderer at once," Talbot said. "At once, without any more stupid delay. He wants this whole horrid matter settled so that he can get on with his vacation. On the whole—can I have some toast? On the whole, he was more moved about Vivian than Mrs. Monfort was last night. He said, it was too bad for Vivian, but of course one chose one's way of life, and if one lived it, one had to take the consequences."

"There's somethin' nice about people like Hector," Asey said. "They decide at birth what they're goin' to be, an' they get to be it. Hector decided he was goin' to be the big-whackingest banker goin', an' he did. There's a sort of holy purpose to the lives of people like that, an' it's all real nice. Only it don't give 'em much insight into the frailties of human nature. It never occurs to 'em that other people like to try side roads."

Talbot lighted a cigarette. "That's probably as kindly a thing as you can say for Colvin. You know, Asey, I resent his attitude. We're not dumb. We've got the hell of a lot done since last night. We've found out the hell of a lot of things about Vivian."

"Like what? Like where she came from?"

"She left Spain last autumn," Talbot said. "Her husband had been killed in the war, and she was broke. Some charitable English people got her to London, and she moved around in the best circles until November, when she just disappeared. Just evaporated. We can't find any trace of her from then until now. I had half a dozen people going into that end of it. Then I got to figuring about passports, and how she got into this country. But as far as the government's concerned, Vivian's not here. No record of her as Colvin, or Garth, or any of the names in between up to the last, Alvarez. And believe me, it wasn't any cinch to find out that much. We burned up the phones. We even called London on her."

"She came in a car," Asey said, "so—"

"We found it after you left, and boy, we've played with that! Second hand coup she bought in New York last week. Fifty bucks down. She paid cash, and then wangled it back from the salesman in a friendly game of craps, later. Used the name of Garth, gave Hector as her reference. Then—"

"Didn't you find her license or registration?"

"It was a boarding house address," Talbot said. "No record of any Garth, Colvin, or anything in between there, either. Her description doesn't fit anyone there. I know some of the boys over in New York, and they did their best for me, but that's all they can find out. There you are. I'll admit it isn't a very spectacular lot of information, but I'd just like to see Colvin get his hands on as much in as short a time, with nothing to work with!"

Asey puffed at his pipe.

"I understand it perfectly," he said, "but of course, all Hector Colvin'd grasp is that you don't know where she come from, or how long she'd been there. Anyway, if she bought a car, she was plannin' to come somewhere, an' most likely it was here."

"I said something like that to Colvin," Talbot returned, "and he said, obviously she'd planned to come here, you didn't just go places on the spur of the moment."

Asey got up and paced around the room.

"Oh, we found out about the Garths, too," Talbot added. "Lewis works for an investment firm, and Carol is a sculptor—well, not exactly a sculptor. She makes bowls and plates and bookends and things. Lives in Connecticut. Lewis lives in New York. Both of 'em perfectly okay, great credits to their businesses and all. The girl pays the thump of an income tax—what are you grinning about?"

"Thinking of Hector," Asey said. "Wait'll I work this out, now. Sit there while I go into the shed."

He appeared later with an armful of newspapers, and at last found what he wanted.

"Listen," he said. "On March twenty-fifth, Hector Colvin, in his Diesel yacht 'Dorinda,' sailed for Mediterranean ports. Here's a picture of the 'Dorinda,' an' an insert of her skipper. He's a Pochet man, by the way. Now, on April twelfth, here's an item about the 'Dorinda' arrivin' at Monte Carlo, after buckin' the storm that—an' so on. Now, Hector's here. Hector says, you don't go places on the spur of the minute. That means that a bit more than two weeks ago, Hector planned to come here. You can carry on the trend of thought from there."

Talbot nodded slowly.

"We morons," he said, "that is, us dopes of coppers, we'll look into Hector. The 'Dorinda' came in about eight, he said. That checks. People saw her. What are Hector and Mrs. Monfort to each other, Asey, and where's that blonde who was at the house?"

"I wouldn't know about her," Asey said, "but Hector and Mrs. M. are on visitin' terms. I'm sure of that. Or was it you in the limousine?"

"Go on, Sherlock," Talbot said. "You interest me greatly. D'you mean that the lady sneaked out under the noses of us dopes?"

Briefly, Asey told him the story of the night's happenings.

"So," he concluded, "owin' to Mr. Smith, I lost 'em!"

"That was a pity," Talbot said. "And they were headed toward Weesit?"

"Yes, that road runs out along the bay. 'Course, it might not of been Mrs. Monfort. Maybe I'm doin' her a great wrong."

"I don't think so," Talbot said. "I'm sure it was Monfort. She inquired for you very solicitously this morning, and hoped you'd had a good night's rest. I said, as far as I knew, you had. She said she hoped so, and she thought you were a very astute man. I concurred."

"Awful astute," Asey said. "Leopold picks my pocket like I was a babe in arms—y'know, I wish you'd find Leopold for me."

Talbot grinned. "Want your wallet back, do you?"

"No," Asey said. "He give me my money's worth in sheer entertainment. But I think it would be fun to look more closely into Leopold Smith. Betsey said that a drunk on a bicycle hailed her near Colvin's, just before she an' Carol swung off the main road last night. I asked her, while I was gettin' those newspapers just now, an' she said the man wanted to know if she'd seen an elephant. She thought he was drunk, and went on. An' the man swerved, an' she says she nearly ran him down. That sounds to me very much like Leopold an' Mr. Romano's son's trick vehicle."

"Give us a description, and that bit of writing on his note to you," Talbot said, "and I'll see what we can do. You think he might have had anything to do with all this?"

"Wa-el," Asey drawled, "you couldn't make any rash statements about a man like that. Anyone who could pick me clean, so neat an' easy, could do most anythin'. But Leopold might have seen somethin'. I'm in favor of almost anythin' that'd help out Betsey an' Carol. You come to any conclusions about them?"

"I do wish they'd stayed home," Talbot said.

"So do I, but what're you goin' to do with 'em?"

Talbot hesitated before answering.

"If you'd only find me a first class suspect," he said, "by tomorrow. Someone we could really take a bite out of. But why in the name of common sense would Betsey Porter want to kill Vivian? She wouldn't. She couldn't. She doesn't even know the woman anyway. Carol Garth has plenty of money. She seems to be perfectly happy and successful, she hasn't seen her mother for years and years, and considering how the girl acted last night, I'd say she was genuinely sorry for Vivian. Why would Carol want to kill her? Why would anyone want to kill Vivian, when you come right down to it? If you can't find me a suspect, Asey, I wish you'd find me a motive."

Asey chewed on his pipe stem.

"And don't," Talbot went on, "say there are two motives, love and money. Vivian had five dollars cash in her pocketbook, and if she'd had money, she wouldn't be hiding away from all her gay pals. And as for love—hell, she's married half the world! From what I've found out about Vivian, she was always ready to marry anyone, and she was open to all suggestions. Why would anyone kill her?"

"You know," Asey said, "if Vivian didn't have money, it's just possible that she was comin' to get some you're lookin' into Mrs. Monfort?"

"Yes, we're—what's going on out there?"

Asey went to the window.

"Frederick," he said, "is startin' off for his new home, an' —my, my, I guess I better help out there."

Frederick, Betsey said, didn't want to go.

"Asey, Frederick shakes hands," she added proudly. "He

just wound his trunk around Pokey and lifted him up off the ground—isn't that shaking hands with an elephant, Talbot?"

"All I know about elephants," Talbot said, "is that I saw Molly, Waddy and Tony when I was eight. At the old Keith's in Boston, and they gave away little coin banks shaped like elephants. And I never cared much for elephants after I found out that you couldn't get the pennies out."

"I got the screw loose in mine," Betsey said, "and stole consistently from myself. So, I like elephants—oh, did he hurt your hat, Syl? He was just playing—Asey, how do you get an elephant to start?"

"What do you think I am, a mahaut?" Asey demanded. "He's your elephant. You start him."

The pastime of starting Frederick enlarged the group in Asey's field, and with the advent of an audience, Frederick decided to show off.

Asey was picking the twins off the end of an elm branch, where Frederick had playfully deposited them, when a cavalcade of automobiles rolled into the drive.

"Hector!" Lewis said. "Good God, it's Hector!"

"Uncle!" Carol looked wide-eyed at the cars. "Oh, Asey, why didn't you warn us—duck, Lewis! Around the ell—"

But before they could escape, they were confronted by the small brisk figure of Hector Colvin.

"I want you two," he said. "Where's Mayo? I want him, at once!"

The automobiles had startled Frederick, but at the sight of Hector, his sense of humor became aroused. Tooting with mirth, Frederick kicked over his water buckets and started out of the field and up the road, with Syl and the Pilgrim Camera Club galloping after him.

"Mayo," Hector Colvin said sternly, "is this any time to be playing with elephants? And Talbot—is that you, Talbot? I thought you told me you were on your way to Boston!"

"I am," Talbot said. "My plane is over at the landing."

"Plane, indeed! Does the state supply you with planes?"

"No, it's mine," Talbot said.

"And what is a man with a private plane doing in the police?"

"Flying it," Talbot said, "and eating. I had to do something, after you closed Bowman's down in twenty-nine. See you later, Asey."

He returned almost at once. "Oh, I forgot," he said. "Max's in charge over there, and the boss said for you to shine up your badge and rally around."

Hector Colvin watched him go.

"Is that Barton Talbot's son?" he said at last.

"Uh-huh," Asey answered. "You wanted me?"

"Yes. Come in your house away from all this crowd," Colvin said. "You too, Carol and Lewis!"

There was something about the way that Hector marched them across the lawn that made Asey think of Dr. Lane and the old Wellfleet Academy filing into class.

"Pupils," Carol echoed his thoughts in an undertone, "will refrain from conversation during walks—"

Two secretaries fell in behind them, earnest young men with thick tortoise-shell glasses.

"Hi, Basil," Lewis greeted the tall one. "How're you—"
Hector glared him into silence.

It took some time for him to seat everyone according to his desires.

"There," he said at last, "there, that will do. Basil, take notes. Carol, Lewis, what are you two doing here?"

Carol and Lewis looked at each other, but neither answered.

Hector repeated his question.

"Frankly, uncle," Carol said, "d'you think it should matter to you?"

"Do you realize that your mother has been killed? Murdered? In my house—"

"Our house," Lewis said. "Our cottage, uncle."

"Don't quibble, sir! What are you doing here?"

"Sir," Lewis said, "it is the custom of our firm to send a man to Boston several times a year, to investigate certain conditions and to—"

"I don't care a fig for your firm! Why are you here?"

"My firm sent me to Boston, sir, and—"

"I said, here!"

"You told us to come in here, uncle," Carol said. "You distinctly ordered us to follow you in. We did. That's why we're here."

The secretary named Basil looked at her in amazement. Hector Colvin stared at her, too. But when he spoke again, some of the bite had gone out of his voice.

"Carol," he said, "I never liked your mother. When she left your father, I promised him that night that I would look after you two children. I did the best I could to bring you up. Possibly others might have done it better, but I did as well as I could. Considering your progress, I think you will have to admit that your bringing up was not a total failure. You were amply provided for by your father. You owe me nothing. You are right, in one sense, in bringing me to task for the way I ordered you about. But you see, this matter concerns you and Lewis and me, not as three individuals, but as a family."

Lewis nodded, and after a second, Carol nodded too.

Asey leaned back in his chair and thought of Bill Porter's description of the first board meeting he ever attended at which Hector Colvin was also present.

"The old buzzard," Bill had said, "he starts out clawing at your throat. If you claw back, then he mellows you. You think what a fine guy this Colvin is, and while you're patting yourself on the back that you know such a fine, upstanding man, he knocks you cold with a rabbit punch."

"The police," Hector continued, "the press, my business, your businesses, our friends—all have to be taken into consideration. My lawyers are coming here, of course, but I want things straightened out. You'll agree with me, I'm sure, that that is the only way."

Asey only half listened while Lewis explained that he and Carol had decided to get some old trinkets and playthings from the cottage, that his trip to Boston provided an ideal opportunity for him to continue down to the Cape. He'd planned his work in the hope that he could take a few days off, the plans had materialized, and Carol was phoned, and she came.

Hector, however, listened interestedly, and then suggested that perhaps they would provide him with an exact list of the things they wanted.

Asey stifled a yawn and poked with the toe of his boot at the pile of newspapers that he had brought in from the shed.

"And then some things in the little wall safe, upstairs," Carol said. "That's all."

"What were they?" Hector asked.

"Mother's wedding ring," Lewis said casually, "and some beads and things of hers. I've got her list here—"

"So!" Hector said. "That was what I wanted to find out! So, you and your mother planned to come here, did you?"

"Why, no," Lewis said. "Not at all. She wrote me from Spain last September—"

"And you just got around to coming here? Oh, no, my boy! That won't do, that won't do at all!"

Lewis turned very red. "If you want to know," he said, "I hadn't any intention of getting those things for mother, at first. And then—well, I'm sort of engaged, and I wanted those miniatures—that is, one of 'em, one of father and mother, and Carol and me. To give this girl. And—well, I didn't want to barge up here alone, and I thought Caro might want things, and she did—"

"And so we waited until we supposed you were safely gone," Carol resented the way that Hector had bullied her brother, "and we came to get our things from our house! And neither of us dreamed that mother was within a million miles of here!"

"Indeed," Hector said, "and where were you going to

send these things that you were going to get for your mother?"

"Here," Lewis drew a folded letter from his pocketbook. "Here, read this, uncle. There's her bank address, and what she wanted, and you can see that the letter's dated—"

Hector Colvin looked at the letter and laughed shortly.

"I see," he said, "that you haven't the envelope—what did you say, Asey? Did you interrupt me?"

"I did," Asey said briskly. "I said, stop all this tommyrot nonsense."

The two secretaries looked aghast.

"You lads run along," Asey said. "Basil an' whatever your name is. Beat it. Run 'em out, Lewis. Carol, you run along too. You—"

"My good man," Colvin said, "have you lost your senses?"

"You," Asey said, "you heard Talbot say that I was to rally around, didn't you? To—"

"You have no official connection with the police—"

"That," Asey said, "is what you think. Close the door behind you, Lewis. That's right. Now, Mr. Hector Colvin," Asey walked over and stood in front of him, "let me ask you a few things for a change. Why are you so awful anxious to prove that the Garths knew all about their mother bein' here, when they didn't know any such thing?"

"I'm not trying to prove any such thing—"

"You're tryin' so hard," Asey said, "to get Carol an' Lewis messed up in this, it just sort of sticks out all over you. It's written in large letters over your head, like a Neon sign. 'Mess them up, before someone finds out about me.'"

Hector, Asey noted with pleasure, was beginning to turn a little white around the gills.

"There is nothing," Hector said, "to—"

"No? Then why did you bring Vivian here from England last November?"

"How," Hector, the indomitable Hector, was almost gurgling with fear. "How—"

"How what?"

"How did you find that out!"

$8.$ THE TROUBLE, Asey thought as he stared at Hector with what he hoped was a stern and malevolent stare, the trouble with bluffing things out of people that way was the complete lack of any follow-up. If Hector Colvin were to ask, "So what?" Asey would just have to fold his tents and steal away as gracefully as possible.

"How do I know?" Asey asked, more to gain time than anything else. "How do you suppose I know? It's my business to know things. Everythin'."

Actually, of course, he didn't know one single thing. The paper he had been kicking with his toe contained the item about the 'Dorinda,' with the picture of the craft and her captain. Underneath had been the simple statement that the 'Dorinda's' last crossing was in November.

But his bluff worked.

He paced around the room while Hector poured out the piteous story of Vivian, and how he had come to her rescue and brought her home.

The last of her money had gone, it seemed. The last of a sizeable fortune. Her last husband was the worst spendthrift of the lot, and their home in Spain had been destroyed. People had supported Vivian on her return to London, but eventually there came a day of reckoning.

"Bad checks," Hector said. "Bills. Bills and bad checks.

It took my staff three days—three whole days, mind you, just to get to the root of the situation. And that was not all. She was involved in some blackmailing scheme. I had to get her out of the country. I did. I gave her money, and told her that I would continue to have a certain amount deposited to her account monthly, and I didn't stint her, Mayo. But I made it clear that if she ran into debt, there would be no further aid forthcoming from me. And I told her that if she became involved in any more unsavory schemes, I would not help her."

"You got her in without a passport," Asey said.

"I had to. I left her in New York, and I have not seen her since that day."

"Didn't you even bother to check up on her?"

"She collected her money at the bank every month," Hector said. "That was enough. More, really, than I cared to know about her. I warned her to keep away from Carol and Lewis. I did not warn them, because I felt my warning might only prejudice them in her favor. I have no doubt that she wrote Lewis as a preliminary step toward sounding him out for money. My sister, Mayo, was not a reputable person. She was boundlessly extravagant. All she ever wanted in this world was money, and men. I bullied the children just now, because I wanted to see if she'd been after them for money—of course they have plenty. I wondered if she had some scheme cooked up to bring them down here and fleece them."

"Why down here?" Asey asked.

"The cottage, old memories, all that sort of thing," Hector said. "Vivian was no fool. If she had intended to get money from them, she would have put on a mother act with all the trimmings. And if she didn't have something like that in mind, I can't imagine what she came here for."

Asey had to admit to himself that Hector's estimate of Vivian, and of her reason for coming to the Cape, was as sound as anything yet advanced.

"You changed your mind about stayin' abroad," Asey remarked. "Sort of sudden, wasn't it, your comin' back?"

Hector sighed.

"What," he said, "this country is coming to—but I won't start off on that. I don't know which is worse, being away and wondering what is going to happen next, or being here and seeing it."

Asey grinned. "An' now," he said, "about Mrs. Monfort. What about her?"

"I feel very deeply," Hector said, "that she should become involved—"

"You know her well?"

"I met her for the first time this morning," Hector said. "She appeared to be a very capable and level-headed individual."

Asey bit his lip.

"Firm," Hector continued, "self-reliant and efficient. Why, some women in her position would have taken to their bed, if a thing like that happened in their household. And she's had a lot to cope with in the house, too, I understand. All sorts of minor accidents. But she keeps her head!"

"She certainly does," Asey agreed. "You—er—let your house to her without knowin' her? How did that happen?"

"I've often wondered," Hector said, "what I should do with the house here. I live almost exclusively on the 'Dorinda,' you know. I find it convenient, and I am not bothered by people. I was discussing the situation with a friend of mine, and he suggested that I rent the place. He is in the real estate business, and he had been approached by an excellent English firm, Pringle, Ponsonby and Thule—"

Hector went on about the excellent English firm of Pringle, Ponsonby and Thule, how his friend had written them, and they had written him, and then cables had been exchanged, finally phone calls had been made.

"You mean," Asey said at last, "you rented the place to Mrs. Monfort through your friend. An' she paid a thumpin' rental, an' paid for the renovations. That it?"

That, Hector admitted, was it.

"And now," he rose, "I must get along and attend to many things. You, I know, are as busy. I'm glad that we have had this opportunity to talk frankly about my sister, and this whole unfortunate affair, and you know that my only desire is to have the matter solved as soon as possible. I shall stay here, of course—my business will just have to get along without me—and of course, I wish to cooperate with you in every way. Every possible way. My staff and I are at your disposal."

"Thanks." Asey felt a little suffocated by all of Hector's benevolence and good will.

"I have the utmost faith in your ability, Asey. I know I can depend on you to bring this trying—er—crisis to a brief and satisfactory conclusion. Do not fail to call on me for anything, anything at all."

There was an aura of virtuous humility surrounding Hector Colvin as he left the sitting room, but it disappeared before he got into his car.

Asey watched the brisk little figure from the window.

Hector, he thought, was pretty perky. Hector was practically cocky.

"Now I wonder," Asey said, "I wonder—hullo, Jennie. Jennie, I wonder if I ain't been given a rabbit punch without knowin' it? I had Brother Colvin worried there, for a moment, but—"

"He certainly didn't look worried when he left," Jennie said. "He was humming."

"Humming, was he?"

"He certainly was, that hymn about bein' crowned with grace," Jennie said. "Did you crown him?"

"On the contrariwise," Asey said, "on the contrariwise. What—will I see the reporters? No, you tell 'em that Mr. Colvin is my spokesman."

"Him?"

"Yup. Say Mr. Colvin's agreed to pass on anythin' I have to say to the pantin' public. That may take a little of his hum out of him."

Alone in the sitting room, he considered Mr. Hector Colvin.

Hector had been worried at first. Badly worried. Hector was downright scared.

But Hector was humming, now.

That meant, Asey decided, that at first he had been warm. He had hit somewhere near something that Hector did not want known. But then he'd wandered away from the hot spot. And once he wandered, Hector realized that Asey had been thrashing around in the dark.

Hector had not called the bluff directly, but Hector appeared to have so-whatted him, anyway. Hector's secrets were still his own.

The cavalcade of cars rolled away.

Hector still had his secret, and Betsey and Carol still had theirs. Everyone seemed to have his own private angle on this, and not one of them gave the slightest indication of breaking down and telling all.

Offhand, Asey couldn't think of any particular method of making them tell, either.

Ralph Budd dropped in after the Colvin motorcade had departed.

"What *I* want to know is, what's become of your friend Warner?" he demanded. "Do you really think that this fellow Warner is still around here?"

"Warner," Asey said, "apparently has his own private angle, too. I don't know where he is. I don't know anythin'. I'm just the man people give elephants to, that's all."

"Aren't you worried about Warner?"

"There's so much more to worry about," Asey said, "than him."

"And you haven't any doubt that he—oh, I asked you that, I know, but it seems so peculiar, this whole business of Warner. The whole damn business is so peculiar anyway. I suppose—well, no matter."

Asey looked at him curiously.

"Kind of bleak today, ain't you?" he asked. "What you been doin'?"

"Oh, I've been over at Colvin's. I took a look at Monfort's green shirt with the wound. He's all right. He'll be up—"

Asey slapped his fist on the table.

"There!" he said. "There's somethin' I forgot to ask Hector about. I meant to ask him if he ever owned an ole nickel-plated .22 among his treasures, before he an' Mrs. Monfort got the chance to get together an' decide that he did."

"I asked him," Ralph said. "He told me it was a relic which he retained solely for sentimental reasons. A slice of his boyhood, or something. In other words, they've already got together."

"Hector," Asey said, "is a very comprehensive sort of feller, ain't he—say, Ralph, what's the matter with you?"

Ralph sat down and swung one leg over the arm of a chair.

"It's that damn house," he said. "I wish you'd wander over there, Asey. Something's happened."

"You mean, like more firewood tumbled on those poor fellers in the green shirts?"

"No, not that. Something's come over the household. It's different, somehow. I can't explain it, but it doesn't seem one bit the way it did last night. Mrs. Monfort was sort of sweeping, and regal, and glamorous, last night. And the servants were—well, you know what I mean. It was all sort of like a stage set. But something's happened. I'd like to know what."

"You're seein' it by daylight, maybe," Asey suggested.

"No, it's more than that. You have a feeling about places, and you know damn well it'd take more than daylight to make that household so sort of commonplace—oh, I can't explain, Asey. You come over and take a look at things, will you?"

Asey laughed at him, but Ralph persisted until Asey gave in and accompanied him over to the Colvin house in Ralph's old sedan.

The place was different. Asey had to admit it.

None of the furnishings had been changed, the servants still wore their green blouses with sashes, and the little curved daggers thrust in them.

But there was not so much heel-clicking or so much bowing or scraping. The men had a spruce, freshly shaved look about them that was very far removed from their suspicious and rather sinister appearance the night before.

And the man who let them in had almost smiled as he threw open the door hospitably.

"You wish to see Mrs. Monfort?" he said before they had a chance to speak. "If you will be good enough to come this way, gentlemen—"

He led them at once to the drawing room.

"There," Ralph said, "see what I mean?"

Asey nodded.

Mrs. Monfort was different, too. Her white hair was done very simply, her hands were bare of rings. Her soft lavender dress with the touch of white at the throat made her seem more like the classic grandmother of the advertisement world, Asey thought, than anything else.

"How do you do?" she said. "I did not see you at church this morning, Mr. Mayo."

Asey allowed that church had slipped his mind entirely.

"So many things to do, of course," Mrs. Monfort said. "I understand. Why, Snapper, you naughty little dog, who let you in here?"

A little wire-hair romped into the room.

"He mustn't come in here," Mrs. Monfort said. "Dr. Budd, will you ring, please?"

"Where's Kublai Khan?" Asey asked as Carl appeared and removed Snapper.

"I'm so very fond of dogs, aren't you?" Mrs. Monfort said.

Apparently she had not heard Asey's reference to the Siamese cat.

"I think," she continued, "that everyone who has a dog is—yes, Carl?"

"The police, ma'am, want Mr. Mayo."

"Thanks," Asey said. "Tell 'em I'll be right along. Uh—I hope to continue our little talk about dogdom, Mrs. Monfort."

His shoulders were shaking as he and Ralph Budd left the room.

"Maybe it is funny," Ralph said, "but—well, what's so funny about it?"

"If she'd said that man's best friend was his dog," Asey said, "I don't think I could of held in. Well, well, they're doin' it up brown, ain't they? Even to switchin' in a nice everyday dog instead of the sleek an' exotic Siamese. I wonder where poor Khan got put—"

"But what's the idea?" Ralph said.

"Oh, I don't know," Asey said. "I haven't got that far. I'm just givin' 'em credit. There's Max, down by the cottage. I'm kind of sorry that Talbot had to leave him. Max means well. He means real well—"

Talbot's trooper greeted them.

"They just phoned down from Boston," he said, "and I wanted you to hear the dope about Mrs. Monfort. Talbot was sure she was something wonderful, like royalty, or something, but he was all wet. She's just plain Mrs. Monfort, an Englishwoman, here for a sort of visit and vacation in this country. She—"

"She wouldn't be a well-known clubwoman, would she?" Asey asked.

"Why, yes, that's just what they said. How did you know that?"

"You can pick it out of the air," Asey told him, "in handfuls. Go on, Max. Who's the blonde, a secretary?"

Anything less secretarial than the descriptions of that blonde, he thought, would be very hard to find.

"Yes, a secretary. Her name is Eda Bailhache. You know, Talbot said he thought there was something queer in her having all these servants, but they told me from Boston that she was just sort of eccentric. She'd got a kidnapping threat once, and afterwards she always had all these servants around."

"Where did Boston get all this information?" Budd demanded.

"Oh, they've probably phoned, and sent men around, and just checked as they always do. I told Talbot this morning, he was crazy to think Mrs. Monfort and her people had anything to do with this killing. Why, I saw her when she went to church, and she was just like somebody's grandmother. Talbot must have had a few last night to keep out the rain. There's nothing sinister about her!"

"A charmin' an' sympathetic woman," Asey said. "That's what. Huh. Got anythin' else, Max? If you ain't, I'll be runnin' along. I—"

"Say, I met Colvin," Max said.

"Did you, now?" Asey returned. "I want to know."

"He seems a pretty good scout," Max said. "Of course, he blew off steam at first, but you couldn't hardly blame him, seeing his sister'd been killed. He told me that he didn't know when he'd ever been so upset. Say, he's just like everyone else, isn't he? I always wondered what a man like that would turn out to be like, but he's just like everybody else."

"A man," Asey said, "of the people, whose childhood years was lean an' full of depr'vations, hard work an' earnest toil. But did this d'scourage young Hector Colvin? No!"

"A thousand times no," Ralph Budd fell into the spirit of the thing. "These very hardships that young Colvin was forced to endure, all acted—what'd they act like, Asey?"

"Like so many goads," Asey said promptly. "So, by his bootstraps—they used t'have bootstraps, in those days—by hard work an' earnest toil, young Colvin hoisted himself to the em'nent position he now occupies. But has that position changed him? No!"

"A thousand times no!" Budd chimed in.

"Goodness me, no," Asey said. "He is just one of us at heart. Just one of us masses. The mind may be that of a great banker an' cap'tlist an' financier, but the heart an' spirit is those of a little che-ild. I thank you, gentlemen."

"Hurray," Ralph said, "huzzah!"

Max stared at them with his mouth wide open.

"Just," Asey said, "a little che-ild. Ralph, let's us get away from here quick!"

Max continued to gape after them as they drove off in the old sedan.

"Asey Mayo," he confided to another of the troopers, "is losing his grip!"

Ralph turned to Asey for instructions at the foot of the driveway.

"Anywhere," Asey said. "It don't matter much. Just get as far away from all that sweetness an' light an' brotherly love as you can."

"What's the reason for it?" Ralph demanded.

"Answers," Asey said, "had to be found for Mrs. Monfort. They found 'em. Mrs. Monfort is a clubwoman, a lecturer, a person well known in charitable circles—huh, I wonder what the charitable circles would of said if they'd seen the way she reacted to that murder last night!"

"But—but is she all that?"

" 'Course not," Asey said.

"I don't quite get this," Budd said.

"All right, you're on a station platform. You wonder about someone. You look at their bags, an' you look at their clothes, an' you look at the lines under their eyes. You put all those things together, an' you get somethin'. Another person might wonder the same way, an' get dif'rent results. But if this person you're wonderin' about has a placard around his neck that says, 'I'm a doctor,' or 'I'm a minister,' why then—"

"Then you look at him and his luggage and all the rest," Ralph said, "and say, of course. And you fit everything in place on that basis."

"Just," Asey said, "like Mrs. Monfort's servants, an' her blonde all get fitted in. An' dear Hector, he's just a dear, dear man who happens to be a millionaire, but you'd never guess, never. I bet you that Hector's staff didn't get a lot of rest last night."

"You think they cooked all this up? But how could they?"

"If they didn't do the cookin'," Asey said, "they stood by with the salt an' pepper an' helped out with the bastin'."

"And where does that get us?" Budd wanted to know.

"I don't know where it gets you," Asey said, "but I'm still just the man who gets given elephants—what you turnin' for?"

"The kids," Ralph said. "They're over at Porter's with that elephant, and mother told me to pick 'em up and get 'em home for dinner. They've got my best Sunday go to meeting camera with 'em, too, and they think that I don't know it. I wish I knew how they learned to open that old safe!"

"Funny they haven't been to Mrs. Monfort an' Colvin's," Asey said. "I didn't think they'd prefer an elephant to a murder."

"I think they went there," Ralph said. "It doesn't seem

possible that they didn't—say, isn't that the bunch of them, over behind Snow's? They don't seem like themselves, on foot."

"Whyn't they get their bikes, I wonder?" Asey said, as Ralph put his finger on the horn and held it there. "The bikes are in the garage at Colvin's—"

The Pilgrim Camera Club dashed over to the car.

"Whew!" Asey said, "if you're goin' to play with elephants, you'll have to warn folks to get to the wind'ard of you!"

"It won't be so bad from now on," Noah said, "we just give Frederick a good bath. He needed it. Say, Asey, we were going for you. We got a note for you."

"Kenny Fisk gave it to us," Pink zipped open the knapsack, "because he had to go away with his father—"

"A man gave it to him," Pokey interrupted. "A sailor, off Colvin's yacht—"

"A sailor—let's have it, Pink."

An odd expression crossed Asey's face as he read the note.

"Some of my guesses," he told Ralph, "are right. Read what Warner has to say about Mrs. Monfort."

9.

RALPH stared at the single sentence.

"No matter what part they decide to build up for her," read the precise script, "you treasure Mrs. Monfort like your mother."

Ralph read it again, but before he could make any comment, Asey had turned to Noah.

"Is my cousin Syl over to Betsey Porter's?" he demanded. "He is? Well, will you take a message to him for me? You will? Wait a sec, an' I'll write it—"

The Pilgrim Camera Club trotted happily off with the slip of paper.

"I hate to dispose of 'em that way," Asey said, "but they had to be disposed of. They had a sort of active look about 'em. I just told Syl to amuse 'em, an' then send 'em with a note somewhere else when he got exhausted. Now, what do you think of Warner's item?"

"How do you know it's from him? And Asey, that's written on Hector Colvin's own personal stationery, from his yacht!"

"I know Warner wrote it," Asey said, "because it's his writin'. It's his style, too. Anyone else would have written somethin' like 'Mrs. Monfort is in deadly danger, guard her with your life. Maybe they will say she is not Mrs. Monfort, maybe they will say she is not in danger—.' An' so on an' so forth. You could run that sentence into a couple of paragraphs, if you wanted to."

"But the yacht paper, what does that mean?" Ralph wanted to know. "Would it mean that Warner was out on the 'Dorinda'? Why didn't Colvin tell you that he was— oh, I see. You think that Warner's been shanghaied?"

Asey chuckled. "Prob'ly."

"Why?"

"Well, Warner's got to be somewhere," Asey said, "an' maybe the yacht seemed a nice place to keep him. Like Hector told me a while ago, people don't bother you on yachts. On the other hand, people might get bothersome an' prowl around the Colvin place."

"You don't seem at all moved. Aren't you going to rescue him?"

"Nope."

"But why not, if he's being held there?"

"It looks to me," Asey said, "like he prob'ly *wanted* to be shanghaied."

"I don't get it," Ralph said. "I don't get this."

"If Warner could get a note ashore to me," Asey said, "don't you think he could get ashore himself? A note to the cops, for example. It'd be easy enough to get him off."

Ralph shook his head. "You may be the man they give elephants to," he remarked, "but me, I'm just a stooge. I don't seem to grasp things."

"In a manner of speakin'," Asey said, "there'd be no nicer place than Colvin's yacht, if you wanted to be right in the thick of things, would there?"

"Go on."

"Well, I just think that Warner decided there was more to be learned from bein' with the crowd than runnin' away from it. If he'd wanted me to get him off the yacht, he'd have mentioned the fact. But he didn't. He just said for me to watch out for Lady Monfort's well-bein'.'"

Ralph was silent for a moment.

"Look," he said at last, "I haven't any doubt that Dr. Cummings would be all up to date and maybe half a league ahead of you at this point, but me, I'm just starting out on my career. I'm just a naïve young man. Let me get things all straight and settled. We decided that Hector was a Baddy—that's one of the twins' best phrases. We decided that Hector was a Baddy, and not on our side."

Asey nodded.

"You're sure, now?" Budd persisted.

"Sure."

"And Hector, if what you think is true, has got your friend Warner tucked away on the 'Dorinda.' That makes Hector still a Baddy, and Warner is a Goody. Warner's on our side. That's right?"

"Right."

"Now," Ralph was warming up, "now—Mrs. Monfort is a pal of Hector's. That makes her on that side. Right?"

"Right."

"Then," Ralph concluded triumphantly, "why does Warner care a hoot what happens to the lady, and why in God's name does he tell you to cherish her?"

Asey shrugged.

"You don't know?" Budd demanded.

"No," Asey told him, "I can't think why Warner should

care, but I think I'd might as well do as he suggests. Drive me back over to my place, Ralph, and I'll pick up my car there."

"Okay," Ralph said. "But just the same, this fellow Warner bothers me. Everything bothers me, but he seems to bother me most. You keep saying that he's all right, and you know him, and all that, but—well, I just hope that Comrade Warner doesn't turn out to be a disappointment to you, Asey. Maybe it's just because I'm young, but practically everything to do with Warner seems queer. And you take him so calmly! If a friend of mine was shot at, or shooting, or shanghaied on a yacht—well," he looked at Asey, "it's your business, thank God."

One of Hector Colvin's fleet of cars was blocking the driveway to Asey's house.

Ralph blew his horn, but the car did not budge.

"Pull over, will you?" Asey stuck his head out of the window and yelled.

Instantly the car was moved to one side, and the secretary named Basil got out and hurried over to Asey.

"Mr. Mayo," he said, "I was waiting for you. So sorry to have been in the way, but the chauffeur and I were both sound asleep. We've had rather a—er—full time lately. Mr. Mayo, could you come out to the yacht, right away? Mr. Colvin wants to see you, if it's quite convenient."

Asey thought for a moment.

"I think it'll be convenient," he said. "Ralph, can you take care of that message I just got, d'you think?"

"I can, and I will," Ralph said.

He threw away his cigarette and started to whistle a

nursery rhyme, just loud enough so that it reached Basil's ears.

"Tell Jennie I'm goin' out to the 'Dorinda,'" Asey went on, "an' have her get someone to send my roadster after me in about half an hour, will you?"

Budd nodded, and continued to whistle.

"An' if Talbot should come back—"

"I'll tell him, too, that you're on the 'Dorinda,'" Budd said. "Shall I tell Mrs. Porter, or Noah and the twins? It wouldn't be a bit of trouble, really!"

Asey thanked him politely, and Budd continued to whistle as Asey walked over to the Colvin car with Basil.

"What's the name of that thing?" Basil asked curiously. "What was he whistling?"

"'Will you,'" Asey said, "''step into my parlor, said the spider to the fly?'"

"How odd," Basil said seriously. "For a doctor to whistle, I mean."

"It would be odder," Asey said, "if he didn't."

Basil made stalwart efforts to keep the conversation going as they drove along, but Asey was strangely unresponsive. Asey, Basil decided critically, was rather a stupid person. Hector Colvin already had him under his thumb. No matter how smart people thought they were, Colvin usually managed to get them under his thumb sooner or later.

"There's the 'Dorinda,'" Basil said. "And the tender is waiting at the club wharf. Quite a boat, the 'Dorinda.'"

"Uh-huh," Asey said.

"This is a new 'Dorinda,'" Basil said impressively.

" 'Dorinda V,' you know. It was put into commission only last August. Two-ninety-four overall."

"That so?"

"You know quite a lot about boats, don't you?" Basil asked in rather a condescending tone.

Asey looked at him as if he noticed his presence for the first time.

"Yachts, you mean? Well, I used to cruise 'round a lot with old Cap'n Porter."

"You were the—I mean, you were an officer, perhaps?"

Basil was annoyed by the audible snicker of the wharf attendant.

"Sometimes," Asey said.

"It was a large yacht?" Basil asked.

"As I r'call," Asey said, "she was four hundred an' eighteen feet overall. This is a nice little tender, what's her speed, around twenty-five miles an hour, Tom?"

"Hi, Asey," the man at the wheel greeted him. "Yeah, she'll do better than that in smooth water—"

Basil sat like a ramrod while Asey and Tom chatted technicalities during the trip out to the yacht.

Another secretary met them at the gangplank, and conferred with Basil in lengthy whispers.

"I'm sorry," Basil said, "I'm so sorry, Mr. Mayo, but Mr. Colvin has gone ashore unexpectedly to see one of his partners. The partner—er—gets seasick, and it was necessary that Mr. Colvin speak with him at once. He asked if you would wait. Will you come to the library?"

"If you don't mind," Asey said, "I'd like to talk with Ridley. Is he aboard?"

"Captain Ridley? Oh, yes."

There was another whispered consultation, and then Asey was taken to the captain's quarters.

Ridley looked at him, and at once took a leather-framed picture from the wall and held it out to Asey.

"Glad to see you," he said. "Sit down. That's a picture of my family."

"A fine lookin' family," Asey said politely. "Quite a lot of 'em, too."

"Three girls," Ridley said, "and four boys. I also have my wife's mother to support, and my father, and there's an uncle in Buffalo who needs a little something now and then. Asey, is it true that there's more unemployment now than there's ever been before?"

Asey grinned. He could almost hear Hector Colvin giving Ridley his orders.

"One word out of you, Captain Ridley, and off you go! One word!"

Hector would have rubbed it in, too.

"You don't need to worry about any bread lines," Asey assured him. "I just thought I'd pass the time of day with you while I waited for your boss. Those secretary fellows mean well, but as Colvin's niece said, if you put 'em all together, you'd just have a bale of thin cardboard."

There was a slight noise outside the door, as though someone were choking.

"Like to see some of the 'Dorinda' while you're waiting?" Ridley asked. "I can't take you through Mr. Colvin's quarters, of course, or his office or library—come," he called, as someone knocked on the door.

"Mr. Frack would like the captain in the engine room, sir, if the captain can come," a steward said.

"Oh, I know. Yes, I'll come—excuse me, Asey, I'll be right back."

The steward paused in front of Asey.

"Mr. Cowley-Forbes asked me to ask you if you'd care for—"

"Mr. Who—which—? You mean Basil?" Asey said.

"Yes, sir. Wouldn't you care for a drink?" the man lowered his voice. "And *he* says," Asey knew he did not mean Basil, "will you get the hell on your job and watch her, and leave the rest to him. Perhaps," he raised his voice again, "a highball?"

"Steward," Asey said, "what time is it?"

"After three—"

"After three?" Asey said in horrified tones. "After three? Steward, you get Mr. Basil Thingummy an' tell him I've got to be put ashore at once. Right away, quick. Why, I've got to see the head of the state police at four!"

"Yes, sir!" The steward bounced out of the room.

Basil took Asey's departure very much to heart.

"But Mr. Colvin," he said, "he'll be disappointed. It was very important—"

"So's my date with the head of the state police," Asey returned.

"It was about a letter in the mail that was brought to Mr. Colvin today," Basil said. "A letter from Mr. Colvin's sister, and he particularly wanted to show it to you himself. He thought it was very significant."

"When he gets back from conferrin' with his partner," Asey said, "tell him to hunt me up. So long."

Basil and the other secretary watched the tender churn toward shore.

"Isn't that boat," Basil said, "going faster than usual?"

Ridley, passing by, heard the question and answered it.

"Asey," he said succinctly, "is taking her in."

One of the yacht club stewards ran out as Asey started along the wharf.

"They're calling for you," he said, "from the Colvin house. Dr. Budd wants you right away. Quick—"

On the deck of the yacht, Ridley put down his glasses and smiled at Basil.

"That car you just saw streaking away," he said, "that was Asey, too."

The only person who watched Asey's performance along the strip of torn-up road was Mrs. Dyer of Weesit, who was taking her usual Sunday afternoon walk over to her brother's. Heart trouble was common in her family, but Mrs. Dyer dated hers from that moment when Asey started his roadster along the shore road.

Unaware of the palpitating Mrs. Dyer, Asey tore along toward Hector Colvin's house, and Mrs. Monfort.

He very nearly collided with two motor cycle cops at the entrance.

Inside the grounds a horde of green shirted servants and blue coated police milled excitedly to and fro.

Asey grabbed Bert Blossom by the arm as he got out of the car.

"What happened?"

"Somebody tried to shoot Mrs. Monfort—"

"Is she hurt?"

"Yes, but not bad. She—"

"Who shot at her?"

"You see, she'd come out on the terrace—"

"Man alive, who shot at her?"

"Well, I wasn't here at the time," Bert said, "but she came out on the terrace and—"

Asey grabbed one of the troopers passing by.

"Who shot at her? Didn't you get him?"

"I was down by the cottage," the trooper said. "She came out on the terrace, and they think—"

"Doesn't anyone know?" Asey demanded.

"Well, they think—"

"Didn't you get the person? All of you people here, an' you didn't get him?"

"We think the shot came from over yonder," the trooper gestured vaguely toward the right.

"I see," Asey said. "Somewhere from that half of the county. Not this half, *that* half!"

He ran along the terrace and into the house, without meeting any of the servants or any more troopers.

"Oh," Asey murmured, "just leave all the doors open, that's all. The hoss is gone—huh! Ralph, where are you?"

Finally he located Dr. Budd and Mrs. Monfort, in a small bedroom on the second floor.

She was sitting in a chair by the window while Ralph dressed a wound in her left forearm.

"Ah, Mr. Mayo," she said. "I could wish that you might have been here half an hour ago."

"I wish so, myself," Asey said, marvelling at her composure. The expression on her face never changed as iodine bit into her arm. "I wish so. Anythin' I can do, Ralph?"

"Nothing, thanks. You know what I think, Asey? I think that Mrs. Monfort and your cousin Jennie Mayo have a lot in common."

"I know what you mean," Asey said. "What happened?"

"Mrs. Monfort and I," Budd said, "started to stroll down to the cottage—does that hurt? Okay. And out on the terrace, someone started shooting at her. They missed, comparatively speaking. One bullet went through my coat sleeve, and seared me, and one went through Mrs. Monfort's arm. And while everyone else went berserk, we withdrew indoors and coped with the situation."

"You coped with it," Mrs. Monfort said, "very well indeed, considering the lack of cooperation from my men and from the police."

"There wasn't much to cope with," Ralph said. "The hardest part was finding a pan to boil water in—you may not know it, Mrs. Monfort, but the smallest pan in Colvin's kitchen holds two gallons. There you are. Does that feel perfectly awful? Your maid can make you a fancier sling, if she ever gets through having hysterics—"

"It feels very comfortable," Mrs. Monfort said. "Thank you, Dr. Budd."

Almost instinctively, Ralph bowed.

"You take this very calmly," Asey commented.

"The novelty of this sort of thing," Mrs. Monfort told him, "has long since worn off. In fact, I find it rather monotonous."

"Those women's clubs," Asey said, "I know how it is. Just bang-bang-bang, all the time."

She smiled for the first time since Asey had seen her the night before. Then the smile faded, and her blue eyes seemed suddenly very tired.

"Who did the shootin'?" Asey asked.

"There are a number of people," Mrs. Monfort said casually, "who might possibly have some reason to try to kill me."

"You think that this might have been some member of your household?"

"Possibly."

"Johann, p'raps?" Asey said.

Of all the green shirted men, he had liked Johann the least.

"No, not Johann," Mrs. Monfort said. "Johann is at present—er—laid away in the cellar. No, I don't feel that Johann is responsible for this."

Asey walked over to the window, looked out and then returned.

"I gather," he said, "that Johann is just temp'rarily disabled, or did you have to kill him?"

"He is just tied up," Mrs. Monfort said. "Johann rather outdid himself."

"Would the little place out there by the garden," Asey said, "would that be where Khan—"

"Is buried? Yes. I do not know what Johann put in my

bedtime glass of milk," Mrs. Monfort said. "It must have been tasteless and odorless. Khan was a very wise cat."

Ralph Budd lighted a cigarette.

"Look," he said, "this, all this isn't real. Now it's getting to be a stage set again. Mrs. Monfort, d'you mean that people are—are sort of sitting down and trying to kill you?"

Mrs. Monfort remarked that such seemed to be the case.

"It—well, I just don't know the word for it," Ralph said. "It's utterly fantastic!"

"It's rather tiresome," Mrs. Monfort said.

Ralph looked at her, and then got up and stubbed out his cigarette.

"If someone's trying to kill you," he said, "and they've tried twice since last night— Asey, she's got to be looked after! Who's doing this, and why? We'll get Talbot to—"

"My dear young man," Mrs. Monfort said, "no one is going to kill me. Not until I have accomplished something which has got to be accomplished. I have a task to do, and I am going to do it. But until I have done it, nothing else is important. I am really sorry for Vivian Garth. I knew her when she was a child. I am sorry for many things which have happened. But until I have accomplished my task, those things are unimportant."

She paused for a moment to rearrange the folds of her sling.

"A number of obstacles," she said, "have appeared in my way. But there is nothing which is going to stop me. There is nothing which I will not do to achieve my end. Does that, Mr. Mayo, answer any of the questions which may have been puzzling you?"

"I admire," Asey said honestly, "your fine disregardin' of Fate. But there's a certain point beyond which you can't disregard it. You can't remove poison from your food by will power alone. You can't stop bullets or turn away knives, just by sayin' no, no matter how forceful you are about it. You got a task to do. That's all right. I got one, myself. I want to know what's goin' on, before anyone else gets killed."

Mrs. Monfort frowned.

"I know nothing," she said, "about the murder of Vivian. I am positive that none of my people had anything to do with it. They swore to me that they did not. I believe them."

"You don't think that someone was after you, an' got Vivian by mistake?"

"No, Mr. Mayo, I do not."

"An'," Asey said, "you don't much care how many people get killed, bein' mistaken for you, as long as you do what you're settin' out to do. I see. Where is your—er— secretary, Mrs. Monfort?"

"I don't know."

"It wouldn't just possibly have been her that was pottin' at you?" Asey asked.

"It might have been," Mrs. Monfort said. "It might have been. Eda was always a very poor shot."

A bullet crashed the glass of the window in front of which Mrs. Monfort sat, and imbedded itself in the wall behind her.

"Always," Mrs. Monfort said. "Always."

10.
ASEY jumped, grabbed at the back of Mrs. Monfort's chair and shoved it away from the window, all in one swift movement.

"Thank you," Mrs. Monfort said, looking critically at the ripped plaster of the wall. "Thank you. Yes, Eda was always a bad shot."

Ralph Budd looked from the wall to Mrs. Monfort, and then back to the wall. Then he sat weakly down on the floor. His little black bag was there, and he touched it tentatively, as though he were reassuring himself that there was nothing wrong with his imagination.

"I think," Mrs. Monfort added, "she flinches."

"Asey!" Ralph said. "Asey, what—where are you going? You're not leaving me—us—"

"The person shootin' *is* yonder," Asey said. "They got the yonder part of it. Someone's got—well, maybe a 30-06 with telescopic sights. No wonder they didn't find anyone before, huntin' under the sundial in the garden an' peerin' up branches of trees!"

"They thought—" Ralph began.

"Oh, no, they didn't. Don't accuse 'em of doin' any thinkin'," Asey said. "Now listen, I'm goin' to investigate. You keep her away from windows, from drafts, keep her away from everythin', hear me? You watch over her, an' if she wants an egg, analyze it first, see?"

"My dear Mr. Mayo, I assure you—"

"My dear Mrs. Monfort," Asey said, "it may seem like somethin' divine was wrappin' a protective veil around your person, but Dr. Budd is goin' to hold the veil in place with adhesive tape. Just to make sure."

He slammed the door and ran out into the corridor, where he nearly tripped over a prostrate maid.

"What's the matter with you?" he demanded.

The girl lifted her head and burst into a torrent of French.

"Mort?" Asey said. "No, she's not dead. Get in there an' work for a livin'—"

He continued downstairs, pausing only to yell at the trooper, Finlay, who was wandering in a bewildered fashion through the lower hall.

"Second floor, left at the head of the stairs," Asey said. "Snap up there, Finlay—she's all right, you an' Budd see that she stays that way!"

Out on the terrace he found Bert Blossom, raptly contemplating the side of the house.

"Say, Bert!"

Bert jumped. "Huh—oh! I thought you might be—"

"There's not a soul lurkin' in that drain pipe," Asey said, "nor anybody hid under that ivy leaf. Bert, find Max and have him follow me—"

Bert blinked a little, and watched Asey race over to the roadster.

He was so relieved to find that Asey was Asey, and not some stranger with a gun, that he had not really listened

to what Asey said. Besides, it always bothered Bert to
have people startle him from the rear that way.

"Now, did he say to follow him—say, did Asey say to
follow him?"

He appealed to a trooper rushing past.

"I don't know." The trooper didn't pause.

"No," Bert said. "No, that's it. He said *not* to follow.
Not to have Max follow him. Find Max, and tell him *not*
to follow—"

With the air of a man on an important mission, Bert
tracked down Max and repeated the message.

"Asey said, you're *not* to follow him."

"Who the hell wants to?" Max said irritably. "I didn't
even know he'd gone. I don't care. That man's in his second childhood, that's what the matter with him is! Tell
Max he needn't follow—who does he think he is that I
should follow him, anyway? The hell with it!"

"Well," Bert cleared his throat, "he told me to tell you,
that's all—"

"And you did. So what?"

Bert shrugged his shoulders and ambled back to the terrace.

Sometimes, what with the Pilgrim Camera Club, and
traffic, and everything, he wished he had not been so eager
to acquire the job of constable. On the whole, it didn't pay.

He sat down on a railing and stared up at the window
which the bullet had gone through. Sometimes, he thought,
it was better to sit down and think things over. A man got
just as far, sitting and thinking, as he did rushing around.

Sometimes a man got a lot more than people who rushed, like Asey Mayo. Rush-rush-rush all the time, that was Asey. Tearing around, driving that car like greased lightning.

The roadster did bear a striking resemblance to greased lightning as it tore along the shore road.

Three figures fled as he swerved around the steam roller, and Asey blew his horn twice at them. Apparently the Pilgrim Camera Club had not been amused by carrying notes, and had taken to the road again.

Asey tried to think, as he sped along, of a direct road to the hillside which he wanted to investigate. Half of the hill, he knew, was a cemetery. He had never been there, but there must be roads.

He found one, and started along it, rather grateful for the slight drizzle, and for the time. Earlier in the day, the sight of his speeding roadster would probably have caused considerable unfavorable comment from those townspeople who made Sunday visits to the cemetery.

He stopped by the covered pump in the center, and studied the roads.

The Congregational side of the cemetery had only a footpath leading off it. The tarred road disappeared into the woods beyond the Methodist side. Probably, Asey thought, turning into an old carriage lane, that would lead about where he wanted to go.

"On the other hand," Asey murmured, "maybe I guess I better not—"

Parking the roadster by the pumphouse, he took the

precaution of locking the car and putting the keys in his pocket.

"Not," Asey said, "that I think for an instant that any of *you* good people—now, let's see."

He walked along the tarred road, which ended, as he had suspected, in a rough overgrown carriage lane.

But an automobile had been through it very recently.

The tire marks were fresh, and one of the scrub oaks was still swinging, trying to return to the position from which someone's fender had pushed it.

And there was only one set of tire marks.

Ten seconds later he came on the car itself.

Two seconds later, an astonished couple goggled at the barrel of Asey's Colt.

"Uh," the boy said, and gulped. "Uh—oh, now, don't be that way, Toots! Don't scream!"

The girl screamed again, and kept on screaming.

"Ssh, don't! Hey, don't—aw, gee!" the boy looked helplessly at Asey as the girl wound herself around his neck and clung there.

"How long you been here?" Asey asked.

"About fifteen minutes—hey, you're choking me! Say, you—"

"Then you didn't hear any shot, did you?"

"Oooh!" the girl wailed, and got a fresh grip on the boy's tie. "Oooh, guns? Guns! I want to go home! I want to go home!"

"I didn't hear any gun," the boy said. "Was—hey, climb down! Was that all you wanted?"

Asey grinned.

"That's all I wanted," he said. "But if you do happen to hear a shot, just take care of Toots, won't you?"

"Somebody after those deer again, huh?" the boy asked. "I heard that there was. They got two Boston men last week—say, wasn't that a shot, then?"

"Didn't he go away quick?" Toots said, disentangling herself. "Where'd he go?"

"Oh, after the fellows, I guess. Don't," the boy said fondly, "you worry about them—"

Asey worked his way through the bushes down the side of the hill.

Possibly, he thought, someone actually was shooting deer out of season, but it was his impression that the deer was a two-legged one, somewhere in the general direction of Mrs. Monfort's house.

There were several small clearings among the scrub pines and scrub oaks of the hillside. From any one of them, a person might enjoy at his leisure an excellent view of the Colvin estate. From any one of those clearings, a person with telescopic sights could have potted at Mrs. Monfort, in the bedroom window.

From one of them, someone undeniably had.

But there was no trace of any person there now.

Asey walked slowly about the first little patch, but he could find no shells, no indication that anyone had been there. It was getting almost too dark for any more shooting. Probably the last shot had been a derisive gesture of farewell on the part of—*was* it that blonde, Eda, who was responsible for all this?

He wondered as he went on to the next patch.

Mrs. Monfort seemed entirely willing to let him believe that it was Eda. But Mrs. Monfort probably would have been equally willing to let him think Annie Oakley was shooting at her, if Mrs. Monfort felt that would keep him from sticking his nose into her affairs.

Purposes as ingrained as Mrs. Monfort's, Asey thought, amounted almost to a disease, and you had to take that into account when you considered her answers. If anyone should ask him, Eda was probably keeping Johann company in the cellar. Eda would not be out on the loose, if Mrs. Monfort entertained any base doubts about her. No matter how poor a shot Eda might be—

He caught sight of something brightly metallic in the sandy soil, and stooped to pick up the head of an aluminum putter. Beyond it, he noticed a rusty ice pick. Both, he thought as he sat down on a rock, both were odd things to find so near a cemetery. But when you came right down to it, there weren't many things that really belonged near a cemetery anyway.

His pipe slipped out of his fingers as he drew it from his pocket.

Just as he leaned over to pick it up, a shot rang out, and something whined through the space where his head had been.

Instantly he tumbled to the ground.

That was not the result of anyone peering from a great distance through telescopic sights. That was someone with a revolver, and most uncomfortably near.

"Dear Eda, or someone," Asey murmured, hugging

closer to the base of the rock, "keep on missin'—"

He hadn't noticed when he sat down what a small rock it was. One of the smallest, stingiest rocks he had ever seen in all the days of his life. The lee of that rock would probably be scorned as a place of refuge by a good-sized cat, although Asey had more than a faint suspicion that a skunk had recently passed by.

Below and to his left lay the Colvin estate. Several of the windows had lights in them, now, and he could see cars coming and going at a tremendous rate.

Someone, Asey reflected bitterly, might have had the decency to follow him, as he'd asked. Someone, from all those carloads scurrying about, might have had the common sense to investigate all this shooting.

"Did you," Asey murmured ironically, "hear a shot? Why, tch, tch, no! That was a backfire. Or someone out shooting deer. Just a poacher. Don't give it a thought—"

He could always stay there until it got really good and dark. By that time, Eda or whoever it was could have packed up their arsenal and departed, and doubtless enjoyed a good dinner to boot.

Asey reached out a hand and felt for his Stetson. He had no intentions of lying behind this rock any longer than he had to.

Gingerly he pushed the Stetson up till the crown stuck above the level of the rock.

Nothing happened.

He pushed it higher.

Still nothing happened.

He waved it once or twice, and then got up and stretched.

"Ho-hum," he said. "How plum silly I'd have felt if I'd—now I wonder, how did she get away? If she had a car here, why didn't she go before? I wonder—"

The couple whom he had disturbed earlier supplied the answer.

He found them back in the cemetery near the pump-house, sitting on a low headstone that said "Bessie and Willie." The girl was weeping noisily, and the boy looked frightened and unhappy.

"A woman held us up!" he said. "She took our car—"

"When?"

"Just now—hey, is this roadster yours? Take us back, will you? That's my father's car, and if anything happens to it—hurry, Toots—"

"You can come," Asey pulled out his keys, "but I won't be responsible for anythin' that may happen—shovel Toots in, feller. I'm in a hurry—"

At the top of the hill, the boy let out a whoop.

"Say, there she is, see? Down there—she had trouble shifting. I thought she would, you got to push the clutch—oh, can you catch her? I just got to get father's car back. I *got* to. He don't know I had it—"

"If you'll hang on to Toots," Asey said, "we'll see "

Half way down the hill, Toots stopped weeping and began to moan.

She had caught sight of the speedometer.

The boy had seen it, too. He stared at it, and his eyes bulged.

"Yes," Asey said, "it's workin'. You take care of Toots, an' let me do the drivin'."

"I guess," the boy said as the roadster swung onto the tarred road at the foot of the hill, "I guess you are Asey Mayo, huh?"

Asey admitted it.

"An'," he added, "you tell Toots for me that either she shuts up, or else she gets tossed plum out on half of an ear—"

Toots subsided a little.

"That's better," Asey said. "Was she a blonde that held you up?"

"Just like a movie star," Toots said. "Just like a movie star, she was. She—"

"Yup," Asey said, "I know. Glamor. What'd she have with her in the line of weapons, feller, or didn't you notice?"

"She had a revolver. That's what she held us up with. And a rifle, too. Was she—was it she shooting deer? Her? I—I guess maybe she wasn't—"

Asey grinned.

"I guess," he said, "that deer is the only thing she hasn't bothered to take a shot at—now, you two hold on. She's headin' for the main highway, an' I can't pass her till she gets there, so I'm goin' to shortcut her. Hang on!"

Their progress through that short cut was one of those things, Asey thought, that he would remember for some time to come.

Toots's lungs alone would have made it memorable.

The first bounce they hit on the rutted road set her off, and from then on, she ran loudly and with gusto through the entire gamut of hysterics.

Asey listened to her with a certain amount of honest admiration.

He hadn't heard such an ear-shattering din since the day that his Aunt Sophy's horse Rover saw a horseless carriage, and promptly rushed into Wellfleet Bay with Aunt Sophy in the buggy behind him. Until now, Asey had never thought that Aunt Sophy's vocal gymnastics could ever be equalled. Given a runaway horse, Toots could probably make Aunt Sophy sound like a gently murmuring stream.

But in spite of Toots and her hysterics, and the road with its puddles and mud, Asey reached the main road in time.

"You're goin' to get her!" the boy said excitedly. "See, she's just ahead! Gee, I didn't know our old car could go that fast! You'll get her, you'll get her sure—"

Asey would have got her with ease, if, just as he started to pass the sedan, two women had not suddenly jumped in front of the roadster, exactly as Leopold Smith had jumped the night before.

11. FORTUNATELY, this time, there was no ditch.

Asey pulled the car back on the road and shut off the engine.

"Get her!" the boy said. "Aren't you goin' to get her?"

"Now?" Asey asked succinctly.

He yanked open the car door and walked over to the two women. If Betsey Porter, or anyone who knew Asey, had seen his face at that moment, they would have scuttled to the nearest hole and cowered.

"Well, well," the woman said brightly, "your car has good brakes, hasn't it? Why, we thought for a moment, you were going to tip over, didn't we, Milly?"

Milly said they certainly did.

"You really were going very fast," the woman said, roguishly wagging her finger at Asey. "Really, you were going terribly fast."

Asey looked at her.

"Dangerously fast," the woman continued, but some of the brightness was gone from her voice.

Asey put his hands on his hips.

"You really should have been stopped, shouldn't he, Milly?"

Milly said gracious, yes, he certainly should.

"You're the sort of person responsible for our tremendous

highway fatalities," the woman said defensively. "You're a menace."

"An' who," Asey inquired with a purr in his voice, "are you?"

"I am Ella Salinas Mell—"

"Mrs. Smell," Asey said, "I—"

"Mell. Mell, not Smell. And this is Miss Block. One of the Lancaster Blocks," she added parenthetically.

Under his breath, Asey murmured something about soft pine.

"We are doing the Cape," Mrs. Mell announced.

"I bet," Asey said.

"We are so fond of the dear Cape—"

"With its bayb'ries," Asey said, "its dear quaint houses, its dear quaint characters—I know. Mrs. Mell, are you by any chance huntin' an elephant?"

Mrs. Mell's laughter tinkled.

"My, no!" she said. "We're hunting Mrs. Monfort—that's why we hailed you."

"So you were hailin' me, were you?" Asey said. "I see. You'd better learn broad-jumpin' before you ever really undertake to stop someone. Do you know Mrs. Monfort?"

"She is one of the best known club—"

"Do you know her?"

"Well, of course, I've never met her personally, but the radio said she was one of the most important club-women—"

"I should have guessed it," Asey said.

"You mean, Mrs. Monfort?"

"No, you. Good night—"

"Oh, but wait! You haven't told us where to find her! We've got to find her. It's terribly important—"

"Got a pencil?" Asey asked. "I'll draw you a map. Now, you'll have to follow this real careful, because the road isn't too good in spots—"

"We will! Thank you so much! We won't forget your kindness."

"On the whole, Mrs. Smell," Asey said, "I don't think that you will."

If they followed the map carefully, they would end up in the swamp near Hell Hollow. And even if they didn't, he thought, they had a good quaint drive ahead of them.

He walked back to the car.

"What'm I going to do about that woman an' our sedan?" the boy said unhappily.

"You're goin'," Asey said, "to have to break the news to father. But I wouldn't worry. I think your car'll be found very soon. I wouldn't know in what condition the cops'll find it, but I think it'll turn up. Now, I'm goin' to drop you off in the village. I feel some phonin' is in order. You can find someone to take—"

"You know what I think?" Toots asked suddenly, as though a spotlight had snapped on somewhere within her, "I don't think you're after the car one bit, I think you want that blonde!"

Asey and the boy looked at each other and sighed as the roadster sped toward town.

"I bet you do!" Toots persisted. "I bet you want that blonde!"

"Me," Asey said sadly, "an' Harpo Marx."

Half an hour later, he completed his phoning.

Dr. Budd and the troopers were looking after Mrs. Monfort. More troopers had started out after Eda and the stolen sedan, the plate numbers were being flashed far and wide. And the Colvin place, Budd assured him, was being guarded within an inch of its life.

"Then," Asey said, "you don't need me, do you?"

"Not unless Mrs. M. needs a chess partner," Budd said. "I feel she's a little bored with whitewashing me—"

"How's her purpose?"

"You'd better come over and take a look at that later," Ralph said. "It's resting now, but I'd hate to have to cope with it alone."

Back at his own house, Asey found Betsey Porter sitting dejectedly on a stool in front of the living room fire. She nodded to him.

"Hello," she said.

She sounded fully as dejected as she looked, and very nearly as thwarted as Asey felt.

"Hello. How're you?"

"Oh, colossal," Betsey said. "Stupendous. Just simply peachy."

"What you been—hey, Jennie, bring my food in here, will you? What you been cryin' for, Bets?"

"Nothing specific," Betsey said. "Just accumulated woe. I've been chatting with my husband. That is, I listened to him while he ran up a bill. It's too bad he does his road-testing so near telephones."

"What did he have to say?"

"Don't let's go into it," Betsey said. "But he'd be jailed if he tried to mail it. Seems that he heard about this on the radio just after something vital had busted on his benighted car."

"Nothing busts on a Porter," Asey said, tackling his meal. "We only own to slight mechanical flaws. What else has gone on?"

"Oh, reporters. Reporters and reporters," Betsey said. "And police. And police and police. I thought the police had been napping a bit, but it seems that they've just been burrowing away like beavers. Or whatever those animals are that burrow. I wish Frederick would burrow, for a change! Dear Frederick," Betsey reached for a cigarette, "is now secured by every large chain on the lower Cape, and I employ more people than Bill does. D'you pick up social security blanks at the post office, or d'you have to write your senator, Asey?"

"You can always give Frederick to a zoo," Asey suggested.

"I've just finished sending off telegrams," Betsey said, "to every zoo and animal farm in the New England states. I called the head of that animal hospital, and he gave me a list. I wired Bill's Aunt Lizzie, too, and asked her if maybe she wouldn't like Frederick."

"Lizzie Strathmore? Why?"

"Oh, I never liked her much," Betsey said. "And she's so crazy over that Peke of hers. I thought an elephant might broaden her. And then there's Lewis Garth. Asey,

THE ANNULET OF GILT 153

you'd better speak pretty sharply to Lewis. He's got this fanciful idea, and Carol and I are worried to death that he'll really do something about it."

"Like what?"

"Oh, he starts in with the premise that Carol and I are in a spot. We are. That's been brought home to us with force today. Then Lewis thinks, he'll confess to the murder, and that'll remove Carol and me from our spot, and then Hector's lawyers can get busy, and he can repudiate the confession—he's got it all worked out. He's spent the day brooding about it. I think he feels very deeply about his mother—"

"Wait," Asey said. "Lewis is goin' to—but what's the idea? Just to save you an' Carol?"

"Yes, from all this unpleasantness," Betsey said. "Lewis is apparently one of those men who gives women a stroke a hole at golf, and throws points at tennis, and opens doors, and carries bundles. You know. I'll call him down and have you go into the matter with him. It's all very well to be noble, but I don't see where he'll get anywhere by burning his fingers and sticking his head into the lion's mouth, just to save our faces—"

With a fine disregard for her metaphors, Betsey went off and returned with Lewis and Carol.

Lewis propounded his theories with considerable enthusiasm.

"Now, last night I went upstairs directly after dinner," he said, "and read a book. I came down later and listened to the radio, and then I went to bed. I was in bed when you phoned me from uncle's, Asey. Now, why shouldn't I confess? That'll take the girls out of it, and Uncle Hector—"

"You'd just endear yourself to him, wouldn't you?" Asey asked.

"He might, at that," Carol said. "I think that uncle would dearly love to have a goat. And he likes sacrificial gestures. He sent Lewis the thump of a check that time that Lewis let some vague linesman make the winning touchdown—"

"I passed to Bobby," Lewis said, "because they were going to get me—"

"Yes, dear, I know. But the papers and Uncle Hector thought differently, and Hector simply loved it. He adores that sort of thing. It would probably be all right with Uncle Hector, but—"

"But you might point out to Lewis, Asey, that there are certain flaws in this mammoth idea," Betsey said. "Like Mrs. Hoyt and the maids and virtually everyone else at the Inn all seeing you, and all knowing perfectly well that you didn't stir from the place. That's just one of those items that some smarty will bring up, you know."

"They can always be confused about the time they saw me," Lewis said. "No one ever really knows what time anything happens, except in books. And there aren't any real clews, those fellows over there admitted as much to me. So if there's nothing that can really convict anyone, then I can't possibly—"

"You'd just better call the whole thing off," Betsey said. "Let it fade from your mind. Your car was in the garage, wasn't it? How'd you have got to Colvin's, with water wings? And if you can explain that belt of mine, and all, you'll be one up on the forces of the law—you want me, Jennie?"

Jennie announced that the twins and Noah Snow wanted her.

"Frederick trouble again, no doubt," Betsey said. "I wonder what he's thought up—Asey, do they have strait-jackets for elephants? I think one would be cute for Frederick. With little ruffles—"

Asey grinned as he followed her out into the kitchen, where the Pilgrim Camera Club were wolfing down some of Jennie's gingerbread.

"Frederick's okay," Noah told Betsey. "You know what? He wanted more food. I guess you better order a lot of hay and carrots, Mrs. Porter. We used up about all there is in town. And he wanted a drier place. We got him into the shed, and he quieted right down—"

"Just curled right up, did he?" Betsey said. "Well, that's a relief. You have been simply swell, you three. I'm afraid that all this mahauting has kept you away from Colvin's, though, hasn't it? Did you get pictures there?"

The twins and Noah exchanged rather grim glances.

"No," Pink said.

"I meant to ask you about that," Asey said. "An' about your bikes. I'll get 'em for you. I should have thought of that."

"Don't bother," Noah said.

"Look, what's happened?" Asey inquired. "Haven't you been to Colvin's at all? What's the matter?"

"We went there this morning early," Noah said evasively. "We'll go back again some time, maybe."

"Were you chased out? Did Bert get after you? Or the cops? Or Colvin himself?"

This defeatist attitude on the part of the Pilgrim Camera Club, Asey thought, had a sinister aspect.

"No," Pink said. "No, we didn't see Bert or Colvin. The cops was all right."

"Who'd you run into? Mrs. Monfort?"

"We saw her," Noah said. "Well, I guess we'll go along now, we got to go. Thanks for the food, Jennie, it wasn't bad at all."

"Maybe you better tell Butch how to make that gingerbread stuff," Pink added. "Hers is too dry. G'night."

"So long," Noah said. "We'll water Frederick in the morning, Mrs. Porter."

"Be seein' you," Pokey said.

Asey frowned as he watched them down the driveway.

"I don't like this," he said. "Somethin' is up."

"D'you suppose Mrs. Monfort scared the pants off 'em?" Betsey suggested. "Her name seemed to bring a reaction."

"I don't think that she scared 'em," Asey said thoughtfully. "Remember, those kids took Hector Colvin in their stride. Not to mention Admiral Ormiston an' the navy. No, I don't think she scared 'em, Betsey. I think Mrs. Monfort infuriated 'em. That's a lot worse. If they've decided to get back at Mrs. Monfort, with that Eda—I wonder if I hadn't better tell 'em to stay away from Colvin's place, Betsey? I don't want those kids to get mixed up in all that mess. It's not safe—"

"I can't think of any more glowing incentive for them to go there," Betsey said, "than your ordering them to stay away because it wasn't safe."

"That's what I'm afraid of," Asey said. "Well, I'll tell Ralph to keep his eye on 'em. I don't worry about those three, they're capable of most anythin'—well, let's get back to Galahad, an' his bright idea. Ord'narily, I'd suspect Brother Garth an' all this confessin'."

Betsey stared at him.

"But I don't," Asey continued, "because Talbot already checked up on him. His car was in the garage, an' he didn't leave the Inn."

Before they had any chance to continue the matter of Lewis and his confession, Talbot himself arrived.

"Come somewhere," he took Asey by the arm, "and let me talk with you. Asey, I've never met up with anything like this, never! That—that fox terrier!"

"Meanin' Colvin?" Asey said, leading Talbot into the dining room. "What's he done?"

"Would I like to know," Talbot said, "boy, would I like to know! Can you guess what my orders practically amount to? I've been practically told to lay off Mrs. Monfort, and Colvin, and this whole business! Now, can you beat that? Never in all my life has anything like this happened before, and we've got mixed up with more politics than you could fill a garbage dump with. She's no prominent clubwoman, and you know it as well as I do, and by God, I called a friend of mine in England and proved it! He's a newspaper man, and he'd know! And he'd never heard of her."

"What do they want done?" Asey asked.

"About this case? No one seems to give a damn. Just as long as Mrs. Monfort and Colvin aren't brought into it. 'Startling developments' have been promised by tomorrow —I don't know where the hell they found any startling developments. I haven't found any!"

"Startlin' developments, huh?" Asey said. "Surrounded by the greatest secrecy, maybe?"

"Sure. Then we'll have developments kept secret. That'll be on page three. And in about four days, you might find a squib somewhere in the classified ads, 'Colvin Case Closed.' Asey, what's all this business of Mrs. Monfort being shot at? Is it a fake?"

"It wasn't a fake that sailed through the air where my head'd been a tenth of a second before," Asey said, and told of his trip to the cemetery hill, and his ride with Toots and her boy friend. " 'Course," he concluded, "there's one fleetin' consolation. If they choose to make Mrs. Monfort a clubwoman, she'll be just as bothered by droves of people like Mrs. Mell, an' Miss Block. On the whole, I don't know but what they might thwart Mrs. Monfort better than Eda's bullets."

"What's this purpose of hers?" Talbot demanded.

"Monfort's, or Eda's? Eda just wants to shoot. As for Monfort, I wouldn't know. The purpose has got a holy sort of ring to it, but that don't mean it's necessarily very benevolent. So you think this whole affair is goin' to be dropped?"

Talbot nodded.

"The old hot cake," he said. "Well, I suppose it's not

the first thing connected with Hector Colvin that got laid away in lavender. And say, what's he been doing, mesmerizing people?"

"You mean Max?"

"I mean Max, and all the rest," Talbot said. "Pretty soon they're going to be calling him daddy. Asey, this gripes me, this does. I'll admit that the chances are that we probably wouldn't have got anywhere, anyway, but I hate to see something like this just shut, bang. Just because we haven't found any clews doesn't mean that we can't, or won't. There aren't any traces of anyone but Betsey Porter and the Garth girl, nor any prints but theirs, and of course the green shirts. We've gone over the whole cottage, and we haven't found anything, but I still think there's plenty to be found. If we could only get a motive, we'd have a lot."

"What about that wall safe?" Asey asked.

"Hadn't been touched. Not a mark on it."

"Looked inside?"

"No, to tell you the truth, I forgot to get the combination from the Garths," Talbot said. "But the safe wasn't touched. Vivian never got to it, if she was headed for it. Asey, what did she come here for?"

"To get money," Asey said.

"Who from, Hector? But she didn't know that Hector was coming. She didn't know—"

"Why not?" Asey said. "We didn't know that he was comin' home, but that don't mean other people might not have. I—Talbot, I hear cars. Look out an' see—"

"Colvin," Talbot said. "There's something funereal about

that cortege, isn't there? All those black sedans—say! Max is with them, and Davis! Asey, something's happening here! What d'you suppose—"

"I don't even suppose, any more," Asey said, getting up from his chair. "But if you really wanted to lay this case on ice, Talbot, what would do it?"

"What? What do you mean, what?"

"Who, then?" Asey started out into the hall to the front door. "Think hard, Talbot, 'cause I got this feelin' that— ah, Mr. Colvin. Come in—"

Carol and Betsey hung over the banisters in the upper hall and watched the men file in behind Hector Colvin.

"The regular Sunday meeting of the choir," Betsey whispered, "will be held at the residence of A. Mayo—say, who're those two with the handcuffs on?"

"They look," Carol said critically, "as though they'd crawled out of the plaster. Betsey, do you seem to smell that smell?"

"Like rats?" Betsey said. "I do. Droves and droves of the smuggest rats—Carol, what's this uncle of yours gone and dug up? I think we'd better do some eavesdripping, you and I—"

Asey met them at the foot of the stairs.

"Mrs. Porter, Miss Garth, I want t'be the first to offer my c'ngratulations."

His drawl, Betsey noticed, was drawlier than usual, and his eyes were twinkling.

"You're cleared," he added, "of all c'mplicity in this terrible, tryin' affair. You're free, free to breathe the pure air of—"

"Asey, what's this utter nonsense!"

"Of God's great out-doors," Asey went on. "Free to come an' go as you please. Free to forget. Maybe you can even get along with renovatin' the Porter house, Betsey, an' gettin' the wing fixed."

"What *is* this?" Carol said.

"Come see," Asey said, "what uncle's got. Nice Hector, good old uncle, if he hasn't gone an' got you two an alibi! Come hear 'em."

Carol's eyes narrowed. She looked at Betsey, who grinned.

"Let's hear the alibi," she said. "It ought to be good, anyway."

Hector Colvin hurried over to them as they came in the room.

"Dear Carol," he said, "I have some very good news for you and for Betsey. My men, working quietly with some private detectives, and of course with some of the police—a special detail," Hector added quickly, as Talbot started to speak, "a special detail. They have unearthed something of the greatest importance to you. You see these two men, here?"

Betsey and Carol had been studying the handcuffed pair with intense interest.

There were a lot of adjectives, Betsey thought, which might be applied to the two men. They were tattered and dirty, for example. They were unshaven, unkempt and uncouth.

But somehow Betsey couldn't bring herself to a point of feeling that they were very sinister.

Carol echoed her thoughts.

"They look terribly hungry to me," she said. "A meal would do them a lot of good, uncle. Have you fed them? I'll call Jennie, she always has food—"

"No, no!" Hector said. "Wait—"

"But really, uncle," Carol said, "you can't let a couple of starved men stand around in handcuffs like this—"

"Carol," Hector said coldly, "permit me to know the proper procedure in this situation. May I continue?"

"Oh, by all means, uncle," Carol said. "Continue away, but I think it's mean not to feed these poor men first. They—"

"Carol!" Hector said.

"Well, do be brief, won't you, uncle? And Jennie can feed them when you're through. I—"

"I'll ask her to make some sandwiches," Betsey said. "She'll love to—oh, by the way, you *are* hungry, aren't you?"

The men admitted, with a cautious restraint, that they were very hungry.

"There, see?" Betsey said. "You men, Mr. Colvin, are so dense about things like that! Wait'll I get back before you begin—"

Hector was breathing hard by the time Betsey returned.

"Now," he said, "if you are quite ready, I will tell you the story. These two unfortunate men were about to rob my house—Mrs. Monfort's house—last night, when they saw you, Carol and Betsey, come over the wall and approach the cottage. They followed you. They—"

"How simply amazing!" Betsey said. "Did they happen to see me lose my belt, too?"

"I am coming to that. They followed you to the cottage. They were peering in the window when you—er—fell in the living room. They saw, by the light of your flash, that you tripped over a body. They stayed there until you put the electric lights on, and simultaneously they heard someone coming from the big house. It was Johann. Before he entered the cottage, he stooped to pick something up. Am I right?"

"The tall guy had a belt in his hand," the scrawnier man said. "My pal an' I, we seen it, didn't we?"

"Surest thing you know. We seen it."

"At that point," Hector said, "these two men decided that it was time for them to leave. Johann had summoned help. They do not know what happened later—"

"But," Talbot said suavely, "it may safely be assumed that Johann shifted belts—"

"That is what happened," Hector's smile was acid. "We have questioned Johann—your man Max did that, and he has finally produced Vivian's own belt, which without question was used to kill her."

"That's right," Max said. "Kimberley's played with it. Powder, perfume, all that. *He* never was so sure of the other, you know."

"An' of course you're sure," Asey said, "that these two had nothin' to do with killin' Vivian."

"We have found the truck driver," Hector said, "who gave them a lift—"

"An' he was listenin' to a program on his car radio," Asey said, "so he knew what time it was, to the dot."

"Exactly," Hector said. "You have guessed it. My men saw these two near the wharf today, thought they looked suspicious, and I consider it very fortunate that they were picked up. Naturally, in view of the service they have performed, I shall intervene in their behalf."

"And what does this do to the case?" Carol demanded.

"I should think," Hector said, "that the medical examiner could give no other verdict than death at the hands of person or persons unknown. The—"

"The startling disclosures—no, startling developments in the murder of Vivian Garth," Talbot said, "have resulted in the complete exoneration of Mrs. Porter and of Mr. Colvin's niece. The case continues to remain a mystery, and—"

"There, Lewis," Carol said hastily, before Hector had a chance to make any retort, "there, hear that? Aren't you glad you didn't confess?"

"What do you mean, Lewis confessing!" Hector said.

"Lewis was going to be noble and sacrifice himself," Carol said, "to save Betsey and me—shut up, Lewis, I'll tell him if I want to. Yes, uncle, Lewis was going to blight his life and jeopardize his future and ruin his good name—"

"Caro—"

"He was going to fake a confession," Carol said. "He had it all planned out, and it took actual persuasion to make him change his mind. He—"

Hector clapped Lewis on the back.

"Just," he said, "just the sort of thing I'd expect from you, my boy! Oh, come along with me, now, will you? There are several things I wish to talk over with you. Well, Asey, I'm glad this is all settled so fortunately. Good night! I must be getting back—"

"Wait, wait!" Betsey said. "Don't forget the sandwiches —here, take 'em, you two. You'll have to eat 'em en route."

Talbot waited until Hector and the rest had departed, and then he clapped Asey heartily on the back.

"Just what you expected, my boy!" he mimicked Hector's voice. "Just what you expected! Boy, doesn't Hector think things up! I'll be seeing you later, Asey—"

Betsey and Carol went over to the window and watched the cars roll away.

"Lewis may make faces," Carol said, "but he's really delighted to be in uncle's good graces, though I don't suppose he'd ever admit it. It's just occurred to me that things impress Lewis."

"My dear," Betsey said, "there are very, very few young men who wouldn't be impressed by Hector, and his shiny cars, and his shiny secretaries, and his shiny yacht, and all the rest. Probably the Pilgrim Camera Club want to be captains of finance, after watching Hector's display. Dear Hector, Hector Protector—isn't there a nursery rhyme about Hector Protector?"

"They sent him to the queen," Carol said, "and the queen sent Hector right back. I dare say it served him right. Yes, Bets, I know what you mean about Lewis and Hector's shininess, but I didn't think that Lewis was that way.

Father took things so light-heartedly, always. He laughed so at Hector. It used to infuriate him. Shall we tell now, Bets?"

"I think so," Betsey said. "The chances of us picking oakum, or putting numbers on license plates seem sufficiently dim—yes, I think we'd better. You go and get it."

Carol returned in a few minutes with a bundle wrapped around by a bandanna handkerchief.

"I think, Asey," she said, "that it's just about time we showed you what we removed before Johann burst into the cottage—"

12. SHE SPOKE quietly

enough, but tears were starting from the corners of her eyes as she passed the bundle to Asey.

"It—it's all so tawdry," she said, as though she were excusing herself. "Oh, it's all so tawdry!"

"Don't cry, darling," Betsey said. "We had to show him sooner or later."

"But I feel so beastly!" Carol said. "I've felt so beastly, hiding things. As though I didn't want people to find out who killed her. And after all, she *was* my mother! I did want things found out, but—oh, dear!"

Betsey tried to comfort her.

"Explain to him," Carol said. "Tell him."

"Asey understands, darling," Betsey said. "He'll understand— Asey, open that bundle! Don't make this any harder than it already is!"

Asey untied the knotted ends of the handkerchief.

Jewellery cascaded to the floor. Necklaces, rings, bracelets, brooches— Asey stared at them.

"You see," Betsey said, "Vivian had those with her. She must have had them in—in her hands when she was killed, because they were all over the floor. We picked them up and put them in my bandanna."

Asey picked up a ring and looked at it curiously.

"She'd been at the safe," Betsey went on. "And *how* I

worried for fear someone might look in it, and find things gone. Carol couldn't remember the combination—she had it on a paper at the Inn. If she'd thought of it, I'd have put the things back. Anyway, we took them."

Carol wiped her eyes.

"I simply couldn't bear," she said, "to have people think she was killed in the act of—well, looting. And that's what it would have looked like. That's what the papers would have said. Did you see her shoes, Asey? Did you notice them?"

"They were wet," Asey said, "an' worn."

"Worn! They were worn through! And her dress didn't fit. And her hair—everything about her simply screamed that she was broke! And mother was always so smart. It seems sort of a queer thing to say, but I used to get a sort of pleasure, while I was at school, of seeing her name in the lists of the best dressed women. I—well, she'd been killed, and there wasn't anything we could do about that. But we could keep from the papers and from Uncle Hector and everybody else—we could keep from them the fact that she'd been killed sneaking away with her old jewellery because she was poor. And that's just what would have happened!"

Asey nodded.

Carol, he thought, was probably right. The headlines almost wrote themselves. "Much-Wed Beauty Slain While Stealing Own Jewels from House of First Husband." "Famous Beauty Now Destitute Killed in Desperate Attempt to Steal Old Jewels." Somehow the contents of that handkerchief, if they had been found, would have cast one final layer of notoriety on the name of Vivian Garth.

"Yes," Asey said, "I think you done right, but what it was you was holdin' back has kind of worried me a lot. An' you took a chance—"

"I think it was worth it," Betsey said. "Very definitely. I'd do it again. Of course, there were some awful moments. Like sitting on that couch in the cottage, so afraid we'd be searched. And Johann glaring at us. And when you marched us into that greenhouse, I was so afraid that things would clank! And Asey, now that you know everything, what about this fantastic alibi tale that Hector Protector told? Those men never saw us! I know they didn't. Hector upheld the story we told, but we didn't tell it right. We—"

"What *is* the right version?" Asey asked. "Just for my own record."

"Well," Betsey said, "it's almost hard to tell you, we've balled things up so. We parked by the wall, and flipped over it, and went down to the cottage. I stayed outside to watch while Carol went in, but she couldn't find the lights, and after about five minutes, I went in. In the living room, we tripped, and I put on my light. We didn't speak. It just was too—well, we both bent down and picked things up, by the flash. Then Carol found the switch and put that on, and it was a long time after—ten minutes, certainly, that Johann burst in. We had found everything in the bundle by then, and we just didn't know what to do. We couldn't seem to think, or talk, but we sort of incoherently agreed we'd better get hold of you, and to confuse things until you got going and saved the day. That's all there is. And now, d'you suppose that Johann *did* find it—I mean, my belt?"

"We can find out. Somehow, that part had a ring of truth to it."

"I'm more interested about uncle and those men," Carol said. "What d'you suppose, he just picked up those poor starving creatures from a ditch, and bribed them to nod as he talked? And how can that yarn get by the police? Talbot didn't believe him, but the rest thought it was simply fine."

"I've no doubt," Asey said, "that your uncle could prove everything he said. Men like Hector don't say things that they can't prove, under the circumstances. If Hector said that a truck driver brought those men to the Colvin place, you can be sure that a truck driver would appear who'd swear that he brought them. Don't underestimate your uncle, Carol. He didn't get where he is today by slidin' over details."

"But the police," Carol said. "They should know when a story is as patently made to order as that!"

"The police," Asey said, "are a little like the captain of your uncle's yacht. They have to eat, an' to feed other people b'sides. The police have been given to understand that the quicker this is smoothed over, the better for everyone. Don't ask me why. I don't know."

"Then, the person who killed mother will go free?" Carol said. "And Uncle Hector— Asey, I won't have that! It's rotten! Why doesn't uncle want—oh, what a lovely opportunity I threw into his lap, telling him about Lewis's confession. Lewis will come back tonight with a lovely new job in uncle's office, and a firm conviction that the family name will be better off if this matter of mother is dropped! That's what's going to come of all that back-slapping, and my-boying. Asey, did uncle kill her, himself?"

"I don't see how he could have," Asey said. "I tried to do some timin' this afternoon, to figger out if one of those power tenders from the yacht couldn't have skipped in ahead of the yacht. An' of course there was that car I followed. I thought it was Mrs. Monfort, but it could of been Hector. But I don't think so, Carol. He'd have a better alibi for things than those two hungry critters. There ain't his finish to the thing."

"You're right there," Betsey said. "Things around Hector do have a certain polish. And I don't think Hector would kill anyone, anyway. I think he'd find nasty things to do, and have them done, and then gloat."

Asey got up.

"An' there's another thing," he said. "I keep feelin' that Hector is terrible worried about somethin'. Even now. I'll give Hector his due. I don't think he wants *not* to find out who killed your mother, Carol. I think, in his way, he wants to find out as much as you do. But I think Hector's worried about somethin' comin' out of the findin'. I think—"

"Stop," Betsey said. "Don't get into any philosophical discussions now. I couldn't stand it—where are you going?"

"To call Talbot. Carol, I want the combination of the safe in the cottage, if you've got it."

"It's in the stuff that was brought over from the Inn," she said. "I'll get it."

Betsey toyed with the contents of the handkerchief.

"It's a funny collection," she said. "I never had a chance to see it, really, before. That ring's not bad, nor that pin. But the rest is pretty cheap. Look at that brassy bit, it looks like a thing that holds insulation on heating pipes. It was black—oh, I know. I suppose when Vivian was Vivian Garth, that was the last word in black neck chokers, but the black's worn down to the brass. Mother used to have a metal thing like it. Asey, this stuff—brass ring, the pins, and all—it hardly seems worth the effort of stealing."

Asey agreed.

"Well, she was, wasn't she?" Betsey demanded.

"That's what I'm goin' to find out," Asey said.

"You certainly can't think that she was going to put those things *into* the safe! What utter nonsense. This stuff might look well in a candle lighted room, but you know and I know that it's not worth much."

"We do," Asey said. "I also know that Talbot says that no one had been upstairs in the cottage."

"What! Well, you certainly must admit, Asey, we've provided you with a new angle to things!"

"You have," Asey said.

Carol returned with a slip of paper.

"Here you are," she said. "It was in some papers that got turned over to me. Lewis has a duplicate. I suppose mother must have just remembered."

A few minutes later, Asey succeeded in getting Talbot on the phone at the Colvin place. A lengthy and complicated conversation followed, with pauses that drove Betsey frantic.

"Get somewhere!" she whispered. "Get somewhere, Asey! Either that combination works, or it doesn't—you can't gabble about it any longer! Oh, you can, can you?"

The combination, Asey reported at last, did not work.

"But it's got to!" Carol said.

"Probably it would of," Asey told her, "but it seems that your uncle had a new safe put there a couple of years ago. Some servant of his turned out to be very handy with safes. So Hector said, let there be new safes, an' the staff got goin', an' put new safes in everywhere, in the big house, in the guest house, in the cottage, an' they topped off with a fancy door for the wine cellar. So, although your intentions of shieldin' her were good, Carol, it looks like your mother hadn't been at the safe."

"Asey," Betsey said, "what are you so upset about? And what car hadn't been found? What were you and Talbot talking about?"

"A car," Asey said, "that they should of picked up a long while ago, an' they haven't."

He knew if he told Betsey about Eda and his adventures of the afternoon, he would never get away and over to the Colvin place.

"That blonde," Betsey said, displaying her sometimes uncanny perspicacity. "Where's that blonde? I bet that she has—oh, someone's knocking, Asey. Is Jennie still here?"

Jennie went to the door, and then bustled back to the living room.

"There's a man says he wants you," she announced. "A thin liverish lookin' thing. Says his name's Smith. Leo—"

Asey was at the door before she could finish.

Leopold Smith stood on the millstone that served as a step.

"How do you do?" he said politely, extending Asey's wallet. "I came to return this to you. It was very kind of you, but I do not feel that I can accept it."

Asey felt his lower jaw dropping. He did not blame it.

"Very kind of you," Mr. Smith went on. "You understood that I was in need of funds, and you wished to assist me. I appreciate it, Mr. Mayo, but I don't feel I should accept so much money from a stranger."

Asey found his voice. "You can't accept—what do you mean!"

"You were very considerate of my feelings," Mr. Smith said, "tucking it in my pocket while I was asleep. That was the gesture of a gentleman. But I don't feel—"

"You should accept so much money from a stranger," Asey said. "I know. You said that before. Will you—er—step inside?"

"Thank you, but I must be on my way. I—"

"Feller," Asey said, "I think p'raps you better step inside, first!"

Mr. Smith wiped his feet very carefully on the door mat, an effort, Asey remembered, that Hector Colvin had not bothered to make.

"Come 'long," Asey said, "I want you to meet Mrs. Porter an' Miss Garth. Bets, this is the gentleman who used to know Frederick. This is Leopold Smith."

"My dear man," Betsey said warmly, "this is a pleasure. What do you say to make Frederick move?"

"'Gee,'" Mr. Smith said. "That is, Mr. Romano used some foreign phrases, but I always found that Frederick obeyed 'Gee' very nicely. Sometimes I said 'Gee-ap,' and he obeyed that too."

"We said a lot more than 'Gee' to him today," Betsey said. "Nothing happened."

"It is the tone of voice you use to Frederick that matters," Mr. Smith said. "Frederick is very sensitive to voices. He used to wave Mrs. Romano around his head after she sang, unless someone stopped him. Frederick didn't like her voice."

"Frederick," Betsey said, "isn't particularly crazy about mine. Now, tell me about food—"

"I hate," Asey said, "to bust into this chummy little chat on the home life of elephants, but I got things to do. Betsey, is this the feller you nearly killed on the bicycle near Colvin's last night, on your way over there?"

"Dear me, no," Betsey said. "*His* voice boomed."

"Didn't he ask you if you'd seen an elephant?" Asey demanded.

"Yes, he did. But it wasn't Mr. Smith, Asey. Mr. Smith's voice is—uh—gently flat. My man's wasn't. No, Asey, it was not Mr. Smith."

Mr. Smith looked very interested.

"What wasn't I?" he inquired.

"The easier way to go at it," Asey returned, "is for you to tell me where you spent yesterday evenin'. From six, say, until eight."

"Would five until nine-fifteen be all right?"

Asey drew a long breath. "Yes," he said. "Where was you from five until nine-fifteen?"

"I don't want you to think," Mr. Smith said, "that I was shirking my hunt for Frederick. I really wanted to find him, but—"

"Where were you?"

"It was wet," Mr. Smith said, "and I was wet, so I stopped in at that barber shop in the village and dried out a little. But my mind turned constantly toward Frederick, and I—"

Asey got up and went to the phone.

"Nellie," he said wearily to the operator, "gimme Danny's saloon. It's Sunday? So it is. Well, gimme the barber shop part, then. Gimme Danny, anyway."

Danny knew all about Mr. Smith. He told Asey about it, not without a certain amount of bitterness.

"I see," Asey said. "I see. No, thanks. Okay, Danny."

He was grinning when he turned away from the phone.

"I'd ought to have guessed it," he said. "Pea and shell, huh? No wonder you flipped that wallet off me so pretty. You seem to've cleaned out Danny's bunch, last evenin' an' today, too."

"I am a chemist, in a manner of speaking," Mr. Smith sounded very hurt. "I don't understand—"

"But when the flavorin' business goes on the blink," Asey said, "you ain't averse to provin' that the hand is quicker than the eye? Is that it?"

"The public," Mr. Smith said cautiously, "always seems to enjoy a game of skill. Sometimes, as I said to Mr. Romano, the older a game of skill is, the better the public seems to like it. Sometimes I think that a game of skill is perhaps more lucrative than something like an elephant."

Asey chuckled. "Your little game of skill yesterday," he said, "was more lucrative than you know. It's placed you at Danny's joint, an' given you an alibi you was rather needin'. Leopold, how many folks did you ask about Frederick, while you was huntin' him?"

"Oh, quite a large number of people. The—er—customers at the barber shop," Leopold said, "felt it was rather amusing, that I should be hunting an elephant. They thought it was funny—"

"Just saw the funny side," Asey murmured. "I shouldn't wonder. Go on."

"They kept laughing and laughing, and asking each other, 'Have you seen an elephant?'—and then they began to yell it at everyone they saw. I didn't mind, because I knew if they kept yelling it long enough, perhaps it might reach the ears of someone who really had seen Frederick, and then I could find him. I think, Mr. Mayo, that if Mrs. Porter was accosted by someone last evening who asked her about an elephant—"

"You think it was one of the boys comin' home from Danny's." Asey said. "So do I, an' I must say, it sort of disappoints me. I'd hoped that—but no matter. That won't work. Leopold, which way are you bound? I got to go out, an' I'll give you a lift—oho!"

He peered into the wallet which he had been holding.

"It's all there," Leopold said quickly.

"Yes," Asey flipped through the bills, "but these are ones an' twos. I had tens an' twenties. I thought this was sort of fatter an' fuller."

Mr. Smith nodded sadly. "Unfortunately," he said, "the customers in the barber shop had only ones and twos. The —er—tens and twenties became mislaid earlier in the day. The public in Orleans is rather astute. Perhaps you'll drop me off at the railroad station, or at a bus stop?"

"Asey is not going to drop you off anywhere," Betsey said, "not until I've found out more about Frederick. In fact, Mr. Smith, you wouldn't care for a temporary job as Frederick's keeper, would you? Until some kindly zoo takes him off my hands? You appear to understand Frederick, and Frederick clearly demands understanding. Just an adolescent problem child, that's Freddie."

Mr. Smith considered.

"In your spare moments," Betsey said, "you might give me some pointers about the pea and shell game. I'd like to teach Bill Porter a lesson. He's a sucker for the pea and shell industry. I have to drag him away from the county fairs."

"You an' Leopold settle his future between you," Asey said, putting on his coat. "You're old enough to know what you're hirin', Betsey. Say, Leopold, how'd you get over here? Your shoes don't look like you'd walked."

"I stopped a car," Leopold said simply.

"Yes, I know how you stop cars," Asey said. "Just a flick of the ankles, an' there you are."

"This car didn't stop as well as yours," Leopold said. "The brakes were not as efficient as your brakes. The woman wasn't very polite about being stopped, either."

Asey said he could understand that.

"But she calmed down when she found out that I only wanted a lift. She was rather a strange woman," Leopold said reminiscently. "I asked her where she was going, and she didn't seem quite to know. You see, I had made very careful inquiries about the roads. I didn't want to get lost again, like last night, and the roads here really are very confusing, with all this construction. So I asked where she was going, because I didn't want anyone to go out of their way just for my sake—"

"I begin to see," Betsey said, "why Frederick would get along with you, Mr. Smith. You are what I call a considerate man."

"Thank you," Leopold said. "I try to be. I always said to Mr. Romano that if he would be more patient, and more considerate of the public—"

"Leopold," Asey paused in the doorway, "what sort of— tell me more about this woman."

"She was lost," Leopold said. "So I suggested that if she would be good enough to bring me over here, I would in turn give her a brief résumé of the principal roads of the neighborhood. She brought me, and I did. I think," he added, "that she was a stranger here. She had rather harsh things to say about the Cape, too. She—"

"Leopold," Asey said, "what did this strange woman look like?"

A dreamy look came into Leopold's eyes. "She was a beautiful, beautiful blonde," he said. "A beautiful, beautiful blonde. One of the most beautiful—"

"You see how she affects people, Asey," Betsey said. "Of

course, it's Mrs. Monfort's missing blonde, isn't it? Was she exotic, Mr. Smith?"

"Boy," said Mr. Smith appreciatively, "boy oh boy, oh boy!"

"With an accent," Betsey said, "and a glove on her left hand. That's Eda, all right. That's the girl. Is she the one the police hadn't found in the car, Asey? She is? And you're going after her—for shame, Asey Mayo, chasing blondes at your age!"

Asey sat down rather suddenly on the arm of an easy chair.

"What's this," he demanded, "about a glove?"

"That glove!" Carol said. "I noticed that, too. Is a single glove the *dernier cri* these days, Betsey? I was terribly impressed by it. Terribly."

"I wondered, myself," Betsey said. "I intended to ask you—"

"What glove?" Asey almost shot out the two words.

"This black glove on her left hand," Betsey said. "I simply couldn't take my eyes off it when I saw her, mad as I was. But if she had it on while she was driving—did she, Mr. Smith? Well, if she had it on while she was driving, maybe it isn't style, Carol. Isn't that odd. D'you suppose it serves any purpose?"

"What sort of purpose could it serve?" Carol returned. "After all, either you wear a glove, or you don't wear a glove, and—"

"Oh, you know what I mean," Betsey said. "Maybe there's something the matter with her hand. Maybe it's scarred, or disfigured, or something. I've got a cousin who always wears a scarf about her throat to hide the mark of a burn. It's one—"

She stopped short and stared at Asey.

"Asey Mayo," she said, "what *is* the matter? Have you seen a ghost?"

"What," Asey said briefly, "amounts to a ghost, Betsey."

He strode across the room to the built-in case and yanked down two books.

Something about the purposeful way he turned pages silenced even Betsey, although questions were almost falling off the tip of her tongue. She had a feeling that Asey wouldn't even hear her questions, anyway, even if she yelled at him.

"So that," Asey said, finally snapping the second book shut, "is what they call that place now. Why in time didn't Warner—" he checked himself, apparently just realizing that he had spoken out loud, "why in time don't people *tell* me these things? Why don't I get told things?"

"You haven't told us very much," Leopold Smith remarked. "Do you know who she is, this blonde woman I just met? Is she a foreigner? It seemed to me that she was a foreigner, by the way she talked. Is she—"

"Asey," Betsey said, "where are you going? Where are you—"

"What's happened now?" Carol demanded.

"Nothin's happened," Asey told her. "I just sort of come to."

"Where are you *going?*" Betsey said.

Asey smiled at her.

"I honestly don't know," he said, "if I ought to go to the public lib'ry, or find a pack of bloodhounds, or just plain hide. I'd like best to hide. Leopold, what a fateful man you turned out to be!"

13. CAROL and Betsey and

Mr. Smith sat in silence in the living room until they heard the roadster pass down the driveway.

"Mr. Mayo jokes a lot, doesn't he?" Mr. Smith said. "I think he jokes more than anyone I ever saw. But do you know, I don't think that he was joking when he said he'd like best to hide. I think that he meant that, don't you?"

"Mr. Smith," Betsey said, "you're a mental colossus if I ever saw one."

He thanked her modestly. "I always used to tell Mr. Romano that—"

"Asey was looking at the atlas, Bets," Carol picked up the books from the chair. "The atlas, and a book about Europe today. Now what in the name of something or other would either have to do with all this mess?"

"Search me," Betsey said. "I wish I knew what he looked at. What page, I mean."

"I know," Leopold said.

"You know—how?"

"Why, he thumbed the pages of the atlas like a pack of cards," Leopold said. "I just automatically counted. Old habits cling, I always say."

Betsey thrust the atlas at him, and Mr. Smith opened it and without hesitation indicated a page.

"This is the one," he said. "I remember all that green in the corner. I always notice green."

Carol peered over Betsey's shoulder.

"Looks like a lot of Balkans to me," she said. "I don't see that this gets us very far."

Betsey agreed. "But he mentioned Warner, and you can't tell what that might mean. He might be connected with anything, even a Balkan. Well, well!"

"Maybe Mrs. Monfort's a Balkan," Carol suggested. "Or Eda. You know, I don't know why they couldn't be. Those green shirted men looked more Balkan than anything else. The whole business is a little Balkany, Betsey, if you stop to think it out. Intrigue—"

"Intrigue in the Balkans," Betsey pointed out, "is all very well, but what would it be doing on Cape Cod? Asey Mayo and Eda, the beautiful blonde spy—no, Carol. Not on Cape Cod. Things like that don't happen on Cape Cod."

"Darling," Carol said, "if you stop and think things out clearly, you'll be forced to the painful conclusion that a vast number of things have happened on Cape Cod since last evening, none of which you could reasonably expect to have happen on Cape Cod."

"Yes, but—"

"No," Carol said, "don't yes-but. You stop and consider. Begin with where the hat gets shot off that man's head, and work through everything up to Uncle Hector's starving alibis. And Mr. Smith, and Frederick. And we don't know all the things that Asey's been mixed up with. Just you stop and do some considering, Betsey darling. Just you ponder."

Betsey said acidly that she had been doing practically nothing else.

"Ponder some more, then," Carol said. "And then explain to me why Asey Mayo, of all people, virtually pales when he finally remembers who that blonde creature is—"

"I suppose you think I didn't notice the way he looked? Carol, I think we ought to go out after Asey."

"Is that so?" Carol said. "You don't think, darling, that you and I have done quite enough of this spur-of-the-minute dashing around?"

"But someone ought to know that he's gone after that woman! I do think we should go, Carol."

"I don't," Leopold said.

"What have you got to do with it?" Betsey demanded.

"Nothing, really," Leopold answered. "But she had that rifle, you know, and at least two revolvers. Right in the car with her."

"What!"

"Yes, she did. I was almost afraid for a moment that I'd made a grave mistake in stopping her," Leopold said. "That's why I don't feel it would be wise, Mrs. Porter, for you to start out after her. But Mr. Mayo will get along. He jokes a lot, but I feel that he is a very wide-awake man. Mr. Mayo will not be caught napping."

Betsey raised her eyebrows. "What about that wallet?" she asked.

Leopold looked very hurt. "That was an error of faith, Mrs. Porter. He was not caught napping."

"Maybe," Betsey said, "but even Asey Mayo isn't infallible.

And I don't think this blonde will be guilty of much napping, either. A rifle and a couple of guns! Does that sound like napping to you? Does that give you the impression that she's not alert?"

"Nevertheless, she naps," Leopold said firmly.

"How do you know?"

Leopold permitted himself a smile. "Mr. Mayo may be guilty of an occasional error of faith, but I think I may safely say that the beautiful blonde—really, she is very striking! But the beautiful blonde naps."

He drew a small gold cigarette case from his pocket and presented it to Betsey.

"See?" he said. "She naps."

"Leopold Smith!" Betsey said severely, "if you work for me, I shall shake you every night by the heels—what a case! Carol, good Lord, Carol, it's even got a crest on it! Lordy, that's a thing, that is!"

"Let's look at the papers," Carol said.

"Papers? What papers?"

"In it, you goose," Carol said. "Open it and fish them out."

"Open it and fish what papers out?" Betsey said. "What are you talking about?"

"You just don't get around, Bets," Carol said, shaking her head. "By rights, there should be papers inside that. Lousy with code. Or a treaty, or something. *Will* you open it?"

Betsey sniffed, and snapped the case open.

"There, little one," she said, "there's glamor for yez. Two mentholated cigarettes, crushed and very stale. Two measly—"

"All right," Carol said. "What about the inner compartment? There's always an inner compartment. Comrade Smith, you see if there isn't."

"If you can find any inner compartment in this," Betsey said, "I'll—"

"Be careful, Mrs. Porter," Leopold said. "There is one, you know. There—why, how did you know there would be a paper in it?"

Carol looked at him, looked inside the case, and then went and sat down on the couch.

"Apparently," she said, "there are just no limits. None at all. Got a feather, Bets? Wave it and watch me bounce."

"But how did you know about the paper?" Leopold repeated.

"She didn't," Betsey said. "She didn't know. She was being funny, and it backfired. Read what the paper says, Leopold. I couldn't bring myself to the point of touching the thing. What's it say?"

"It says, Vivian, El—I don't understand this, Mrs. Porter. You better—"

Betsey had the paper in her hand before he finished speaking.

" 'Vivian,' " she read. " 'El 4-9768. Ask for Mrs. Garth.' Carol, do you hear that? Carol, do you hear that! Leopold, did you swipe this case from that blonde tonight? No, don't fence and parry. Did you take it from her just now, when she brought you over?"

Leopold sighed and said that he had.

"She knew mother!" Carol said. "Betsey, let's—"

"Let's start right out after Asey!"

"No, let's go at it the sane way. Let's call Talbot, and let the police—"

"Really," Leopold said, "I regret this. Truly, if you will return the case to—"

Betsey looked at him with scorn. "You," she said, "are the last person we're bothering with. You don't think I'm calling the police because *you* took that case, do you? The only thing—"

"Then perhaps," Leopold said, "I may go—"

"Go where?"

"And look after Frederick. Perhaps I'd better go right now. Frankly, I should prefer not to come in contact with the police. Last week, Mr. Romano and I had some unfortunate experiences with them, and I think it might be better if I did not see them just now."

"Then you depart and look after Frederick," Betsey said. "Jennie's husband will take you over and find you a place to sleep. Do I need to warn you that the long arm of Asey Mayo is a lot more potent than the arm of the police? Okay, run along."

"Should you," Carol said after Leopold hastily left, "have—"

"Let him go? I don't know," Betsey said. "But he has to go somewhere, and he might as well be making himself useful with Frederick. And somehow, I don't think that Leopold will try to beat it. Leopold is not dumb. Carol, think of that blonde having your mother's phone number— don't you really think that we'd better try to find Asey?"

"No!" Carol said. "You'll go out of this house over my

dead body! Whatever's going on, it's nothing for you and me to leap into. You go call Talbot, and let him do things."

"You're so sensible," Betsey said with some irritation. "Just so contained, and so sensible—it's *bad* for you, you'll be an emotional wreck—"

"Betsey, go call Talbot. I'm not going to fall for any more of your extravert thoughts."

"Oh, all right," Betsey said, "all right! I'll go call him. But if Asey only knew! Wouldn't I like to reach out and put my hands on Asey Mayo!"

As a matter of fact, she almost might have.

Asey was sitting out back in the stacks of the local library, not half a mile away. At his feet and on the table before him were piles of magazines, American magazines and English magazines—mentally, Asey blessed the Misses Sanderson, who presented the library at intervals with their outdated surplus.

He found the face he was hunting in a picture of the guests at a state ball in London. From then on, his work was comparatively simple.

Half an hour later he put the magazines back in their compartments in the stacks, and, ignoring the 'No Smoking' sign, lighted his pipe.

Some things were beginning to clear themselves up in his mind, although they didn't begin to be as clear as he would have liked them to be.

That little yellow spot on the map that looked like a drop of spilled orange juice was a place he had never expected to hear about again. He couldn't even pronounce the name it had now, there were too many consonants in the wrong places for his tongue to manage. But it had once been Festenburg, and Warner always referred to it as Little Graustark.

It was Warner's fault that they had landed there. Warner had lost the train, and it was the last train for many days to come. Train service in the time of Bela Kun was invariably strange and intermittent.

At the start, Asey remembered, Warner had considered the whole thing a tremendous lark. They'd been doing a routine errand for General What-was-his-name, the one with the eyeglass, and Warner had welcomed that little revolution. Warner had been particularly delighted with the blonde girl who seemed to be running it. Warner thought she was the most beautiful thing he'd ever seen.

"A countess or something," Warner had always been patriotically vague about titles. "Anyway, she's the daughter of a count they ran off his estates and killed, but she's with this crowd now. Just a kid, but boy, she's making things hum!"

At home, Asey thought, the girl would have been in boarding school, letting mice loose in the chapel and smoking cigarettes behind the teacher's back. In Europe, at that time, she had greater scope. The thing that had always appalled him about that business was the number of things a girl that age had been able to think up. That she thought them up was, on the whole, a little worse than that she caused them to be done. For twenty-four hours, she had held Warner prisoner. After the first hour, Warner had not thought it was such a tremendous lark. He had been very nearly dead when Asey finally got him out of her clutches. He

emembered thinking at the time that it might have been
etter if she had killed Warner outright.

She wore the glove on her left hand even then. Asey had
never personally cared to investigate, but someone had said
hat her hand had been mangled in an accident. At any rate,
t served the purpose of identifying her now; Asey couldn't
emember the names she had called herself in those days,
but she had never been known by anything as brief and as
imple as Eda.

And here she was, glove and all, pot-shotting at Mrs.
Monfort.

He was a fool, Asey thought, not to have guessed that
Mrs. Monfort's regal manner was no pose. But she had been
born an American, in spite of the titles she married. And
her husband, who had died recently, had been one of the
men who put Little Graustark back on its feet. The magazines gave no clew as to what official part she now played
in running the place, but from the way her face popped up
in pictures with this big shot and that big shot, at one state
function after another, in one country after another, Asey
guessed that Mrs. Monfort had more than the tip of her
finger in the pie.

That much was all right.

But what was she doing over here at Hector Colvin's,
and why had she let that blonde bit of nitroglycerin loose
in her household?

Of course, Asey thought as he puffed at his pipe, there
was something to be said for allowing Eda the run of your
household. She would be in a place where you could keep

an eye on her, if you suspected that she was up to mischief
Perhaps, on the whole, Eda was less of a menace in the
bosom of Mrs. Monfort's household than she was, for ex
ample, on cemetery hills.

Eda and Mrs. Monfort, between them, must account for
Warner's presence. But, Asey thought grimly, he certainly
wished that Warner had enlightened him on a few things a
the start. He'd straightened out a few items with all thi
home work, but there were still plenty of things that couldn'
be answered.

He remembered Ralph Budd's suspicions about Warner
and wondered—but that was impossible. Warner was al
right. He had to be.

"He *is* all right," Asey said, as if to reassure himself. "He's
no Baddy."

If he started to worry about Warner, he'd never get anywhere.

There was still the problem of Hector Colvin. And there
was still this purpose of Mrs. Monfort's.

The purpose was easier to guess about than Hector. If
those magazines were to be believed, Mrs. Monfort's purpose probably concerned itself with her little orange juice
drop of a country. What Hector Colvin might have to do
with it, Asey couldn't imagine.

He could, he supposed, try to find out.

He snapped off the green shaded light, and groped his
way to the library's front door, which he locked. Then, re-
membering Miss Hopkins's instructions, he tried the door
handle to make sure it *was* locked. Miss Hopkins had not

really wanted to give him the key, not until he murmured things about a new encyclopaedia.

The Hopkins house was dark, so in accordance with still more instructions, Asey went around to the back door and left the key under the pail on the back steps.

An upstairs window squeaked open.

"Is that you, Asey? Did you—"

"Yes'm," Asey stifled a laugh. "Yes'm. I locked the door, an' tried the handle, an' the key's right here under the pail. If you'll buy those books, please, an' send the bill to me—good night!"

He hurried away before she could give him any more instructions.

As he got into the roadster, he wondered just what Miss Hopkins would say if she knew that a woman like Eda was running around loose in her vicinity.

Asey chuckled at the thought.

But of course they would have picked Eda up by now. That was the great advantage of the Cape. Once people got on the Cape, they had to stay there or return the way they came. Or take to boats, which wasn't likely in this case. You could bottle people up on the Cape. Eda had already been lost, and Asey didn't think that Leopold's information would have enlightened her to any great extent. At this time of year, with roads so torn up that main highways looked like side roads, it wasn't at all hard to get lost.

At any rate even Max, even Bert Blossom, Asey thought, ought to have got hold of Eda by now.

Of course, she might have left the sedan and picked up

another car. But he had enough faith in the police to feel
that they had coped with her. There was so little traffic, they
couldn't have missed.

Just outside the village of Pochet, he caught sight of the
sedan in a ditch to his right.

There was no mistaking that sedan, even in its crumpled
condition. That was the sedan which he had followed from
the cemetery, the car that belonged to the father of Toots'
boy friend.

Asey drove past it without stopping.

About a mile further along, he turned off to the right on
a side lane, and started back in the same direction from
which he had come.

It didn't seem humanly possible that the police could have
failed to pick up Eda. But if they hadn't, Asey was not
going to take any chances. He was going to proceed in a
very cautious circle.

The distance between the two roads was not great. Parking the roadster, he took the keys and started across lots.

He congratulated himself, as he neared the sedan, that he
had not touched a single branch. Not a single twig had
snapped under his feet. No ramping tiger could have been
stalked with any greater care than he employed in stalking
that ditched sedan.

"Stalkin'," Asey said, "de luxe."

He even paused for a good quarter of an hour under the
shelter of a pine tree, near the side of the road.

During that time, a coupe and a truck had passed by. The
drivers of both cars slowed down and peered into the wreck-
age before they drove on.

Certainly if Eda had been lurking around to pinch another car, she either had done so already, or she would have done so with those two.

"Mayo," Asey murmured, "you're an ole sissy. Hiding behind pine trees. An' this afternoon, you hid beside a rock, remember."

He strode over to the sedan.

It was empty, but in the back seat was the rifle she had used that afternoon.

As he opened the door to reach for it, something jammed into the small of his back.

"Dear me," Asey said, "an' after all the care I took, too!"

14. "STAND still. Fold your arms behind your back."

"Hi, Eda," Asey said conversationally, "where were you, up a tree?"

He had talked himself out of a similar situation with this blonde, in the days gone by, and he hoped that he might be able to do it again.

"Fold your arms behind your back!"

Asey folded them.

"I don't think," he said, "this is any way to treat an ole friend. First you shoot at me, now you jam guns into me—"

"Keep still."

"As I r'call," Asey continued, "you was doin' the same thing the last time we met. The years ain't taught you a thing, have they? You just don't seem to be able to learn a bit by experience."

"Where are the keys to your car?"

"I swallowed 'em," Asey said.

"This is no time to joke!" the throaty voice was just as ominous as it used to be, Asey thought. "I want those keys."

"That's pretty silly of you," Asey said. "That car'll mark you. With my roadster an' your black glove, Eda, you won't have a chance. Say, why did you kill Vivian Garth?"

"I did not kill her!"

"Eda," Asey said, "I know just enough about you to know

that if anyone's killed, an' you're around, you are responsible. 'Member that wall in the courtyard by that inn, where you used to stand 'em up an' mow 'em down, with your machine gun? Whyn't you take a machine gun to Mrs. Monfort? You might of had some better results, Eda. A machine gun at twenty paces is one of the most efficient things—but you know all that. That courtyard—"

"If you say another word," Eda said, "I shall shoot."

Asey waited. If she had been going to shoot, he thought, she probably would have shot by now. On the other hand, you couldn't make any predictions about what Eda might do.

Expertly, she removed the car keys from his pocket.

"Now," she said, "I shall dispose of you, and then I shall dispose of your friend Warner—"

"You said that once b'fore," Asey reminded her. "But you didn't."

"This time I shall not be so foolish as to let you talk."

"So," Asey said, "you learned somethin' with the passin' of years, after all, huh? Well, b'fore you begin your disposin', I do wish you'd tell me why you killed Vivian Garth —how did you happen to get mixed up with her?"

He did not really think that Eda had any connection with Vivian Garth, nor did he think she had killed Vivian, he was simply making a strenuous effort to take up Eda's mind while he worked his feet out of the gummy mud without her being aware of the fact. A good swift kick would take that gun out of the small of his back, but he had to be sure of his footing.

"How did you know that I knew Vivian!" Eda demanded.

She sounded a little startled, but nowhere near as startled as Asey felt.

"I'm the feller that knows things," Asey drawled so that she couldn't guess how startled he was. "Don't you remember anythin', woman? Somehow I'd of thought that part would of stuck in your mind."

"You don't know a thing," Eda said. "Not a thing."

She answered without any hesitation, and she sounded properly scornful and incredulous. But at the same time, Asey felt that Eda was beginning to have a doubt or two.

He laughed what he hoped was a very meaning and foreboding laugh.

If Eda continued to talk, then he could be reasonably sure that she was worried about how much he knew. If she dropped the matter, then it was just about time for him to act. Eda might, as Mrs. Monfort insisted, always miss; she might be as bad a shot as she seemed. But on the whole, Asey preferred not to be the exception that might prove that she was.

He wondered what in thunder she was waiting for, anyway. She had the car keys. He couldn't think of any reason for her dallying around. Eda was not the sort to dally, unless she had a purpose. And now that he thought of it, why hadn't Eda got away from the Cape while she still had the chance?

She had failed in her attempts to kill Mrs. Monfort. Why hadn't she packed up and departed? If Eda still wanted to take a whack at Mrs. Monfort, why didn't she get to it? What was she larruping around in old second-hand sedans for, just to kill time? There was something faintly ridiculous in the thought of Eda just killing anything as bloodless as time.

"How—" Eda stopped and began again. "So, you made Johann talk, did you?"

"Johann? My dear girl, we never even bothered with Johann," Asey said easily. An occasional item of pure fact, he thought, always lent an air of reality. "Johann? Pooh."

Apparently the little item of pure fact bothered Eda a lot. It bothered her far more, Asey felt, than anything he might have made up.

His feet were all set now. He was all balanced and ready, and he could get her any time he wanted to. But first it might be wise to dally with Eda and see if he could find out what she really knew about Vivian and Vivian's death.

"If you knew," Eda said, "why didn't you arrest him? Why did you not stop him before he killed her?"

"We are waiting," Asey said darkly.

"You don't know!" Eda said. "You are trying to trick me. You don't know!"

"In this country," Asey said, "we do things so dif'rent, Eda. We find out things first before we take steps—you know, that'd of curtailed your goin's on a lot, wouldn't it? Havin' to know things first. On the other hand, maybe you'd of been satisfied with lettin' mice loose in the chapel if you'd—"

His sentence dangled in mid air.

Quickly, so quickly that it hadn't seemed possible and it didn't seem possible even now, Eda's hand had flashed under his corduroy coat and removed his Colt from the shoulder holster.

Eda's throaty laughter was, he thought, pretty nasty.

"Thank you, Mr. Mayo," she said. "Thank you. I have dropped the small stick now, and I have your gun—I have learned something after all, you see, with the passing of the years. I have learned to make use of a small stick, as you did once when you had no gun. I have learned to let other people do the talking. You and I, Mr. Mayo, know who killed Vivian, but you will never find any opportunity of availing yourself—"

Asey kicked and jumped backwards in one swift movement.

His lashing foot must have achieved its purpose, he thought, for although the Colt barked, the bullet went whining far to the left.

Asey scrambled to his feet.

"Yah!" he said. "Missed me again—oh, no, you don't."

He struck the gun up and out of her hands, just as she fired again.

Instantly she turned around and started to run, and Asey started after her.

He grabbed her, but she wriggled loose and darted ahead again through the woods.

This was the time, Asey thought grimly, that he had her.

She was wearing pyjamas under her short coat, the pyjamas that everyone had so unfailingly mentioned whenever they spoke of her. And although she was ripping along fast enough now, those pyjamas would slow her down in the woods, if they didn't just plain out and out trip her. He himself had had trouble enough stalking through the

nderbrush, even when he had time to feel where he was
tepping.

That ground was treacherous and boggy. Old branches
ay among the network of hog cranberry vines. Someone
ad trimmed them, but had never picked them up. And if
he heel of her pumps once caught in the hog cranberry—

The heel of his own shoe caught.

He stumbled and clutched at the branch of a tree to keep
rom falling.

The branch came off in his hands, and he went hurtling
orward. His head hit against a tree stump with the sound
of an egg breaking against the side of a bowl.

He felt like a broken egg when he came to.

"Like all the broken eggs in—like an omelet," he muttered.

It was raining again, pouring pitchforks and barn shovels,
and he had been out long enough to have become as sodden
and boggy as the ground on which he lay. There was a
lump on his head that felt like a grapefruit. His ear stung,
and then sent the little pains down the left side of his face.
They stayed there a moment and romped around, and then
went back to his ear and stung again.

His first effort to rise almost convinced him that it might
be simpler to lie there and die of pneumonia.

But after he got up, it wasn't so bad. Most of those shooting stabs had been due to a blackberry vine that was wound
around him. After he divested himself of that, he felt definitely better.

He walked slowly and with great care back to the nearer
road, where the sedan still lay crumpled by the ditch.

The Colt was, he supposed, kicking around there somewhere in the mud, but he made no attempt to try to find it.

"What's the use?" he said bitterly to himself. "What good's it do for you to have a gun, Mayo? Seems like the only reason you carry a gun is to let blondes take it away from you, you big cheese!"

Wrenching open the door to the back seat, Asey got in. The angle wasn't so bad after you accustomed yourself to it. And at least it was dry.

He had no idea what Eda might be up to. He had no idea what might be going on now. Perhaps a sturdier soul might walk through that downpour, over those roads, and find out. Perhaps he should.

Asey yawned, pulled a blanket that smelled of clams from the floor of the car, draped it over himself, and went to sleep.

It occurred to him as he dropped off that he couldn't be more faithful about sleeping in ditched cars if he were making a survey of the situation.

Noah Snow's father said as much when he waked Asey the next morning around nine o'clock.

"Make quite a habit of this kind of thing, don't you?" he inquired.

Asey blinked at the sun, and felt the side of his head.

"Is that blood?" Snow demanded suddenly.

"Is what blood?"

"All over the side of your face—say, what're you doin' here, anyway? You look, say, you look terrible! What happened to you?"

Asey grinned.

"I was bein' foiled," he said, "by a beautiful, beautiful blonde. An' if you was to ask me where my car was, Harry, I'd have to break down an' tell you that I think she took it with her."

Snow looked at him suspiciously.

"Say, what is this, Asey? Yesterday, you were havin' your pocket picked by a man named Smith!"

"Leopold F. Smith," Asey said, and yawned. "F for Fate. Huh. I wonder if Eda's got a middle name. Harry, the time has passed when I could sleep in ditches night after night an' not feel it."

"You look awful," Snow told him candidly. "You really do. You look terrible. You look like ten nights in a bar room, or something."

"I feel like scrambled eggs," Asey said, "left a long time on a plate. An' you know, Harry, you don't look so good yourself. You seem sort of perturbed—who sent you to get the car?"

"Nobody. I was just goin' to ask you whose it was," Snow said. "It looked like Ed Butterfield's, but I see it's got New York plates on."

"New York plates, huh?" Asey said. "Huh! I never noticed that last night. Seems like Eda learned a good deal, with the passin' of years. Wonder where she picked them up. Well, I'll give her credit. 'Course, it does sort of seem that the cops might still have picked it up on principle. Does Ed Butterfield have a son, a weedy boy with pimples? An' he's got a girl friend named Toots who yells all the time."

Snow said that was Ed Butterfield's boy, to a T.

"Then this is Butterfield's car," Asey said. "You better yank what's left of it away—oh, you haven't got your wrecker with you?"

"No, I wasn't out on business. I wasn't out to get this car. I just saw it an' stopped, to see whose—as a matter of fact," Snow said nervously, "I was headin' over your way to get you. But I won't bother you with that now. Don't you want me to drive you home? You *are* sort of bunged up."

"If you didn't take me," Asey said, crawling out of the sedan, "I don't know as I wouldn't of burst into tears. I've had my fill of cars in ditches. Did you want me for anythin' special, Harry? You look upset."

"I am," Snow said. "Say, are those your guns in the car? That rifle an' the others?"

"Nope, mine's in a puddle over yonder, see?" Asey picked it up and thrust it into his belt.

Snow stared at him. "What's been goin' on, with your gun in a puddle, an' these here—these are all empty, Asey!"

"Uh-huh."

"Don't you want to look at 'em?"

"I pretty much guessed they'd be empty," Asey said. "If they'd been loaded—well, don't let's go into that."

"What's been happenin'?"

"I told you," Asey said, "I got foiled by a blonde. Same sort of thing you used to see in the movies. Pearl White in the 'Iron Claw'—"

"Somebody clawed your cheek, all right," Snow said. "There's a thorn in it—lean over. Asey, don't you want a doctor?"

"If I didn't know I was clawed," Asey said, "I guess I

don't need doctors. Harry, I want to know what the matter with you is. It's nothin' about the kids, is it? Noah an' the twins?"

"What made you think that?" Snow asked quickly. "Why'd you say that? Did you know they was up to something? Did they tell you—oh, but I'll wait till you get fixed up an' feeling better. I guess you got problems enough, from your looks."

"Harry," Asey said with some annoyance, "stop this yappin', or I'll go back to that sedan. An' I do want to get home, an' get to a phone—look, what's happened to the kids? What have they gone an' done?"

"I'll tell you," Snow said, "after I got you home—honest, Asey, it's too long to tell you now. Wait'll you get home, an' get that bump an' those cuts all fixed up. Then I'll go into it."

Asey was irritated by his absolute refusal to say another word during the ride home. But the silence did give him a chance to do some quiet thinking. He had a lot of things to look into.

Before he could get to the phone, Betsey and Carol jumped on him.

"So," Betsey said, "that's how you look after you chase beautiful blondes, is it? Asey, we've practically gone crazy, and we found out the most amazing thing—"

"After I've phoned," Asey said. "Not now."

He looked so utterly weary that Betsey almost crept away.

Talbot had left the Colvin house, but Asey talked with Max.

"Is Mrs. Monfort okay? Good. What about the blonde? *What* blonde? No matter, Max," Asey said, "if you'd met her, you wouldn't ask what blonde. Have you seen my car? Car? C-a-r. No, you haven't. Vandals? You want me to see vandals? Max, I seen too many. I—oh, all right. I'll be over, if Colvin wants me. In a little while."

Asey yelled for Betsey. "Now," he said, "what did you find out?"

"After," Betsey said severely, "you've had a nice bath, and some food, and got your wounds attended to, and clean, dry clothes. Not now!"

The bath and the food and the dry clothes all did wonders in repairing Asey's looks.

"There," Betsey said, "if it weren't for that lump, and the iodine streaks, and the adhesive tape, no one would guess you'd been cavorting around with blondes— Asey, I can't hold in any longer. I've got to tell you what we found out last night. Leopold swiped the blonde's cigarette case, and in it was a paper with Vivian Garth's phone number! There, what do you think of that?"

Her face fell.

"Asey," she said, "you don't seem surprised! You don't even look pleased!"

"I'm not surprised at anythin', right now," Asey said. "An' I'd be a lot more pleased if she'd jotted down the name of the person that killed Vivian, instead of Vivian's phone number."

"Where's Eda now?"

Asey shrugged elaborately. "An' I don't care," he added, "if I ever see her again."

"Look, Asey," Snow said uncomfortably, "I guess I better run along. You got a lot to do, an' all this business—"

"Sit down," Asey said. "Got any more to tell me, Betsey?"

"Nothing important. Only that we spent the night shuttling Leopold between here and my house with a lot of books," Betsey said. "We found out Eda's family from her crest on the cigarette case, and we found out lots of details about her ancestors. She had one that was quartered by the king in person and then thrown to the dogs—isn't that a piquant bit? And they all had names like Paul the Bloody, or Hubert the Butcher. Her grandfather was The Mad Count—of course, we didn't find anything awfully up to date, but it's nice background."

"There never was any question in my mind," Asey said, "but what she come by her habits natural—see you later, Bets. I want to talk with Harry. Harry, what's the matter?"

"I don't know where to begin, even," Snow said. "I—you know, they been tearin' up the roads with the cutters, don't you?"

"I certainly do. Steam rollers, like, with the spikes that gouge. There's one I know intimately," Asey said, "beyond the Colvin place. I've sashayed around it till I'm sick an' tired. It wouldn't of hurt the road committee one bit to have their men leave things at the side of the road instead of the plumb center of it. I—"

He remembered suddenly that Noah and Pink and Pokey had been over by that cutter the previous afternoon, when he was starting off to the cemetery hill.

"Asey, did you ever see any of the kids playin' around that cutter—oh, I don't suppose it matters if you seen 'em or not." Snow got up and walked around the room. "Everybody else in Christendom's seen 'em, an' that's what matters.

But they say not. An' if they say not, then I believe 'em."

Asey looked sharply at Snow's face, and changed his mind about commenting on the way in which Snow told a story.

"That roller up by Colvin's that was left there," Snow went on, "wasn't steam, but a diesel. It's been in my shop a lot, an' the kids have played around it there. Asey, those three are a wearin' bunch. They pester the life out of people to get pictures, an' they've taken a lot of pictures that have got 'em into plenty of trouble."

Asey agreed.

"But those kids, they're not bad," Snow said. "I admit they get into scrapes, I'll admit they can get you so mad you want to whale 'em, but they tell the truth. If they say they didn't, I know they didn't. I don't care if all the world saw 'em this morning at five o'clock!"

Asey reached for his pipe. "The way I get this," he said, "the steam roller that's a diesel has got played with, an' the boys say they didn't. That right? Now, where were they at five this mornin'— Harry, don't tell me that they were at Hector Colvin's!"

"Hector Colvin!" Snow said hotly. "I don't care what he says he's goin' to do. I believe those kids. An' look, Asey. I know you're a busy man, but you'll help me, won't you? Hector Colvin can't talk like that to me! He's not goin' to put my son into any reform school!"

"Oh," Asey said, "oh, don't tell me they been harryin' Hector again! An' with Hector in the mood he's in—"

"You can't tell me anything about his mood!" Snow said. "I just see red when I think of that little squirt. But it wasn't Hector Colvin the boys were mad at, Asey. They were mad with that Mrs. Monfort. She had one of her servants beat 'em. Now, I'll be fair!" Snow banged the table with his fist. "There's been many the time that I've whacked 'em. But this woman's servant used a real whip! That's what happened yesterday mornin', an' it was the whip that got 'em mad. The idea of it, more."

"I understand," Asey said. "A razor strop or a hair brush is one thing, but a whip's somethin' else again. Now I'm caught up. The kids tried to take pictures yesterday mornin'. Mrs. Monfort had them whipped. An' the kids planned to get back at her."

"That's where the cutter comes in," Snow said. "See, I told you it was a long story. They planned to run it over and block her drive."

"Tearin' the drive, en route."

"No. And the road outside's goin' to be cut, anyway. They were just plannin' on leavin' it there in the drive. That was all. It was enough, an' it was wrong, but it seemed a fine idea to them. You know, like cows in belfries. I did that once, myself," Snow said. "I thought it was just as smart! Well, the kids got up early this mornin', an' sneaked over to Colvin's place—this is their story, mind you. When they got there—"

"They saw all the cops—"

"Oh, they knew the cops were there. But you don't think that would've kept 'em away, do you? That just added. Look, Asey, you'll just have to go over an' see what the kids found—but I don't suppose you feel like it, do you? I guess you got too much to do."

Asey reached for his hat.

"That's white of you," Snow said, "to bother with the kids, when there's all this business of Vivian Garth going on."

Asey pointed out that he had to go to the Colvin place anyway, and that he was considerably overdue, as it was.

"Why didn't Ralph Budd snap to?" Asey added. "He was over there. If the twins were in trouble—"

"He got called away around four. Someone had to be taken to the hospital, an' Budd's about the only doctor functionin' here, right now. I wish he'd been over there, myself!"

"Look," Asey said as he walked out and got into Snow's car, "just sort of prepare me for what to expect, will you? What did the kids *do,* really?"

Snow sighed.

"Asey, that's just it, that's just the whole point! *They* didn't do anything. They just went there. But the minute they were seen, they got grabbed—"

"By the cops?"

"By everybody! By the cops, an' the servants, an' Hector Colvin, an' that Monfort woman—the whole kit an' caboodle jumped on 'em, an' said look what they'd done, an' this was the time they were going to get theirs, an' Colvin began shooting off his mouth about this reform school notion of his, an'—"

"But what happened?" Asey asked. "What had happened? What did the kids get booked for?"

"Don't you see, Asey," Snow said, "don't you get it? Everyone thinks *they* were in the steam roller—the cutter—whatever you want to call it. But they weren't, don't you see? It was someone else that'd taken it before they got there!"

Before they reached the Colvin place, Asey had formed a pretty good mental picture of what to expect.

And his mental picture proved to be reasonably accurate. It was the other things that turned up, however, that impressed him far more.

15. THE FRONT part of the Colvin estate was as sleekly impressive as ever. But the grounds at the rear reminded Asey at once of Betsey Porter's new wing, and the ensuing shambles.

Not, he thought as he examined it critically, not that this was anywhere near as picturesque as Betsey's. No one would ever want to photograph it as the bombardment of Shanghai. But this was a great deal more final. Hector Colvin's pride and joy, those winding tar roads, were wrecked. They were demolished. There wasn't enough left to mend. About the only thing Hector could do was to have people sweep up the remains and start in fresh.

"Look," Snow said bleakly, "at those tennis courts, will you?"

"I see them," Asey said. "They wouldn't do for any bombardment pictures, either, but you might be able to work a nice rice field out of 'em."

Snow's voice failed at the gardens. He just pointed and then turned away from the sight.

"The new orchard, too, huh?" Asey said. "Just took that in his stride, this steam roller lad. Harry, has anyone explained to you why someone didn't *hear* all this? My experience with steam rollers is kind of limited, but I should of thought that the whole household would of been out here before he was fairly inside the rear gates. I take it he come in the back way."

"That don't make a lot of noise," Snow said. "An' then there was that rain, remember, about that time. An' the wind was blowin' a gale. An' this is a good distance from the house. A good city block."

"I'll never believe," Asey said, "that someone couldn't have heard this. Good Lord, man, this house was guarded by servants an' cops—don't tell me that not one of that bunch heard that cutter goin'! I think that I'll look into this."

After spending half an hour looking into the situation, Asey came to the conclusion that two brass bands and a couple of cheering sections could have entered the house without anyone being the wiser. After Ralph Budd had left for the hospital, the guard had broken down entirely.

"What a chance," Asey said, "for Eda! Why she didn't take it— Max, can you stand there on your two feet, an' tell me that you went to bed!"

Mrs. Monfort herself had suggested it, Max announced. And none of them had had any sleep since God knew when. And there were always the servants.

"And all this business of people trying to kill Mrs. Monfort," Max continued angrily. "I'm sick of it. I'm sick of that talk. They tell me—that is, Bert Blossom says, a lot of people have been shooting deer out of season. Probably that was a hunter over on the hill or something, yesterday. And this blonde, this Eda, I'm sick of the sound of her name. I don't know what you and Talbot got on your brain, Asey. Like Mr. Colvin said to me last night, this was a perfectly simple case—"

"What you mean is," Asey said, "you an' everybody else

went to bed the minute that Ralph Budd left. Oh, I know. A couple of the boys stayed up an' played a little pinochle. Get me that Alex, or Carl, or any of those lads with the green shirts. Let's hear their version."

Three of the servants had remained up. One had heard a noise, and thought it was the rain on the tiled roof. Another had thought it was one of the police having trouble starting a car. The police, it appeared, had been having trouble starting one of the cars. The third man heard nothing at all. It seemed that he was slightly deaf.

"There's not a thing," Asey said, "that I can say. Nothin'. Nothin' at all—"

"There's Colvin," Snow interrupted. "See him, spluttering over there. Golly, he's mad! He's madder now than he was when I was here before."

"He's got more of an audience," Asey said. "He—well, well, well!"

He watched with narrowed eyes as the figure of a tall man in baggy tweeds detached itself from the group hovering around Hector Colvin, and started across to where Snow and Asey were standing. You couldn't mistake that figure and the pipe, and the silly pork pie hat.

"Hi, Asey," Terence Warner said.

"Hi," Asey returned.

"Asey," Warner removed the pipe from his mouth, "wouldn't you have derived a tremendous amount of pleasure from doing anything that infuriated Hector like this? If only I'd known about this cutter, I'd have got to work myself."

He and Asey grinned at each other.

"As a matter of fact," Warner continued, "I think the fellow overlooked a bet. See that damn fool ornamental cannon? It's pointed toward the greenhouse. Very little work would have set that off. I've noted it for future reference."

"Do I gather," Asey said, "that you're a little sore at Hector?"

"No," Warner said promptly, "revenge is the Lord's, but if I am given any slight opportunity to assist Him, I shall work my fingers to the bone. In case it's worried you, I'm on the right side, you know."

"When'd you get off the yacht? An' how?"

"Last night, with banners waving and flags flying," Warner said. "I spent the night here as an honored house guest. Invited specially by Mr. Colvin. I hoped you'd drop over— under the circumstances, I didn't want to leave. Tell me about your face," he added, looking interestedly at the adhesive tape and the iodine. "Did you get all that in the line of battle?"

"A beautiful blonde," Asey said, "she—but see here, Warner, if you were in this house last night, you can settle the cutter problem—what about it?"

"I don't know," Warner said. "I personally spent the night in Mrs. Monfort's closet—she doesn't know it, of course, and I'd hate to have her embarrassed by the knowledge. But all those coppers and everyone, except that young doctor, they all just took things so lightly. Anyway, I was in the closet, and that's on the front of the house. I didn't hear a thing. But I was terribly pleased about the results. I consider that cutter a stroke of genius, pure and unadulterated."

"But the kids!" Noah said. "We *got* to do something about them, before Colvin—"

"They're nice youngsters," Warner said. "I've been talking with them. Yes, I think we should shut Hector up, Asey. I think that Hector has talked enough. For a man with his money, what's a bit of road-laying and tennis-courting? Bagatelle. Will you shush him, Asey, or shall I?"

Asey smiled. "You was here last night, wasn't you? Wa-el, maybe we better cooperate, like. S'pose we go see Hector—no, we won't need to. Hector's comin' to us."

Hector was bristling as he marched across the torn-up lawn.

"Snow," he said curtly, ignoring Asey, "I've spoken with my lawyers, and I shall press charges—"

"Mr. Colvin," Asey said, "I think it's about time you learned the truth. Warner did this, you know."

"What?" Hector stared at him. "You! What do you mean, Warner did this?"

"What he said, Mr. Colvin," Warner answered. "I did it. Now, you run over and apologize your head off to those youngsters, and apologize to Mr. Snow, and call up someone and tell them to make you new roads and things, and just you forget the whole business. I'm tired of hearing you talk about it."

"You? I don't believe it! You didn't do it. You—"

"Mr. Colvin," Warner said, "you had it coming to you, don't you think? Do I have to go into all that dreary business of the yacht?"

Hector's tail, figuratively speaking, was between his legs as he walked away.

"Mister," Snow said to Warner, "I don't know how you did that, but if he—"

"Thank Asey," Warner said, "not me. It was his inspiration, I just provided local color. Now, you make Hector apologize. Don't be soft. People are too soft with Hector. And tell your son and the twins that I'll show 'em that camera of mine when I find the rest of my bags."

"Well," Snow said, "well—Asey, I—"

"Hustle after Colvin," Asey said. "Make him grovel."

Snow hurried off.

"And in another second," Warner said, "he would have wept over you, Asey—Asey Mayo, I want to have a nice long chat with you—man, don't you ever grow old? Come over and sit on Hector's ugly green settee. It won't be any less uncomfortable than the chairs in his house. I don't think I ever saw such uncomfortable chairs! What's the use of being Hector Colvin if you can't have a comfortable chair to sit in! Asey, you old scout, I'm so damned glad to see you!"

"I'd be gladder to see you," Asey said with entire honesty, "if you'd just let down your hair a little more in the beginnin'—*why* didn't you let me know about things!"

"On my word of honor—this is just like sitting on an iron railing, isn't it? On my word of honor, I didn't know, Asey. I did not know. D'you think I'd have made any secret of Eda, if I'd known about her?"

"You knew you were coming here—"

"Two weeks ago," Warner said, "I decided I'd come and spend a summer on the Cape, being lazy. I got as far as Boston, and met a lad I know, and he asked me if, since I was going to the Cape, I wouldn't keep an eye on a lady that people wanted an eye kept on. He said her name was Monfort. Didn't tell me who she was, but I gathered she was a sort of unofficial ambassadress. I said sure, and because I connected the Porters and the Cape, I sat down and wrote Betsey and asked her to look me up a place."

"You might have written me."

"I set out to, and then I thought that house hunting was more in Betsey's line. I hoped to see you if you were about, and I stuck in that bit about the annulet to see if I'd get a rise out of you. Say, whose idea was that password, do you remember? Did we ever use it?"

"I wouldn't know," Asey said, "who invented it, but I don't think we ever used it. That's why it give me sort of a violent shock. I couldn't imagine what would be goin' on, if you had to drag that word out, an' write me by way of Betsey."

Warner sighed. "And I thought it would be good for a laugh! Just as I thought this would be a nice lark, sort of sitting on a hotel veranda, keeping an eye on an elderly female. Just a nice lark, and maybe I'd make a bit of money. What did you say? What did you murmur?"

"I said, I'd have thought you'd got over this larky thinkin'."

"I got over it," Warner said grimly, "shortly after I drove down here. I got confused by the roads, and I asked a man and a woman where you lived, and where Mrs. Monfort was staying. And guess who I asked."

"Eda and Johann," Asey said. "Thus beginnin' your troubles."

"Exactly. And it didn't occur to me for some time who that couple was. I just got this feeling that a number of un-

THE ANNULET OF GILT

pleasant people were pursuing me, with no good purpose. Eventually I landed at your house—I'm going to buy Jennie Mayo *more* Christmas presents this year! Was Jennie upset?"

"She was even trussed up like a fowl, but she loved it," Asey said. "I think I begin to get this straight. You grabbed my hat at my house, an' left when those fellers come, an' headed for Porter's—did you drive?"

"Yes. Jennie said you were over there, so there I went."

"An' on the beach, people shot my hat off your head, an' you shot back—"

"Well, wouldn't you have done the same? I got him, too, but Eda and Johann had too many people around. They corralled me, and did me up, and took me here to this house. They brought all my bags along but one, but I haven't any idea what they did with my car. I thought it was so kindly of them, to bring my things, but they just wanted to paw through them. Asey, guess how I felt when I spotted Eda's glove, and remembered things."

"Prob'ly," Asey said, "about the same way I felt, last night, when Betsey an' Carol brought up the glove item, all casual an' incidental, like. It sent shivers rompin' up an' down my spine. Tell me, did Monfort know all about this, an' you?"

"Not right away. She found out later, and instantly leapt to the conclusion that I was the nastiest kind of enemy. She took me on board Hector's yacht that night. Say, was it you who was following us on that trip?"

"Over that road, at half a mile an hour?"

Warner laughed. "Oh," he said, "I felt it must be you,

and I kept wishing for the sight of your face. That funeral procession! The driver was scared pink. And it's just as well that you didn't try to catch up with us, Asey. You disappeared just as we'd drawn up to snare you, too."

"Leopold F. Smith," Asey said. "F, for Fate. I think I'll give Leopold a lot of Christmas presents, too, if he don't make away with my wallet, first. What happened on the yacht?"

"They didn't know what to do with me!" Warner laughed so hard that tears came to his eyes. "They simply couldn't figure me out. By then, Eda'd beat it, and Johann had put on an act, but Monfort and Colvin didn't know what tag to put on me. They just didn't know what to do with me at all! 'Member what that big Prussian said, that I was the hardest person to kill in cold blood that he ever knew? I think that Monfort and Colvin felt the same way. They finally tucked me down in a stateroom, and that was duck soup. The first chance I'd had, really, to get oriented. That steward used to work at my club, so after I caught on a bit, I wrote you that note. Last night, Hector got his confidential report on me, and Hector's ears are still red. I came ashore—now it's your turn."

Asey's side of the story made Warner's forehead wrinkle.

"So Eda's still loose! Oh, I don't like that, though it won't do her any good to get Monfort now, except just pure spite. Hector asked me what to do about Johann, and I suggested that Johann be held onto for a while, and then deported as a nasty alien. By the way, Johann did switch that belt on Betsey Porter, if that clears anything up. Without Eda, Johann is a bit of a reed. He sways very easily. Well, that's that, Asey, and now I'd like to look into this Vivian Garth business. That's something I'd like to get settled. That, from the bits I've strung together, has all the earmarks of dirty work."

Asey looked at him.

"You," he said, "may have got to Vivian, but I'm back at Mrs. Monfort. What's this holy purpose of hers? What's she doin' here?"

"That got me for a while," Warner said. "She comes from Little Graustark—what was its name?"

"Festenburg. Say, it's a state now, I looked it up in the atlas last night."

"One of those places," Warner remarked, "where one statesman said, I'll give you these two villages for those two villages, and when they got through, Little Graustark was left over. So it got to be a state. And Mrs. Monfort's husband, the late Prince, he was a worthy and patriotic soul who really did a job on it. And after the Prince died, the restive element rose. And guess who helped the restive element? Yes, sir, Eda. She just never got over those delusions of grandeur. A Cleopatra complex, or something. Does the film begin to clear?"

"Not a bit," Asey said truthfully. "And Hector is wavin' at you—"

"Hector can sit on a tack," Warner said. "He can sit on this bench, that's worse. Asey, Mrs. Monfort wanted to keep her little state whole. But it's poor, and she needed money. She was an American, and she knows where money comes from. She used to know Colvin. Colvin is a banker. So—"

"But it's a poor, benighted little state," Asey said. "I know

all about the place. I got to be almost an authority on it last
night at the lib'ry. How could Monfort wring any money
out of Colvin? On her good name?"

"Little Graustark had hills, remember?"

"You bring up the dumdest things," Asey said. "I lugged
you over half those hills, an' you lugged me over the other
half, an' you ask me if I remember 'em!"

"We didn't know it at the time," Warner said, "but there
was minerals in them thar hills. Not gold, but nice minerals
that Hector Colvin can form companies about, and sell, and
just make money over, hand over fist. And Mrs. Monfort
can get Hector's nice cash, and go home and put the restive
element on relief, or something. See? And the hilarious part
of the matter is, both Monfort and Colvin have played their
cards so well, each thought the other was all set to back
out. That's why Monfort was so grim, and why Hector was
so fussed about this murder. They don't want this deal to
get around. What's the fun of a deal if it gets around, see?"

Asey nodded. "Yup. So that's why Hector pretends to go
to Monte Carlo, an' then comes back boundin' over the
waves, all mysterious, an' why Monfort—what's her title?"

"When I called her Princess," Warner said, "she answered.
But she doesn't seem to mind plain Missis."

"Well, that's why she's so hush-hush. An' Eda, I know, is
the restive element. An' Eda knows if she can stop Monfort, she can stop the deal. An'—"

"And pig won't get home tonight," Warner said. "There.
It's all so damn simple, but they've gone at it so violently the
hard way, that it seems hard. Of course I see their point in
coming here. I can't think, offhand, of any place in Europe

where they could have chatted very safely, or with much peace."

"Yeah," Ascy said. "They got so much peace here! A murder, odds an' ends of shootin', an' some first class vandallin'."

Warner laughed. "At that," he said, "it's probably a dove nest compared to what they'd have run up against, abroad. I was over all last winter, wandering around in my aimless fashion, and I must say, time doesn't teach people a thing."

"Quotin' that sage, Mr. Leopold Smith," Asey said, "the older a game of skill is, the more people seem to fall for it. Have Monfort an' Colvin settled their deal yet?"

"I rather think they got to it last night, here," Warner said. "Colvin stayed here, you see. And when she finally got to bed, Monfort slept what I should call the sleep of one whose mind was at rest—Lord, how *could* I have heard that cutter, with her snoring? I do think that's genius, that cutter. Think of it. If that isn't a thumb to the nose, I never saw the gesture." He got up from the bench. "I can't sit here another minute, on that thing. Is everything all settled in your mind?"

"There are little lapses, like," Asey said. "Like about Budd bein' called, an' then sent away, an' stuff like that."

"Eda was countermanding Monfort's orders. The green shirts were all confused. Eda was beginning to get out of hand—d'you know how Monfort controlled her? Took away her clothes. That's a fact. I heard Monfort talking with her maid. They swiped Eda's clothes, except for a lot of those fancy lounging pyjamas. Pretended they'd got lost in transit, or something. Monfort decided that a woman in exotic pyjamas was pretty well confined to the house—"

"I wish," Asey said, "that Monfort could have seen her in action last night. It might have seemed a nice idea at the time, but it didn't work last night. Tell me, did the servants know what was going on?"

"They're a wooden bunch," Warner said, "except for Johann. He was the major-domo. I think they were, and are, loyal to Monfort. And Eda was always adept at confusing men. If the servants, any of 'em, ever wavered, I'd lay it to Eda. Monfort didn't know much about Johann, but when she began to get wise, she acted quickly enough. Asey, there isn't possibly another thing to settle. I want to see that cottage and find out about Vivian Garth."

"Okay," Asey said, as they started to pick their way through the cut-up turf. "Come see the cottage. I gather you're just puttin' Eda out of your mind?"

Warner walked a few steps without answering.

"No," he said. "I try not to think of her. That's not quite the same thing. Do you know, I think I'm afraid of her. I had a little more intimate contact, of course, than you—"

"Now you're braggin'," Asey said. "Besides, you wasn't with me last night. Hold up, Warner, there's Mrs. Monfort —I think she's startin' after us—"

"You know," Warner said as they paused and watched Mrs. Monfort walk along the covered terrace, "I admire that woman's courage. It couldn't have been easy to nurse a thing like Eda in the bosom of your household. I should not have had the courage, myself. Of course, she knew all about Eda, but a lesser woman than the Monfort would have kept Eda just as far away as possible."

"Thus," Asey said, "givin' Eda every op'tunity to carry on all sorts of dirty work—"

"At long range, and in comparative comfort. Exactly, Asey. Instead of that, Monfort royally commanded Eda to come here with her. Companion secretary was the official title, I gather. Eda couldn't refuse. It was too golden a chance to pass up. She didn't seem to realize that she was being curtailed. Yes, I give Monfort full credit. I only wonder if her droplet of a state is worth it. Or worth her, either."

Mrs. Monfort, Asey thought as she approached, had a little of the chameleon in her. She was regal this morning, but not as regal as she had been Saturday night. Probably the black dress and the cape helped. She was cordial, but it was not the assumed cordiality of Mrs. Monfort, the fake club-woman. She was calm, but it was not the ominous calm of the afternoon before.

Asey asked how her arm was.

"Quite well, thank you—" she glanced at Asey's cuts and bruises, but she made no mention of them. "Mr. Mayo, I am very concerned over those three boys with the cameras. I've just found out that they were whipped yesterday morning by one of my men. I simply told Louis to remove them. The whipping was his idea entirely. The boys have gone now—will you explain to them, and ask them to return and see me? I'm truly sorry that it happened."

She sounded as though she meant every word of it.

"I'll tell 'em," Asey promised.

"Under the circumstances, I think I can understand why they might have—but Mr. Colvin tells me that *you* claim to be responsible for this—er—damage, Mr. Warner."

"I have a steam roller complex," Warner told her. "The minute I see a steam roller, there I am, driving it around and around. I suppose it does puzzle Hector, but then I don't think he ever was a boy, do you? I mean, he may have looked like a boy, but he had nothing like steam roller complexes. I don't suppose he even wanted to be a locomotive engineer, or a fireman, or anything like that."

Mrs. Monfort smiled, and then turned to Asey.

"Do you know where Eda is? And—and what is going to be done about Vivian Garth?"

"Both of those questions," Warner answered for Asey, "have been bothering us. We were about to go to the cottage. I wanted to take a look around. Perhaps you'll accompany us?"

Gallantly, Warner offered her his arm, and led her around the chopped-up swath of the cutter.

Asey followed them slowly.

It was all very well for Mrs. Monfort to take this sudden interest in Vivian Garth, he thought, and in Eda, too.

Now that she had wangled her deal with Hector Colvin, she could afford to show a little interest. That Hector Colvin, in trying to hush up the deal, had also completely obscured the murder—that was something which did not seem to bother her at all. Probably it never even entered her head.

And it was all very well for Warner to say that everything was settled, and explained, and cleared up, and generally solved, except for Vivian. Except for Vivian! Except for her.

"Except," Asey said. "Except. Huh!"

The door to the cottage was ajar. Asey looked at it and shook his head. Probably that was more of Max's work.

Mrs. Monfort noticed the door, too.

"These police," she said, "seem rather careless about some things. I should have imagined that this cottage would have been locked very carefully."

"It should be," Asey said briefly. "Come in, Warner, an' I'll show you what there is to be shown. Betsey Porter an' Carol Garth, they came in the back way. An' here in the livin' room—this way. Here in the livin' room, they found— they found—"

"Aren't you glad," Warner spoke from the hall, "that the steam roller vandal didn't turn up on Saturday night, Asey? I've just been thinking, what a superb way to erase your tracks. In here, was it? Asey! Asey Mayo!"

On the living room floor, almost exactly where Vivian Garth had been found, lay the body of Eda.

16.

FOR SEVERAL minutes, Warner and Asey and Mrs. Monfort stood and stared down at the limp figure in the stained and bedraggled brocade pyjamas.

Warner spoke first.

"I still think," he said slowly, "I still think even now, that she was one of the most beautiful women I ever saw in all my life."

Mrs. Monfort nodded. "That is true," she said. "And it is probably the kindest epitaph she will ever have. Perhaps it is kinder than she deserved. She was one of the most beautiful women, and she was probably one of the worst."

"She heads my list," Warner said, "and the list is quite long. You know, it seems superfluous to say that she had this coming to her. The wonder of it is that she's escaped this long. She was strangled, wasn't she, Asey?"

Asey pointed to the gaily colored chiffon handkerchief that lay near her on the floor.

"Havin' no belt, someone took her handkerchief, an' twisted it like a cord."

"Such an innocent, frivolous handkerchief," Warner said. "Isn't it amazing, that Fate should catch up with her here, of all places? And with something as flimsy as that bit of silk. Isn't it amazing!"

"It's amazing," Asey said, "that Fate should catch up with

her for knowin' a murderer, instead of bein' one. That's the amazing part."

"You mean that she was killed by the same person who killed Vivian Garth?" Mrs. Monfort demanded. "How did she know? How would Eda know?"

Asey shrugged. "But she did. Mrs. Monfort, when did Eda leave your house?"

"Saturday evening. I rather stumbled onto a scene—"

"I was the scene," Warner said. "Eda and Johann had brought me back to the house, Asey, and as they were getting ready to compel me to talk, as the saying runs, Mrs. Monfort strolled in. Eda said I was Public Enemy Number One—did you believe her, really?"

"I didn't know what to believe," Mrs. Monfort said. "After all, you *had* shot one of my men."

"I can't see why that shooting impresses you and Asey so much," Warner said. "After all, I was shot at. I shot back. I don't believe in turning the other cheek, particularly after someone has shot the very hat off my head. Even when it's someone else's hat. What happened to Eda after our little scene, Mrs. Monfort? I know she left, but did she just slip out, or what?"

"She said that the whole affair had made her very faint, and she was going to get a drink of water," Mrs. Monfort said. "I've not seen her since. I don't know how she went, or where she went, or where she stayed, or what she did. Except that she shot at me several times. Foolishly, and rather inefficiently. I had no time to think of her that night. After we left you in the cellar, Mr. Warner, Johann saw lights go on in the cottage here. I think you may understand that the rest of the events that night rather precluded any investigation on my part into the affairs of Eda."

"You weren't worried about her bein' loose?" Asey asked.

"Yes, and no. I knew she had no clothes," Mrs. Monfort smiled briefly, "and no money. I couldn't tell whether or not she had friends outside, but I doubted it. We came to this place by a very roundabout route. I knew Eda had been getting desperate at being so—er—"

"Bottled," Warner suggested.

"Exactly. She had found out that Mr. Colvin was coming, and she knew if she wanted to get rid of me, she would have to get rid of me quite quickly. That was difficult in the house, with the servants around. I really feel," Mrs. Monfort said, "that I made things quite hard for her. Much harder than if she had been allowed to follow me on her own."

"Where'd she get the guns?" Asey asked.

"I think she got them from Colvin's gun room. I think she investigated that room shortly after we arrived, before I had any chance to look at it. She was always a poor shot, you know. She flinches."

Warner looked at Asey and suppressed a grin.

"It looks, then," he said, "as though Eda might have had every chance to know who killed Vivian. I—Asey, shouldn't we break this to the law?"

Asey sat down on the bench in front of the piano.

"If you think," he said, "that it would do any good. Max is in charge here at the moment, and Max, he don't think there is a blonde. He thinks Hector Colvin is an awful nice man—no, what's the use of callin' Max? He'll run to Colvin, an' before we know what's happened, Colvin will have three witnesses who'll say that the Pilgrim Camera Club rode in here on that steam roller, an' killed Eda for the sole purpose of gettin' some pictures of a real, honest to goodness murder."

Mrs. Monfort looked at Warner, and then at Asey.

"I'm afraid I'm the reason for those other witnesses," she said. "Mr. Colvin did not want attention drawn to me. He wanted—"

"To make you a clubwoman," Asey said.

"I can understand that part," Warner said. "And the powers that be, they didn't want Mrs. Monfort advertised, either, Asey. If Mrs. Monfort were revealed as—well, what'll I call you, the Norman Davis of Little Graustark?"

Mrs. Monfort smiled.

"Will that cover it?" Warner said. "Well, if she had been advertised as such, Asey, so many complications would have arisen. For example, there's already a perfectly good ambassador over here, and people would have screamed around and wanted to know what was going on that Mrs. Monfort was here. Restive elements—isn't that a good phrase? Restive elements would have popped up, and made causes out of everything. There's no end to what might have gone on. That is why Hector was allowed to soft pedal. I can't begin to tell you all the people Hector's talked with. That yacht simply buzzed."

"An' just as everythin' gets fixed," Asey said, "here's Eda. It'll be a pleasure to see how Hector an' the higher-ups cope with this."

"I wouldn't want to accuse you of smirking," Warner said, "or even leering, but you certainly have a combination of the two on your face."

He got up from the arm of the chair where he had been sitting. Asey watched him curiously as he walked over to the couch and picked up the blanket with which Ralph Budd had covered Vivian on Saturday night.

"You are very kind to her," Mrs. Monfort said, as Warner put the blanket over the still figure. "I think you are sorry for her."

"It's not that," Warner said. "I just can't seem to think very clearly with her there—Asey, go into this business of Vivian Garth. Let's see what we can see before someone else takes official charge of the thinking."

"What I should like to know most of all," Mrs. Monfort said, "is why Vivian came here. Why she came here at this particular time. I am almost more curious about that than I am as to the identity of the person who killed her."

"Vivian was broke," Asey said. "At least, everything points to that. Colvin was keepin' her on an allowance, an' Vivian wasn't the sort who could understand allowances. Vivian planned to come here. She got a second hand car, an' she came. Then there's that jewel'ry that the girls hid."

He told them briefly about the trinkets which Betsey and Carol had made off with on Saturday night.

"Now that," Warner said when Asey finished, "that's strange. That's damn peculiar. She had these things with her, but she couldn't have taken them from the safe upstairs because she couldn't have got into it. What do you make of that, Asey?"

"I wouldn't know," Asey said. "If Vivian Garth needed money, why didn't she hock those things in New York, instead of trundlin' 'em down here? I don't know the answer. Your guess is as good as mine. She wrote Lewis Garth a long time ago that she wanted to get certain things out of the safe here, or at least that she wanted him an' Carol to get them for her. None of the things that the girls picked up was on that list. There you are."

Warner frowned. "Let's go back to the original thought," he said. "I always have to take this sort of thing slowly. Now, Vivian was broke. If she was broke, she wanted money. You could go a step farther and say that if she was broke and wanted money, and if she came here for it, she wanted to get money from Hector Colvin."

Asey pointed out that Hector Colvin was off on his yacht.

"You see, Warner," he continued, "this is the time of year that Hector goes abroad. Everyone knows it. I knew it. Carol an' Lewis Garth knew it. That's why they picked this particular time to come here."

"I see your point," Warner said. "It should follow that Vivian Garth knew it, too. But maybe she knew that Hector was going to return here."

Mrs. Monfort shook her head.

"The only people who knew that Hector was coming here," she said, "were Hector Colvin and myself. Not one of my men knew exactly what our destination was. None of Hector's staff knew. Naturally, those on the yacht knew they were returning to the states, but they did not know where the yacht would put in."

"You came Friday, Mrs. Monfort?" Warner said. "Well,

a pal of mine knew you'd come here, when I met him in Boston on Friday night. It was his intention to barge down and keep an unofficial eye on you, but then he delegated the task to me. I bring that up only to prove that maybe more people may have known your destination than you think."

"Almost anyone might have known after Friday," Mrs. Monfort returned. "After we got here. But I do not feel that Vivian Garth could possibly have known that Hector was coming Saturday night. Even I did not know it. I did not expect him until Sunday, at the earliest. I did not know that he had arrived until one of his secretaries phoned me. He telephoned, Mr. Mayo, just before you and Mr. Talbot went to the gun room."

Warner sighed. "It looks," he said, "as though maybe Vivian didn't come to see Hector. Maybe she came to see her children."

"I don't think so," Asey said. "They barely knew Vivian. They didn't know she was within a million miles. Why, Carol told me that she saw the letter that Lewis had got from Vivian, an' Vivian spelled his name 'Louis,' an' hers 'Caroline,' instead of 'Carolyn.'"

"That certainly wouldn't indicate any terms of fervid intimacy," Warner commented. "Well, if she didn't know Hector was coming, she couldn't be trying to get money from him. And if she doesn't know how to spell her children's names, I guess she didn't drop down to see the kiddies. And if you eliminate Hector as her goal, you eliminate her getting money from him—Asey, it's being borne on me that I am just a man of action. You are the man of thought. Where does all this get us?"

"Back," Asey said, "to the question of why Vivian came. Of course, she might have come to see our friend Eda."

Mrs. Monfort and Warner both thought that was an impossible solution, and they said as much.

"I don't know," Asey said, "I think from what Eda said to me, an' from what she didn't say, that she knew Vivian. Eda had Vivian's phone number written on a piece of paper in her cigarette case. It's just possible that might be the answer—did you stay very long in New York, Mrs. Monfort?"

"About ten days, and of course it was not possible for me to keep my eye on her every minute. In fact, during some of my preliminary negotiations with Hector's partners, I went to great lengths to keep Eda out of my way. Mr. Mayo, tell me about the Garth children. Why couldn't Vivian have come to see them, if they planned to come here?"

"They planned to come, but the exact time wasn't settled until the last minute," Asey said. "Vivian bought her car last week, though. In my mind, that hooks her up more with Eda's bein' in New York."

"Now what possible connection," Warner said, "can you think of between Eda and Vivian Garth? What have they got in common? What possible link might there be between them?"

Asey grinned.

"Well, what?" Warner demanded.

"They was both blondes," Asey said. "They got that in common—"

"You mean, Vivian was killed by someone who thought she was Eda?"

"Warner," Asey said, "you know yourself that no one could mistake anyone for Eda. No, that angle of it never entered my head. You just asked for somethin' they had in common, an' that was all I could think of, offhand. As to what link they might have—I don't know. Did Eda have a lot of husbands? Maybe they had one in common."

Warner snorted.

"Well," Asey said, "you asked me, an' I'm tryin' to answer. I wonder if Hector couldn't cast some light, maybe. I got summoned to the yacht to hear about a letter from Vivian that he'd just received, but with all the excitement of his two alibis, he didn't remember to tell me last night when he was over at my house. I'll wander off an' get him, an' tell him—"

"Asey," Warner said, "let me break this to him, will you? Please? It would give me so much pleasure!"

"Bring him here," Asey said, "an' we'll pump, an' then we'll break the news publicly. Kind of a commentary on Max that we've dallied here so long without bein' asked why, when an' wherefore."

Mrs. Monfort went to the window and watched Warner as he strode along.

"I understand," she said, "that you and he both knew Eda, Mr. Mayo."

Asey nodded.

"Mr. Warner," she said, "could not possibly have had any motive for killing Eda, could he?"

"I think so," Asey said. "I think you prob'ly have the same motive, an' I suppose I have it myself. I should imagine that mighty few people who knew Eda wouldn't have some motive for killin' her. I should think that in your little," he stopped himself from adding "neck of the woods," and coughed to cover up his pause, "your little country, there'd be any number of folks who'd be willin' an' anxious to kill Eda. There are lots more reasons why anyone would want to kill Eda, I should think, than reasons why anyone should kill Vivian Garth."

"Mr. Warner was here last night," Mrs. Monfort remarked. "Here, at the house."

Asey smiled. "I think he'd probably be able to prove to your entire satisfaction," he said, "that he had nothin' to do with this."

"I don't understand."

"If," Asey said, "you happened to hear a mouse in your bedroom closet, after you went to bed last night, that was Warner. Guardin' your well bein', accordin' to instructions. An'," he added hurriedly, before Mrs. Monfort had any chance to comment, "an' besides, didn't you have Warner tied up in the cellar, or somewhere, durin' the time that Vivian was killed?"

"Yes, but—"

"Mrs. Monfort," Asey said, "you can figure it out for yourself. Whoever killed Vivian also killed Eda. If Warner didn't kill Vivian, he didn't kill Eda. An' he couldn't have killed Vivian. That ought to be reasonably clear."

Mrs. Monfort made no reply.

"Just put Warner out of your mind. If anyone's responsible," Asey said, "for your bein' here alive an' hearty today, it's Terry Warner."

"You seem so very sure, Mr. Mayo, that the same person

is responsible for both murders. Why could Eda not have killed Vivian, and in turn been killed by someone else? Isn't that possible?"

"There's just about one thing we got to work on here," Asey told her patiently. "That is, that Eda was killed because she knew who killed Vivian. Both women were strangled, both were strangled with things they owned. Both were strangled here. A person who's committed a murder that is what you might call a successful murder—"

"Possibly I quibble," Mrs. Monfort said, "but aren't all murders successful?"

"Rhetoric'ly speakin', yes," Asey said. "Actually, no. A murderer who doesn't get found out is inclined not to change his method. I could quote you cases by the dozens, where people got caught for just that reason—excuse me, I think I hear Warner comin'."

He got up and went to the front door.

Not, he thought, that Warner couldn't have let himself in perfectly well, but because Mrs. Monfort was beginning to wear him down.

Asey was surprised to find Lewis Garth with Hector Colvin and Warner.

"Perhaps I shouldn't be here," Lewis said. "I won't stay. I was sent over by Betsey and Carol to check up on you. Betsey says you should be in bed with a couple of aspirin, and I promised I'd view you in person, and report back on your state of health. This—this new development is terrible, isn't it? I—"

"Don't go, Lewis," Hector said. "Stay. I'm sure Asey and

Mr. Warner won't mind. Asey, what does *this* mean?"

"To be perfectly honest with you," Asey said, "I don't think my survey'd be accurate or informative. Did you get that letter from Vivian, or can you get it?"

"One of those invaluable secretaries," Warner said, "had it in his brief case. Here."

He passed over an envelope, and Asey drew forth six purple sheets, heavily scented, and covered with Vivian's sprawling handwriting.

" 'Dear'—dear what?" Asey said. "Does that say, 'Dear Theater'?"

" 'Dear Hector,' " Colvin said. "Perhaps I'd better read it —or Mr. Warner can, if you prefer. Vivian's writing is very difficult to read."

Warner read it, with many pauses and many promptings from Hector.

"Huh," Asey said when he got through, "I don't see but what she could have boiled that down to one sentence, 'I want money, and I will have money, and I will have money soon!' What was that part about the manager?"

"The bank manager," Hector said. "She was very abusive to him. I had someone check on her visit. She threw an ink well at the manager, and knocked over a water cooler. And I had told her, very definitely, that her allowance was ample for her needs, and that it would not be increased or augmented."

"The letter was written last week?" Asey said. "I see. Now, Vivian couldn't have known that you were comin' back here, could she?"

Hector was just as definite on that point as Mrs. Monfort had been. Vivian simply could not have known that he was returning.

"We had no idea ourselves when we'd get here," Hector said. "Ridley thought Sunday. How could Vivian have known? She couldn't have."

"Do you know what is in the safe upstairs?"

"Talbot asked me about that," Hector said. "Basil has the inventory—will you run up and get it, Lewis?"

Before Lewis returned, Talbot himself breezed in, in plain clothes.

"No court," he said, "so I popped—for the love of God, what's that on the floor? Not Vivian—it's not Vivian, it can't be! Asey, what's this?"

Asey told him, gently.

"An' please, Talbot," Asey concluded his recital, "take charge. Just stick Max in an ice box—an' look, Talbot, I bet that you could find a car. What do you think?"

"That sedan? The one last night?"

"No, my car. My own roadster."

"Your roadster? Your Porter? Why, I passed it on my way over here. Two women in it."

"Betsey an' Carol?"

"No," Talbot said, "two women I never saw before. I took a good look at them, because I thought it would be Mrs. Porter and Miss Garth, and I waved at them, and it wasn't."

"Two women? What—Talbot," Asey said, "if you said that the roadster was bein' driven by Frederick the elephant, I don't know that I'd be so very much surprised. What did these two women look like? *Two* women—not one, but two!"

With a certain callous accuracy, Talbot described the two.

"The one that wasn't driving," he added, "looked just like a block of wood, if you know what I mean by that. A block of soft pine."

17.

"I GATHER, Asey," Warner remarked, "that you know these ladies. And if they're half as unattractive as Talbot makes out, they must be awful. Simply awful—what are you murmuring to yourself about?"

"The dear quaint Cape," Asey said, "with its dear quaint windmills, and its dear quaint characters and its dear quaint —yup, I think I know who that couple is, all right. They stopped me last night as I was about to lay my hand on Eda. That was just after she got away from the cemetery hill. So they've got my car, huh? I think I'll take a look into them—"

"Have they any connection with this?" Warner demanded. "How did they get your car?"

"I don't think they have any connection with this business here," Asey said, "but if they've got my car, they must have had some dealin's with Eda. I think they might fill in some spaces. Now, Talbot, you get Ralph Budd, an' rally your men around, an' get to work. Look into that safe, too—"

"Wait," Talbot said. "Before I forget, what happened outside? All that mess. It looks like a spiked steam roller'd been having a field day."

"It did," Asey said. "Look into that, too. See if you can find out who's responsible for it."

"I understood that Mr. Warner was responsible," Hector Colvin said. "I understood that—"

"Me?" Warner said. "Me? You thought that *I* did that? Really, my dear Mr. Colvin, how—why, how eccentric of you!"

"You said—"

"And you believed me? Dear me, Mr. Colvin, where's your sense of humor! Asey, go on with your orders," Warner said. "What can I do?"

"You," Asey said, "are to keep on doin' what you been doin'."

"I don't just get what you—"

"You heard," Asey said. "Mr. Colvin, at this point, with this business of Eda, an' all that it involves, how long is it goin' to take you an' Mrs. Monfort to finish your business?"

"That is not anything which concerns—"

"Mr. Mayo is quite right," Mrs. Monfort interrupted. "We've very little left. I think we'd best see to it at once. It may be possible to gloss over one murder—"

Hector sighed, and then slowly nodded.

"Then get goin', you two," Asey said. "That'll clear up any complications arisin' from you two, an' all your finaglin'. I don't want any more starvin' wayfarers thrust down my throat. Warner, you see that they settle this, I'm goin' after my car an' them women."

On his way from the cottage, Asey met Lewis Garth coming from the house with the safe inventory.

"Take it to Talbot," Asey told him in response to his question. "Tell Talbot to check everythin', an' tell him to talk with Betsey an' Carol, if he gets the chance, about that other stuff. An'—say, have you got a car I could take? I don't want to romp around in one of those bereavin' lookin' black sedans of your uncle's."

"I've got Carol's coup," Lewis said. "I'm sure she wouldn't mind your using it—could I come with you, or help, or anything? I was ordered by Betsey to watch over you."

"Thanks," Asey said, "but I'd rather you stayed here. Talbot can use you. There might be—"

"Look, I know you're in a hurry," Lewis said, "but there's one thing I don't dare bring up to uncle. It's about mother, and—and a funeral. We've left everything to Hector, but he hasn't said a word about a funeral, or anything. I don't know what's done in cases like this, but I'd like to know— oh, you know how I feel! Will you ask him about it?"

"Why," Asey said, "why sure, only why don't you? I thought you an' Hector had sort of come together—"

"He's offered me a swell job," Lewis said, "and we do seem to get along better than we used to, but the subject of Vivian is one we avoid. We just don't mention her—would you ask him?"

"I'll ask him later," Asey said, and went along to the dark blue coupe that was parked on the front lawn.

He'd had no time before to notice Carol's car particularly, but he decided now as he set out that the girl did herself very well. Of course it wasn't a Porter, but it was the only car that he, personally, would accept as a substitute. It was a special job, too, and it had more gadgets even than Betsey Porter's roadster, which carried the gadget record to an all time high. There was even a fancy rack for eating meals in the car, and built-in shelves in the back.

"Very fancy," Asey said, and started in a serious search for his own roadster and the two women.

He went religiously and without success to every quaint tourist spot he could think of in the town. Finally he found them prosaically parked by the horse trough which commemorated the War of 1812.

They didn't look very pleased to see him, and Asey thought he knew the reason why.

"Mrs. Smell," he said, "I'm afraid I'll have to trouble you for my car—God A'mighty, woman, what you done to that radiator grille?"

"You directed us into—and the name is Mell, *not* Smell! I told you that last night!"

Something in the tone of Mrs. Mell's voice made Asey decide that he had better begin again.

"Mrs. Mell," he spaced the two words carefully, "that is my car. Owin' to a number of—uh—quaint circumstances, an' without at all reflectin' on your character, d'you mind tellin' me just how that car come into your p'ssession?"

"How do I know it's your car?" Mrs. Mell demanded. "We don't know, do we, Milly?"

Milly said they certainly did not.

"If you'll just ask someone," Asey said, "they'll tell you it's my car. My name is Mayo."

"Mayo?" Mrs. Mell said. "Mayo. Now where have I— why, are you Asey Mayo, *the* Asey Mayo, the Asey Mayo you read about in the papers? That Asey Mayo?"

Asey sighed. "Yes'm. Now, if you'll tell—"

"Milly, he's that Asey Mayo, isn't that perfectly marvelous! Now, Mr. Mayo, I'm president of the Thursday Club. *The*

Thursday Club, you've heard of it, of course. And Miss Block is secretary, aren't you, Milly? And in the name of the Thursday Club, I hereby extend to you our most cordial invitation to be—"

"I'm afraid," Asey said, "that you got your wires crossed, Mrs. Mell. Wasn't it Mrs. Monfort that you wanted? Now, listen. If you'll just tell me how you got that roadster of mine—"

"But Mr. Mayo, we want *you* to be our distinguished guest, don't we, Milly? I'm sure if there's anyone who can tell us about the dear Cape, you are the one—"

At the end of half an hour, Asey admitted defeat, and promised to be the distinguished guest of the Thursday Club.

"Now," he said, "about the car—"

"But first, the date," Mrs. Mell took a small notebook from her pocketbook. "The date—Milly, you have a pencil, haven't you? Milly just always has pencils, she's so efficient. The date. It's on a Thursday, of course—"

"I'll bargain with you," Asey said. "You answer all the questions I put to you about the car, an' how you got it, an' where you got stove in, an' all the rest, an' after that's over with, we'll settle a date. Now, I gave you a map last night, an' you set out with it, in your car. Take it from there."

It was a little like pulling cactus spines from the sole of your foot, but by degrees, Asey got the story.

Mrs. Mell and Miss Block had set out with the map, optimistically expecting that it would take them to the doorstep of Mrs. Monfort, that renowned clubwoman. To their disappointment, the map did nothing of the sort. They decided that they had gone astray, and even Asey could not figure out where they had gone in attempting to get back on the track again.

Then a woman had waved to them from the side of the road.

They stopped, and this blonde woman in pyjamas had thrust a gun into their faces, and ordered them out of the car.

"Under our very noses!" Mrs. Mell said. "Didn't she, Milly?"

"Go on," Asey said, before Milly could say yes, she certainly had.

They didn't, Mrs. Mell continued, know how they did it, they were just so frightened they could hardly move. But they got out of the car. The blonde tossed some keys at them and pointed to a car up the road, and said that they could take that one, and she wished them well with it.

"And off she went, in our car! Now why do you suppose she did that? We thought it would probably have a flat tire, or something, but it was all right. It went just as well as our car, though of course it's a lot longer, and I had some trouble turning it at first. Do you know why she wanted our car, Mr. Mayo?"

"Because no one knew your car," Asey said, "an' the car that she had was mine, an' a great many people know it."

"I guess they must," Miss Block said. "A lot of people waved at us. I wondered why."

The whole experience had shaken Mrs. Mell and Miss Block to some considerable extent. But they decided to have one last hunt for Mrs. Monfort's before they returned to their hotel. It had occurred to them that they ought to report the incident to the police, but they didn't know where to find the police. They didn't even know where they were, with any remote degree of exactitude.

"I see," Asey said, "but you had a map that should take you to Mrs. Monfort's, an' you relied on it even then. That right?"

"Well, yes," Mrs. Monfort said. "And then I'll tell you what I thought, Mr. Mayo. I thought that possibly a little story such as we had to tell of our strange experience might —well, break the ice, as you might say. It gave our visit a certain purpose, a certain urgency. Mrs. Monfort could not fail to welcome two women who had passed through such an experience, and who wished to call the police. Even at that hour. We thought it would add."

"Uh-huh," Asey said.

"And really, this is quite a pretty car," Mrs. Mell said. "Quite sporty, in fact. Don't you think we were wise to continue to Mrs . Monfort's, Mr. Mayo? What do you think?"

"I think, Mrs. Mell," Asey returned, "that you could demolish an aviary with one shot. So, you followed the map—"

And the map had taken them, Mrs. Mell said, to this bog. Once they got in the bog, they simply could not get out.

"The car is so long, you know. That's how I dented the front, backing. When I came forward again, I mean. And then it began to rain, so hard! I don't think I ever heard such rain. So we stayed in the car all night long, think of that!"

In the morning, they had walked and walked, and finally phoned for a garageman to pull the car out for them.

"I didn't think we should leave the car right there in that ditch," Mrs. Mell explained.

"That car," Asey said, "is gettin' used to ditches. So the garageman pulled you out."

"And he was *so* long coming," Mrs. Mell said, "we just thought he'd never come. His name was Snow, and as I said to Milly, it ought to be Slow."

"What did Snow say about the car?" Asey demanded, grinning.

"He said that nothing surprised him any more. He was rather a strange man, we thought. He asked if our name was Smith, and had we ever been blonde. There were three boys with him, they had cameras, and they took pictures of—"

"The rest," Asey said, "I know. At least, I can guess. Now, tell me about this woman who held you up."

Mrs. Mell said she had hardly noticed her, she was so frightened to death. Then, with the aid of Miss Block, she gave a minute description of Eda's looks, pyjamas, hair, eyes, and the color of her fingernail polish. She also mentioned the glove.

"Did she say anythin'?" Asey asked. "Besides orderin' you out of the car, an' offerin' mine?"

He expected a long discussion of the point, but Miss Block rather amazingly crashed through.

"She said, 'Get out of that car, you. Quick. Hurry.' And we did. And she got in, and then she tossed the keys at us and said, 'Here are the keys to that roadster. May you have a pleasant trip!' And we said, we didn't want any other car, we wanted ours, and she said, 'Take it! It is the first car I ever gave away, but after tomorrow, it will not be the last!' And then she went away. I'm quite sure," Miss Block added, "you will find that quite accurate. I'm the secretary of the club, you know, and I pride myself on my reports. I—"

"And well you should!" Mrs. Mell said heartily. "Well you should! I'm sure there's not a finer set of reports in the whole league than yours, Milly!"

"I cert'ny bet that's so," Asey said. "Now, where were you aimin' to go in that car of mine?"

"We just got through with that garageman," Mrs. Mell said. "After he pulled this out, it didn't go, so he had to bring it here and fix it. Something I did, he said. There were quite a lot of knobs I didn't understand, you know, but I understand them now. We were going to find a policeman, but we stopped to read the inscription on the trough—isn't that a quaint trough! We thought of asking Mr. Snow what to do, but—well, he looked at us so strangely, we thought maybe we better not. Now, about that date for the Thursday Club, Mr. Mayo! You promised!"

"February twenty-ninth," Asey said promptly. "That's a Thursday, an' I have to be in Boston around then. Look, you keep that roadster until I find yours. I'll see to the police for you. When they find your car, I'll send it—where are you staying, at the Inn? I'll send it there, an' the man'll bring the roadster back to me."

He yearned to remove the roadster from Mrs. Mell, then

and there, but he couldn't give her Carol's car, or leave Carol's car for his. He consoled himself by thinking that the Porter probably needed a good tinkering after all those ditches, and a little more Melling around couldn't hurt it much.

"I'll be terribly careful with my backing," Mrs. Mell said, "I really will, Mr. Mayo! I've only bumped the new car twice—look, you can't go, you mustn't go yet! You haven't told us about the woman and—"

"Sorry," Asey said, "I've got to run along."

"Well, we'll see you again, of course, before we leave the dear Cape—and in the meantime, don't forget to put a red mark around February twenty-ninth, will you?"

Asey hoped that she would not see him after she had consulted a calendar.

On the whole, he thought as he drove back, Mrs. Mell and Miss Block had been well worth the effort involved. They hadn't known it—Asey thanked God for that—but they had provided the first common denominator he had been able to discover for Vivian and Eda.

"'The first car I ever gave away,'" Asey murmured to himself, "'but after tomorrow it will not be the last.'"

So, after tomorrow, Eda was going to be able to toss cars around, was she? And he didn't know what that meant unless it meant that she was going to have money. Mrs. Monfort said that Eda had no money. Eda, therefore, was going to get money.

And money seemed to be Vivian's underlying problem, and passion.

That was little enough, but it was something.

And it was about the only thing that was found out that day which gave Asey any satisfaction at all.

"I don't see why you're so discouraged, Asey," Betsey Porter said to him that evening. "It seems to me that volumes of things have got found out. Talbot, and Ralph Budd, and everybody, they've just been flipping around all day, finding things out. So've you."

"An' what've you got?" Asey demanded. "What does it amount to?"

"Oh, they've followed Eda from haystack to haystack, so to speak, after she left Monfort's. And they've straightened out the cars she swiped, the cemetery one, and that Mrs. Mell's—where did they find that?"

"In the woods, behind Colvin's," Asey said.

"And she got her food at Harpers'. The Harpers are going to be sore, their house was broken into last year, too. Everyone knows they leave stuff around. Eda got those New York license plates there, from their jacked-up beach wagon. Don't you think that Eda's got solved enough? Where she went, and all? And we know that Vivian never got to the safe, and that stuff she had with her really belonged to her. Though," Betsey said, "I will never understand how she could have bought that brass neck thing, ever. And Mrs. Monfort and Hector are purring, they're all settled—why, Asey, it seems to me that huge quantities of things have got all smoothed out. Those carpenters actually got to work on Bill's new wing. And Frederick is happy, even. He only broke away once today. What more do you want?"

"Everything is just peachy," Asey said.

"What do you want?" Betsey demanded. "Rome wasn't built in the twinkling of any eye! The trouble with you is, you've dashed around so much, you're bored with just sitting. I don't see how you can sit there and say that nothing has been done!"

Asey looked at her. "All right," he said. "Vivian came for money. Whose? Eda expected money. Whose? How did they get together? Did they get together first over here, or abroad, an' when? That's a fair sample of what I should like to know!"

"I wonder what you'd have in common with Vivian Garth," Betsey said thoughtfully. "Oh, I don't mean you, personally, I mean 'one.' I wonder—"

"An' if you wonder 'husbands,'" Asey said, "I shall open my mouth an' preen my tonsils, an' yell out loud."

"Well, that's a thought!" Betsey said. "Husbands! After all, what would be easier to have in common with Vivian! Did you look into it? You didn't? My dear man, that's the answer!"

"What makes you so sure?"

"The common bond between Eda and Vivian, you goop, could only be men! Men and money. I've been itching to contribute something to the cause, Asey, now I'll get to work and contribute the link between Eda and Vivian. You don't mind if I use your phone quite a lot, do you?"

Asey yawned.

"Did you ever hear the story of Rosamund an' the purple jar?" he asked.

"That child with the horrid mother who made her go shoeless because she bought the purple jar instead of shoes.

Oh, I know Rosamund," Betsey said. "Aunt Prue doted on her. And what about Rosamund?"

Asey chuckled. "The point, if you remember it," he said, "was that the purple jar looked swell, but when she poured the purple stuff out, it was just a jar."

"Pooh!" Betsey said. "You wait and see, Asey Mayo!"

An hour later, out in his dining room, Asey found Carol and Betsey sitting at the table with the extension phone between them.

"Writin' a book?" he asked, pointing to the papers that littered the floor.

"Just numbers and things," Betsey said absently. "Nellie, try that operator twenty-one again, will you? And joggle Paris, the slowpokes—"

"Betsey, who are you callin'?"

"She's just calling people," Carol said. "Society editors, and plain editors, and friends, and—"

"An' their friends, an' their friends' friends—"

"You wait," Carol said. "We've got places, we have."

Asey sat down and listened to Betsey's determined conversation with someone—he hoped it was operator twenty-one's call, and not Paris.

He was dozing when Betsey let out her war whoop.

"There, smarty pants," she said. "Your phone bill is going to look like a box car number, but here you are. Listen. Vivian's husband before the Spaniard was a Hungarian. Not a Hungarian really, now, it's that place that Eda came from. What it amounts to is Hungarian. And the Hungarian was Eda's cousin. And Eda and cousin were pals. That's the nicer way of putting it. And Eda stayed with Vivian and the

Hungarian a lot, in Paris. There was talk that Vivian was going to divorce him, but he got killed in a plane crash. And after that, Eda and Vivian lived together in Paris until Vivian marched off with the Spaniard. There!"

"I take it all back," Asey said. "I forgive you the phone bill. Your contr'bution to this cause is most welcome, an' most gratefully received. Betsey, I thank you."

"Any other little problems," Betsey inquired, "that you'd like Carol and me to solve? Now that we're in the mood, we might do a job for you."

"Wa-el," Asey said, "I could do with a clew. They're always handy."

"Clew," Betsey said. "Footprints? Fingerprints?"

"They gone into those," Asey said. "Old Stockin' Feet was cagey. He didn't leave fingerprints, either."

"Collar buttons?" Carol suggested. "Cigarette butts with that elusive lipstick—"

"A Florentine dagger that has been used as a paper cutter," Betsey said. "How's that for a suggestion? I always love Florentine daggers that have been used as paper cutters. How's for a small gold cigarette case, with a crest? It says, 'Triumpho morte tam vita,' which Carol and I translated after laborious hours as 'I triumph in death, as in life.'" She tossed Eda's case across the table at him. "That help you any?"

Asey snapped open the case. "Nope," he said, "I want a big clew. Those are awful picayune suggestions."

"Hm," Betsey said, "a big clew. Big. Large. Something that bulks. How's for Frederick, Asey?"

"Or that steam roller?" Carol suggested, as Asey put the

case in his pocket. "You can't ask for any bigger clews than an elephant and a steam roller! If you want anything bigger—"

Asey looked at her and smiled. "Those'll do," he said. "They'll do very nicely. They—"

"They're so wonderful," Betsey said, "that you're going right straight out, and investigate them—Asey, you've got that roaming look in your eyes!"

"As a matter of fact," Asey said, "I'm goin' right straight up those stairs to my bed."

And he did. But he only sat on it for perhaps fifteen minutes, and then he climbed down the drain pipe with great care. Even with the knock that Mrs. Mell had left in the roadster, Betsey and Carol did not hear the car slide down the drive.

18. MONDAY was not movie night, consequently the only light on Main Street belonged to the drug store, and the druggist was yawning when Asey entered.

"Sure, you can phone," he said in response to Asey's question. "I'm not goin' home for a couple hours yet. I shut up early every night for the last week, and I been routed out of bed the minute I got into it. Phone to your heart's content."

"Thanks," Asey said, "this may take me some time."

But he was out of the phone booth before the druggist located his cigar stub and got it lighted.

"Line busy?" he inquired.

Asey nodded. "They run into a snag. Look, I got an errand to do, so I've told 'em to call me back here in fifteen minutes. If I don't manage to make it, will you answer for me, an' make 'em wait? I'll hustle."

Noah Snow's father was considerably annoyed when he found it was Asey who had waked him by pounding on his back door.

"You, huh? I suppose you're in another ditch, and a man sold you a gold brick, huh? Or—"

"Harry," Asey said, "this is what is known as the real McCoy. Stick somethin' on an' come over to your garage. I want to know things."

He was back at the drug store in time to get his call.

"More snags?" the druggist asked as Asey came out of the booth. "You look sort of upset."

"I'm not upset," Asey said, "it just sort of gets me riled to be thwarted the minute I get a bright idea. Sister Jane, there, she says she'll get my potty just as soon as she can. Mind if I stick around? There's a hundred thousand things I want to do, but—oh, gimme a soda, or something! I might just as well wait!"

Warner, Talbot and Lewis Garth all roared with laughter when they came in.

"What do husky detectives eat?" Talbot said. "Strawberry sodas. Get your strawberry soda today, and grow up to be a great big detective like Asey Mayo. Asey, you're a fraud. We've just been to call on you. We couldn't see a light in the house, so we decided you'd gone to bed. We—"

"We crept away," Warner said. "Crept, like thieves in the night. Of course, it didn't do much good to creep, after all the banging we gave that knocker—what *is* that thing you're consuming with such relish? I think I'll have one."

Asey looked up at him.

"You really knocked at my door, Warner, an' no one answered?"

"I beat a tattoo," Warner told him, "and nobody came. Should someone have come?"

"Betsey Porter an' Carol Garth," Asey said severely, "ought to be spanked, an' will be."

"What've Caro and Betsey done now?" Lewis asked. "Rushed out into the thick of things?"

"Fortunately, there's no thick for 'em to rush into," Asey

said. "Warner, what was I bein' called on for? Anythin' important?"

Warner laughed. "We've been investigating steam rollers," he said, "believe it or not. I stood it just as long as I could, and then I investigated. We made a test case, Asey. You cannot hear that thing in the Colvin house. Not even tonight, you couldn't. It wouldn't have been possible for anyone to have heard it last night, with the wind blowing, and the rain beating down on that tiled roof. And pop goes the Warner theory of the steam roller."

"What was it?"

"It seemed to me," Warner said, "that that roller must have a purpose. To have someone revenging themselves on Hector out among the grounds, while someone else killed Eda in the cottage—that seemed to me to be stretching the long arm of coincidence altogether too far."

Asey agreed.

"Besides, the steam roller would scare the murderer off," Warner said. "Thus you've got one person, and not two, responsible for both."

"Then you sat down and asked yourself why," Lewis said.

"I did," Warner returned. "Talbot, won't you and Lewis have one of these pink things? One minute they taste like mouth wash, and the next minute they're lovely cherry—"

"Strawberry," Asey said.

"Oh, well. To get back to my theory—I've brooded over this till I've got light-headed. My next idea was, you ran a steam roller to make noises to distract someone's attention. That went pfft when we found out that it didn't make much noise to speak of, at least in the house where it mattered. Someone wasn't using it as a distracting element, and I wouldn't know what anyone wanted to distract for, anyway. Then you come to the transportation angle, and I think you can cross that out. Anyone who would want to be transported in one of those things is simply insane, and, furthermore, it had been left just outside the rear entrance. In brief, Asey, I'd still like to know the reason for that steam roller."

"Does it have to have a reason?" Lewis asked. "I mean, why couldn't all that have been done to spite uncle, or something? That just seems the easiest way out."

"That's just the trouble," Warner said. "That's why it worries me so. It's too easy. On the other hand, I cannot think of any possible reason why a murderer should kill someone, and then race around in a steam roller."

Asey grinned as he rubbed a paper napkin over a spoonful of strawberry soda that had spilled on the marble topped table.

"Well, Sherlock?" Warner said. "Well?"

"Maybe," Asey said, "he's achieved his purpose, don't you think?"

"What do you mean?" Talbot asked.

Asey grinned. "He's got you thinkin' more about the roller than the murderer, ain't he?"

"You're right!" Warner said. "That's true enough. But does it seem likely that anyone would take the risk of being caught rolling around in a steam roller, just so some poor copper or detective would go frantic about it later?"

"How much of a chance was he takin'?" Asey answered his question with another. "None."

Warner waved to the druggist. "Give me another one of those pink things, please," he said. "Apparently they do exciting things to the brain. I can see clearly, Asey, you're on a higher plane. What do you mean, man? D'you mean that X, having murdered Eda, takes no chance of being found out when he forthwith proceeds to tear up Hector Colvin's grounds with a steam roller? What do you *mean?*"

"X kills Eda," Asey said. "X goes out an' gets the roller. X rolls. You admit that he can't be heard at the house. S'pose the cops hear him? They chase, an' find an empty roller. Answer, vandals. Now, s'pose that X wants to know how thoroughly he got away with this killing. S'pose X wants to know if someone suspects that he's around. All right, he'll find out. X rolls around. No one hears, no one cares, no one sees. X is perfectly safe, isn't he? He knows beyond any shadow of a doubt that he was not seen."

"Do I gather," Warner said, "that you, too, have spent the day brooding, Asey? Talbot, will you listen to him? Did you think of that side? No, neither did I. Go on, Asey. Go on!"

"Well," Asey said, "if X is suspected, he'll know better than to be bluffed into anything. Everyone finds out about the rollin' this mornin', an' what happens? The Pilgrim Camera Club is arrested. Eda wouldn't have been found for hours, maybe, everyone's so busy with the Pilgrim Camera Club, the little vandals. X has just distracted everyone, he has, an' you yourself have proved how few chances he took. There you are, as far as I can figger."

Talbot looked at Warner. "I guess," he said, "I'd better

have a pink thing, too. Asey, how did you—say, there are Mrs. Porter and Miss Garth, stopping outside!"

"You'll be told a few things now, Asey," Lewis said. "They've got fire in their eyes. You can see it from here."

And Betsey Porter did express herself very forcibly on the topic of drain pipes and humbugs.

"You're a humbug," she said. "That's what. Getting us all worked up over Frederick, and here you sit, eating sodas —Carol, I want a banana split, do you? Two banana splits, please, Mr. Addison. D'you know, Asey Mayo, we've been way over to the house, and examined poor Frederick from head to toe!"

"What," Asey said, "ever give you that idea?"

"Elephants and steam rollers! You lighted up like a beacon at the sound of them. You did so! And I got to thinking of that jewellery of Vivian's, and that funny neck ring thing, and I decided it was the ring missing from Frederick's tusk. Leopold Smith said we should get a new one, or the tusk'll split from the place where it was cut off. Leopold was worried, because Frederick thumps around so. And you sit here, Asey Mayo, grinning and eating sodas!"

"My soda," Asey said, eyeing the plates the druggist put on the table in front of the girls, "at least appealed to the eye, Betsey. But those things of yours!"

"Revolting," Warner said. "Look, bring me one of them, will you? I want to see what that's like. About this business of the elephant's ring, now—"

"Ring," Betsey said, "or annulet. What a superb pun! The annulet of guilt. It's got a certain ring—"

"Be careful, Betsey," Warner said, "or the contents of that plate will decorate you on the outside. A certain ring! Asey, I found a sort of hoop-like thing today. I showed it to you, remember? It was while we were fiddling around, over where Eda left Mrs. Mell's car."

"I remember it," Asey said, "an' I wondered about it at the time. There's no tellin' where Frederick might have wandered. He might have lost his ring there as well as the next place."

"Then that brassy ring in the jewellery isn't Frederick's!" Betsey said. "Oh, dear, I was so certain that it would be! But I suppose it's too small. What did you do with the ring you found, Asey?"

"It's with the collection of stuff we picked up, just on the chance it might come in handy," Asey said. "I honestly don't think that it will, though."

"I'm crushed," Betsey said. "Somehow I had the idea that someone prodded Frederick up to Hector's wall—did I tell you that we'd been to Hector's?"

Asey reminded her that most of her conversation had concerned elephants.

"Well, we went there, and no one had seen you, but they said Warner and Talbot and Lewis had gone to the drug store—"

"Those pills!" Lewis said. "Mr. Addison, give me some of those pills that Uncle Hector gets. He said you'd know. Thanks, Betsey, for reminding me that we had a purpose in coming here. My good name would get muddy if I'd gone back without 'em."

"Blue box," Warner said. "He was very insistent about the blue box. You'd better get yourself a pad, Lewis, like Basil has."

"What's Hector want pills for, anyway?" Betsey said. "I thought he was looking unusually chipper. I never saw him so gay. Probably his bargain with Mrs. Monfort, I guess."

"Have they got that all over with?" Asey asked.

"All done," Betsey said. "Hector's going back to New York early in the morning, he said. For a short time—no, I'm paying for these, Asey. After your cracks, I pay for my own. Oh, my pocketbook! Lewis, will you get it? Where are you?"

"Playing with kittens," Lewis said. "There's a basketful behind the counter, here. Where's your pocketbook?"

"Behind the seat in the car. Thanks. No, Asey, I had this all figured out in terms of Frederick—"

"I helped," Carol said. "I decided that after the person was lifted over the wall at Hector's by Frederick, Frederick was given a bag of carrots—"

"Frederick, you may wait!" Warner said.

"Exactly. And then X went to the cottage, and then came back, and mounted Frederick, and trundled away. Bets," Carol said, "I begin to feel that you and I do our best work when we sit at Asey's dining room table with a telephone—"

As if it were waiting for a cue, the phone rang in the booth.

"My potty," Asey said. "I'd begun to give up hope of ever gettin' my potty."

After his first five minutes in the booth, Betsey began to make faces at him through the glass doors.

Asey opened them a crack.

"Go 'way, Bets. I ain't got 'em yet, an' it's a punk connection, anyways."

"You'd better get him some change," Carol suggested at the end of ten minutes. "It'll take all the silver among us to pay for this, unless he's been smart and reversed the charges. Where were the—oh, I see the basket. Woozums, you sweet things!"

Betsey surveyed the kittens, and then strolled around the store, reading aloud such labels among the patent medicines as interested her. Talbot leaned back in his chair and dozed. He had had a hard day. Warner, out of sheer boredom, drank another soda.

"Terry Warner," Betsey said, "you're going to die a horrible death. Before you die of acute appendicitis, or something, what's Asey up to?"

"He's phoning," Warner said, "and he's taking an infernally long time about it, too."

"You know as well as I do that Asey is up to something! When he purrs, he's up to things. What has he found out?"

"Personally," Warner said, "I don't think he's found out anything. I never tried to follow the trends of that man's thoughts in the old days, and I'm not going to start in now."

"But—"

"Betsey," Warner said, "I have had a long, hard day. A long, hard day. After a succession of dittos. And those pink things have poisoned my stomach, and I want to be alone."

"But all I want to know—"

"Leave Asey alone," Warner said. "Let him be. If anything was up, I think I'd have guessed."

"What," Betsey said, "a perfectly splendid lot of sleuths and assistants you all turned out to be!"

"Hear, hear," Warner said.

"I mean it! You start in with all the glamor of Eda, and Mrs. Monfort, and the dear Lord knows what else besides, and now you snooze all over drug stores! Isn't it disgraceful, Caro? Look at the mugs!"

Carol didn't look, but that did not faze Betsey. She kept on talking.

"I call this an anticlimax," she said, sitting down at a table apart from Warner and Talbot. "An anticlimax. It's simply preposterous. What a comedown! From Hector's renovated ark with exotic blondes, and men with daggers in their sashes, to a drug store. A drug store with patent medicines. Where the syrup has to be ladled. It doesn't even squirt. Carol, isn't this silly?"

Betsey enlarged on the silliness of the situation.

"Carol," she said at last, "come out from behind that counter and say something! Carol, where are you?"

She crossed the store and leaned over the counter where Carol had been. One of the kittens blinked at her sleepily.

"Talbot!" Betsey said.

Talbot was snoring.

"Talbot!" Betsey went over and tugged at his arm. "Wake up, goop! Listen to me, you! I tell you, Carol has gone!"

"Say good night to her for me," Talbot said, with a drowsy politeness.

"Oh, oh you lumps!" Betsey said in exasperation. "Warner, wake up!"

She ran out to the back of the store. The druggist was sleeping in an old Morris chair whose filling oozed all over the floor.

"Mr. Addison! Oh, you're no use—"

She went back into the front of the store and pounded at the door of the phone booth.

Asey had his back to the door, and he refused to turn around.

"Asey! But Asey—"

He waved her away without looking at her.

"Okay," Betsey said. "Have it your own way, comrades. Have it your own way. You know best. You just know everything, you do!"

Grabbing her jacket, she rushed out of the store.

When Asey emerged from the phone booth, Talbot was sleeping with his head on the table, and Warner was sleeping with his silly pork pie hat over his face.

Asey stared at them for a split second, and then raced to the front window and looked out.

There should have been three cars out there, at least.

There were none.

Asey turned on his heel and darted out to the back of the store.

"Addison," he said, "wake up—wake up and listen to me! Where's your car? Out back? Gimme the keys!"

"They're in it," Addison said. "They—what—"

"You hustle an' wake up them two in the store, an' tell 'em to follow me to Colvin's—I ain't got the time to waste yellin' at 'em, even—"

There was, he thought, as he slid in behind the wheel of the druggist's car, just a chance that he could get to the Colvin place in time.

Warner flung himself onto the running board as the car swung onto Main Street. Asey let him scramble in as well as he could. There wasn't time to slow up.

"Where's everyone gone? Where're the cars?" Warner fanned himself with his hat. "What—Betsey was talking— what's up? Is something happening again? Where at? Colvin's?"

"Who left the store first?" Asey demanded.

"Garths." Warner was almost completely winded. "Garths, I guess."

"Which one?"

"Which? Does it matter?"

"Only," Asey said, "that if Lewis Garth left first, you may just possibly have seen the last of Mrs. Monfort."

19.
WARNER, still breathing heavily, stared at Asey.

"Monfort—now? What? You mean, Monfort, *now!*"

"Well," Asey said, coaxing the last possible reserve of speed from the druggist's car, "there's even the possibility you've seen the end of Hector Colvin, maybe. Dependin' on—"

"Wait. Let me guess," Warner said. "I've just had one of those blinding stabs of light. Depending on whether Hector has paid over to Monfort the down payment on their little deal, or whether Hector's still got it on his person. You think young Garth is after that money—and it's a thump of a lot! Bonds and cash—Asey, why is he racing after it now?"

"*I* got a blindin' stab of light, too," Asey said, "when I came out of that phone booth an' found folks gone, includin' Lewis Garth. I've been doin' some guessin' about Lewis tonight, Warner. That phone call made me pretty sure. But things didn't really begin to percolate in my head until just now."

"What set him off? What inspired him?"

"I think," Asey said, "that Lewis got a blindin' stab, also. From Betsey's talk about Hector Colvin's goin' back to New York—that was when he begun to look edgy. An' also—"

"Good God!" Warner said. "What an ass I am! Why, Asey, Hector and Monfort discussed that part right in front

269

of Lewis and me, this afternoon! Guardedly, of course. Not in so many words. Very guardedly. But I got the idea. After the deal was settled, Hector was to turn this sum over to Monfort. Monfort was to sit and mull things over, make some decisions as to what was going where, and then Hector would take the stuff back to New York, and see to it for her. It's my impression that Little Graustark's almighty poor, and lots of credit items needed bolstering. But Asey, I didn't think that Monfort would settle her part for several days, anyway. I thought they'd have to wait for things to be brought from New York, too. The cash and bonds, that is."

"Apparently Lewis felt the same way," Asey said, "but Betsey chánged his mind in a hurry when she said that Hector was goin' tomorrow. Lewis was edgin' around. I s'pose he figgered the money'd come, an' Monfort'd settled things, an' it was now or never for him. Prob'ly the quickness of this settlin' business shocked him into action. How he did jump for the chance to get Betsey's pocketbook!"

Warner sighed. "I thought so, too," he said. "But I never suspected—why, I've been suspecting Hector himself, all along! Lewis—Asey, Lewis has just been given a job by Hector! You told him to play around with Talbot today. It never entered my head that Lewis had anything to do with all this!"

"D'you think," Asey inquired, "that it entered mine? I think, Warner, that maybe our talkin' tonight helped get him started. We talked a lot about things. We rambled considerable, but we was gettin' warm, an' it scared him. He knew that he'd over-reached—golly, this car!" Asey said.

"This cussed, cussed car! We'd of made better time on snow shoes!"

"Lewis won't be fool enough to kill Monfort," Warner said. "He couldn't—why, he'd lick his goose right at the start. Asey, where did Betsey and Carol go? Where are they? They couldn't have figured any of this out."

Asey set his jaw. "That's one of the things I'm prayin' about," he said. "My only hope is that they may of guessed wrong an' gone to the yacht, or to see Frederick. Anythin'—"

"Things look all right there," Warner interrupted as they finally came in sight of the Colvin estate. "No excitement—Asey, there aren't any cars out in front!"

"None?"

"Not a one! Maybe we've pulled a false alarm, Asey. Maybe something just turned up—"

"That took Lewis an' Carol an' Betsey off, each one in a sep'rate car? I don't think so!" Asey said. "Warner, how'd you leave that house, by the rear drive or the front? Tell me quick—"

"Rear," Warner said. "The road's chopped, but it's as quick to the main road as the front drive is, and there's no gate to block you at, and less chance of being seen—"

"Then you get ready to jump out at the corner," Asey said. "Follow the wall, an' rush around back. I'm headin' straight for the house an' Monfort. Shoot Lewis to a stop if he comes—an' don't," he added as he briefly slowed the car down, "mistake the girls for him—"

"How'll I know which car?" Warner yelled after him.

"Instinct," Asey yelled back.

He sniffed at the absurdity of the question as he started

up Hector Colvin's front drive, but a second later he was faced with a similar predicament when the lights of a car appeared around the side of the house.

It was Carol's coupe. He could tell by the fancy side lights and the illuminated fender guides. But whether Carol or Betsey or Lewis was driving, he did not know.

"Huh!" Asey said, and jammed on the brakes of the druggist's car.

Betsey or Carol would stop at the sight of the car blocking their way. Lewis would probably circle around and keep going.

The coupe gained speed as it came down the drive.

Asey reached for his Colt, and opened the car door.

He had one foot on the running board when the figure of a man appeared from the bushes ahead and jumped directly into the path of the oncoming coupe.

"Leopold!" Asey said weakly. "God A'mighty, it's Leopold up to his old tricks—"

He fully expected to see Leopold meet Fate, then and there, but the driver of the coupe automatically braked, as vigorously as Asey himself had braked on Saturday night.

Carol's car rocked for a second, veered to the right, and turned over twice.

Asey gasped and started to run. He gasped again when he saw Leopold, whole and uninjured, trotting over to the coupe.

"Leopold!" Asey said. "Keep away from that car—you'll be hurt if he's still—"

"How do you do, Mr. Mayo," Leopold said. "I'm afraid

these brakes on this car aren't as good as yours—why, it's Miss Garth's car, isn't it? Oh, dear! I do hope she—"

"Stand aside," Asey said. "Let me open—look out, Leopold, he's got a gun!"

And by the look on Lewis's face, Asey thought, he was going to use it. His own fingers started to squeeze the trigger of the Colt, but Leopold got in his way.

"Why, Mr. Garth!" Leopold said. "You look out, Mr. Mayo, I'll take care of him. You might get hurt—"

Something flashed from Leopold's hand, and Lewis screamed as his gun fell to the ground. While he gibbered like an animal at the knife piercing his hand, Leopold followed up with a competent right to the jaw.

"I'm awfully sorry to hurt him," Leopold said. "I used to have a knife act, you know. But he did seem quite insane—"

Asey drew a long breath and presented Leopold with his Colt.

"I s'pose," he said, "you taught Buff'lo Bill how to shoot—"

"He taught me," Leopold said. "I used to be in his show at—"

"Then," Asey said, "I'll leave Lewis to you, Leopold. I've got a job in the house. Are those brief cases beside him? I thought so. He's our murderer. You guard him—"

The green shirted servant who answered the front door was perturbed when Asey demanded Mrs. Monfort.

"She's in the library, sir, very busy. She—was that a crash I just heard outside, sir?"

"That was a crash," Asey said. "Take me to the library—"

"But—"

"If you want Mrs. Monfort," Hector Colvin appeared, "she's busy. Can't possibly be disturbed. Was that an auto crash I heard—"

Asey shoved the servant aside, pushed Hector out of the way, and started on a dead run for the library.

The door was locked. He had rather expected that it would be.

"Mayo," Hector panted after him, "you can't go—"

"Shut up," Asey said. "Help me, green shirt. I'm breakin' this door down."

The sight of Mrs. Monfort on the floor was enough to silence Hector.

She was not dead, but as Ralph Budd said when he arrived, there was little reason why she should not be.

"He was in too much of a hurry," Asey said. "He—"

"Who," Mrs. Monfort demanded, "who was it? I never knew. Just all of a sudden, something hit my neck—"

"Who was it?" Hector asked. "How did he get in?"

"It was your nephew," Asey said, "an' he come in the window, an' he took those brief cases full of bonds an' cash with him that—"

"Where is he now?" Hector interrupted.

"Leopold F. Smith," Asey said, "is guardin' him—"

"Don't you mean, 'was'?" Ralph Budd asked. "Asey, you never left Leopold—"

"Don't underestimate Leopold," Asey said. "I look on him with respect. Go bring 'em in. You've got a job to do on Lewis's hand. Watch out for him, too, you an' the green shirts. He's in a state—*has* anyone seen Betsey Porter, an' Carol?"

"They've just come in the back way, with Warner," Hector's voice was like granite. "And Talbot has just come. Asey, you are sure—but of course, you must be. Oh, Lewis!"

Hector bit his underlip until, when Lewis was brought in, the lip was bleeding. Carol sat rigidly on the edge of a small gilt chair, blinking back her tears. Hector reached over, suddenly, and took her hand. He had never, Asey thought, seen two more completely miserable people.

"What—" Betsey said, and then she looked at Hector and Carol, and stopped.

"Go on," Hector said. He sounded very tired. "Go on. While Dr. Budd is busy, Asey, tell us how—oh, Dr. Budd, is he badly hurt?"

"That clip on the jaw knocked him out, and he's still groggy," Ralph Budd said. "Asey, what a clip!"

"Not my clip," Asey said. "Just you keep Leopold with you!"

"Come into the living room," Hector said, "and explain—"

"Explain everything!" Carol said. "It's—it's too incredible! Asey, tell us, and get it over with!"

"Talk," Betsey whispered in Asey's ear, "before they break down entirely! Talk!"

"I'll tell you what I can," Asey said. "Only, first, I wish you an' Warner would help Ralph, Talbot."

"He sent us out," Warner said. "Begin with that lengthy phone call, Asey."

"Eda's cigarette case," Asey said, keeping one eye on the door, "had a phone number in it. Presumably Vivian's. My phone call was all about that. It just occurred to me that if there was a number that Eda could call, an' ask for Mrs.

Garth, I could call it, an' be enlightened. I called it, an' after a lot of dallyin', because no one answered, I found it was listed in the name of Lewis Garth. Then I talked with janitors an' apartment superintendents, an' everyone else. It seems that Vivian has been livin' with Lewis."

Carol and Hector stared at each other.

"Go on." Hector's voice was granite again.

"Vivian," Asey said, "wanted money. I guess we got that point settled. Eda wanted money. An' Lewis did. That last was somethin' that stuck me, until I routed Harry Snow out of bed an' looked at Lewis's car. It was in the garage again, bein' fixed. It was a mangy, ramshackle car. Carol's wasn't. Talbot, you said that Carol paid a big income tax. You didn't mention Lewis. It seemed to me that Carol an' Lewis prob'ly should have had about the same amount from their father's estate. I begun to wonder if maybe Lewis didn't need money, an' want it, too. He was willin' to coddle up to Hector. He seemed impressed with Hector, an' monied things."

"I noticed that," Carol said. "I spoke of it to Betsey." She turned to Hector. "Uncle, had you any idea that Lewis was— well, broke, or anything?"

Hector nodded slowly. "I feared it, but I never really knew. I had heard that he lived expensively, that he had expensive friends, and expensive tastes. I thought he was a little like Vivian, in that respect. But—but this afternoon, Lewis talked with me about funeral arrangements for his mother!"

"That put me off, too," Asey said. "So did that fake confession. He was so disarmin'. I thought he really wanted to save Betsey an' Carol from pickin' oakum, but of course, he wanted to find out if he was suspected. But it took me—Leopold!"

He jumped to his feet as Leopold paused uncertainly on the threshold.

"Mr. Mayo," he said anxiously, "Dr. Budd sent me for hot water. More hot water, that is—"

"Well?"

"I've just brought it, but he and Mr. Garth seem to be gone—"

Ralph Budd rushed into the room.

"Asey, my God, where is he? I went in to see Mrs. Monfort, and when I came back—"

"Listen a second!" Asey said. "Listen—"

He could pick the sound of that Porter engine starting, out of all the sounds in the world.

With Warner following, Asey raced to the dining room and threw open the French doors.

"Betsey left the keys in your roadster," Warner said. "There he goes, by the greenhouse—"

Asey raised his Colt and fired. But almost as he squeezed the trigger, the roadster left the torn-up road.

In fascinated horror, Asey and Warner watched the car plough crazily across the rutted tennis courts and hit against the wall beyond. It bounced off, then hit again.

"He got thrown clear," Warner said when the sound of breaking class and grinding metal stopped. "Against the stone wall. See? Your shot—"

"My shot," Asey said, "never got there. It was the road he ploughed up himself that got him, Warner. I have this feelin', somehow, that if it hadn't been for his steam rollin', Lewis would of got away—"

Nearly two hours passed before the group congregated again in the living room.

"Asey," Betsey said, "I still don't understand this connection. Vivian, Eda, Lewis—what about them, Asey?"

"That's where we'll have to guess," Asey said. "Carol, Lewis suggested your comin' down here, didn't he? It was all his idea."

"He said that letter from mother—"

"That was a nice fake, like the list he had of hers," Asey said. "An' the misspellin' of your names. Look, let's figger it this way. Vivian an' Lewis want money. They can't get it from Hector. But Carol has money—"

"Asey!" Carol said. "I never thought— Lewis has written me for money, several times. I gave him—oh, a few hundred dollars. Do you suppose—was this trip down here for the family trinkets some sort of game?"

Asey nodded. "I think so. Lewis tried you out. You gave him money, an' you responded to the family trinket idea. Now, Vivian was goin' to put that jewel'ry in the safe. The more trinkets in the safe—say, didn't Lewis say how sorry he was that things would have to be sacrificed at such small prices? An' even worse, to go out of the family?"

"He made quite a point of it at first," Carol said.

"Let's figger, then," Asey said, "that Lewis an' Vivian intended to work on your family pride to make you buy the contents of that safe. Vivian was puttin' in more stuff, because the more stuff, the more you might be persuaded to part with in the line of cash. The value of 'em didn't matter.

They had sentimental value. You were goin' to pay for your sentimental family feelin's. You told me, Colvin, while we talked about Vivian, that you always was afraid she might try to wangle things from the children, an' what a mother act she'd put on. So—"

"But where does Eda come in?" Betsey demanded.

"Eda knows Vivian, as you found out. Eda comes to New York, finds Vivian—she an' Lewis lived in the apartment part of Mrs. Monfort's hotel. I seen the baggage tags in Mrs. Monfort's room yesterday, but I didn't think anythin' of 'em till I talked on the phone tonight, an' found Lewis's apartment had the same name. Now, Eda finds Vivian, tells her an' Lewis about this deal that's goin' on, an' all that. All that she knows of it. What would be Vivian's reactions, considerin' that letter she wrote you, Colvin? I think, she'd undoubtedly want some of the money herself. She just seems to of wanted any money that was goin'—"

"I think," Warner said, "that I begin to see things. From what I know of Eda—yes, Eda might have set out just to stop this deal that would hurt her restive element at home. But it wouldn't have taken much persuasion from Vivian, or anyone, to make Eda think of herself. I'd imagine that the more Eda thought about the money involved, the less the restive element mattered, and the more Eda herself did. A large sum of money would have satisfied Eda much more than thwarting Mrs. Monfort, I think."

Asey nodded. "I guessed, Vivian persuaded Eda that if there was a deal, they should try to grab whatever money might be forthcomin' that they could handle. Lewis was in a position to dispose of what they might get. An' prob'ly,

Vivian would get a nice cut for thinkin' of it. I think they had some plan like that."

"How," Hector demanded, "could they possibly have known about this place? That Mrs. Monfort was coming? That I was coming?"

"Lewis an' Vivian might almost have guessed," Asey said, "that you'd come to the Cape. Anyway, Eda most likely let Vivian know, right off after Mrs. Monfort come. An' Vivian let Lewis know. He in turn called Carol—didn't he, on Friday?"

"Yes," Carol said. "But why would I be—"

"It was a nice excuse, the Garth children comin' back after all these years. But—Eda wasn't goin' to let you in, remember. I think that's where the first catch came. I think that Vivian wanted to go through with the plan of gettin' money from you, anyway, Carol. I think that Lewis had his mind on bigger things. I'm sure Eda did. An' I also think that Lewis an' Eda were beginnin' to feel that Vivian was in the way—"

"Of course!" Betsey said. "He is—was—such a marvelous looking thing! Eda adored him, probably. And she—well, that sounds logical."

"I think, Mrs. Porter," Leopold Smith said, "that it is quite logical. I think Mr. Mayo is right. Because, you know, Mr. Garth kept saying 'Eda, Eda,' when he was coming to."

Asey looked at Leopold. "I still say, F for Fate," he said. "Tell me, how'd you happen here tonight, anyways?"

"Why, Mrs. Porter and Miss Garth were so excited when they came to the house. I got curious," Leopold said. "And it was rather dull over there, all by myself. Much as I like

Frederick, he sometimes becomes monotonous. So I got a lift over here—"

"An' broke the monotony," Asey said. "Yup. I see. You're one of the finest monotony breakers I ever met, Leopold."

"Thank you," Leopold said. "I try—"

"Lewis came to the cottage—how?" Betsey interrupted. She was in no mood to be sidetracked by Leopold.

"Wait'll we get some more guessin' cleared up," Asey said. "I hate havin' to guess about things, but we can't do much else. An' when you come right down to it, we know enough about Eda an' Vivian to guess pretty accurate about 'em. You can sort of fill in Lewis. Now, he come to the cottage to meet Vivian—didn't he get some phone calls that afternoon, Carol?"

She nodded. "I asked who was calling, and he said a real estate man, and his business in Boston. But now that I think of it, he changed the subject very quickly."

"Let's say he came to meet Vivian," Asey said, "an' finds she's stubborn about puttin' that jewel'ry into the safe. Vivian is goin' to be sure of some money, you see. An' I think that Lewis keeps thinkin' of Eda, an' how much nicer if Vivian wasn't there. P'raps Vivian says so, accuses him of tryin' to sidetrack her. P'raps she says she'll doublecross the two of 'em, an' tell Hector, or Monfort. You can figger the scene. Lewis kills her."

"But Eda kept on trying to kill Mrs. Monfort," Talbot said. "She didn't seem to give up that idea—"

"Colvin," Asey said, "if anythin' had happened to Mrs. Monfort, would you have dealt with Eda instead?"

"I think," Hector said, "that perhaps I should have carried

on some negotiations with her. I had no idea that she was other than Mrs. Monfort's trusted companion."

"You see," Asey said, "Eda stood to gain if she could kill Mrs. Monfort. No matter what way you look at it. Now, come to last night, when Eda meets Lewis—Lewis was stayin' here in the house, wasn't he, Warner?"

"Yes. He was a favorite son," Warner remarked, "by then."

"All right. Lewis has disposed of Vivian, an' he knows perfectly well that he's got us all fooled. There's somethin' about killin' someone an' gettin' away with it that goes to people's heads. An' remember he's dealin' with Eda, who's got her mind so fixed on money that she tells people like Mrs. Mell about it. I think that Lewis suddenly realized what he was up against with Eda. She wasn't just greedy for money, like Vivian. Eda was greedy for it, but she was used to bein' boss, too. I'd say that durin' that argument, Lewis decided he had the strength physically, an' that was enough to put a stop to Eda's brain. There you are. You know about tonight, when Betsey spilled the beans about Hector's leavin' with the money. You know the rest."

"Yes?" Betsey said. "What about the elephant and the steam roller?"

"Lewis's car," Asey said, "was in the garage on Saturday. He hired a bicycle from Snow. Lewis felt pretty safe about all that, to toss his confession in our laps. Remember he said that the people in the Inn didn't matter, you could always confuse people about time? An' remember, Talbot, you checked up on Lewis, an' everyone said he never left? He did, of course. Right after he had dinner. On that bicycle.

You met him comin' back, Betsey. He was the bicyclist you nearly killed. That's the point about the elephant. See?"

"No," Betsey said, "I don't."

"Everyone in town an' the surroundin' countryside," Asey said, "knew that a man on a bicycle was huntin' an elephant. Huntin' an elephant was a sort of byword. Lewis used it, an' you dismissed him as drunk. So did I. I said, he was one of the boys from Danny's place. I thought so."

"How are you so sure he wasn't!" Betsey demanded.

"You r'call that thing you found, in among Vivian's jewel'ry, the thing you spoke about?" Asey asked.

"What I hoped was a tusk ring, but it was too small—what of it? Carol didn't think Vivian ever—"

"It was a pants guard," Asey said. "A cyclist's pants guard. He got an old pair with the bike, at Snow's. Snow said they used to be black, but the black'd worn off, an' they was just brassy. It came off, Saturday night, an' landed on the floor among Vivian's things. So, in a kind of way, Betsey, you got an annulet after all."

"What about the steam roller?"

"We gone into that," Asey said. "We dug that down to its very marrow. Just as everyone knew or heard about the man that was huntin' an elephant, everyone in town had seen the Pilgrim Camera Club, playin' around that roller. Lewis sneaked from the house, last night, to the cottage—"

"How would he know that Eda was there?"

"Remember, Eda was on the loose, an' out of our sight," Asey said, "quite a lot. So was Lewis, though the times he bobbed up meant an awful lot, if you stop to think. Anyway, there's no reason why they couldn't have met an' arranged things, like a meetin'. Now, after Lewis kills Eda, he begins to think. What can he do to mess things up? Well, he did."

"God knows," Warner said, "he did. And you're right, Asey, he could be just as cocky as he wanted to. As you said, he ran few chances, and he had the great pleasure of knowing that no one had seen him leave the house, or go to the cottage. Why, I just assumed it must have been someone outside the household here, because the roller was left down by the road, as if someone had jumped into a car, or gone off somehow. Lewis knew he was safe— Asey, why did he lick his own goose by coming here like this tonight, and trying to kill Mrs. Monfort?"

Asey smiled. "He didn't, did he? The servants didn't know he'd been here. Colvin didn't. No one knew. If we'd come five minutes later, we wouldn't have known any more about who killed Mrs. Monfort than we did about who killed Eda an' Vivian."

"But he had Carol's car—how would he have explained things?"

"Very likely," Asey said, "he'd have come back to the drug store, an' explained that he forgot somethin' Hector wanted done, an' he come back for those pills. He'd have explained. We weren't likely to pounce on him. Even if we did suspect, we'd have had fun provin' he came here an' killed Mrs. Monfort. Or tried to. She herself didn't know who it was."

"Why'd you follow him, Carol?" Betsey asked.

Carol shrugged. "I can't explain. There was just something so furtive about the way he got into my car. Why did you follow me?"

"Someone," Betsey said, "had to find out what had become

of you, and I was the only one available. That's something I'll take up later with Warner and Asey and Talbot. By the way, I went to the yacht club, did you? We must have missed each other by— Asey, something's going on out by the front door. What *is* that noise?"

Asey hurried to the front door.

The Pilgrim Camera Club grinned at him, and three flash bulbs went off.

"Thanks, Asey," Noah said. "We won't bother the rest till tomorrow. Father's waitin'—"

"How'd you get here at this time of night?" Asey demanded. "How in time did you kids find out—"

"The twins called me when Ralph got called," Noah said, "but I was just going to call them, because they'd called father about the cars. We got a good tie-up, a doctor an' a garageman. Er—don't you want to take a look at your roadster? What's left of it?"

As Asey stood in the glare of the wrecker's spotlights, more pictures were taken of him.

"There," Pink said. "We got you an' your car—it's a new angle on the car, too. We got you at the peak of your triumph. If that isn't the scoop to buy us a Leica! Geeps!"

Snow yelled at them to hurry.

"Well, so long, we got to go," Noah said. "You know, father thinks you're a little crazy."

"I can see where he might," Asey said. "Night after night— what d'you think, I'm crazy, too?"

The Pilgrim Camera Club looked thoughtfully at him.

"We think," Noah said, "you're about the most newsworthy person we know."

Warner arrived on the scene in time to hear Noah's remark.

"You know, we had a lot of complimentary adjectives for you in the old days," Warner said, "to which I subscribed whole-heartedly. But—"

"Warner, go climb a tree!"

Warner laughed.

"But it's taken the Pilgrim Camera Club, Asey," he continued, "to hit the nail on the head!"